Brotherhood
OF
SHADES

DAWN FINCH

authonomy
by HarperCollins*Publishers*

authonomy
An imprint of HarperCollins*Publishers*
77–85 Fulham Palace Road
Hammersmith
London W6 8JB

www.authonomy.com
www.harpercollins.co.uk

First published as an ebook by HarperCollins in 2012
This paperback edition first published in 2013

2

A catalogue record for this book is available from the British Library
ISBN 978-0-00-752359-7

MIX
Paper from
responsible sources
FSC C007454

FSC™ is a non-profit international organisation established to promote
the responsible management of the world's forests. Products carrying the
FSC label are independently certified to assure consumers that they come
from forests that are managed to meet the social, economic and
ecological needs of present and future generations,
and other controlled sources.

Find out more about HarperCollins and the environment at
www.harpercollins.co.uk/green

For my two biggest fans – my daughter Eden and my dad

Chapter One – Abbey Boy

A Benedictine Monastery in Hertfordshire – 1534

The small dark room was filled with the stench of bodies, a harsh, acidic smell of unwashed flesh and decay that clung to all those who passed through. A bare flame guttered and spat on its fatty candle as two men, clothed in black robes with a white cord binding their waists, leaned over the two ragged bundles on the floor.

'The mother is dead?' The older man spoke.

'She lingered long enough to hear my words, but the pestilence was too strong in her.'

'And the boy?'

They both turned their attention to the sweat-stained rags that loosely covered a body-shaped bundle, unconscious and yet still clinging to his dead mother.

'He sickens as his mother. I cannot say if he will clear the night.'

'He has no one?' enquired the older man.

'None have come here, and it is too late to find kin tonight. We do not even know his name.'

The older man straightened his back and winced as it clicked straight.

'Put him with the others in the huts, and tell Father Dominic he shall need three to pass this one over.' He walked towards the door, turning back just before he left. 'And order the gates closed: we shall have no more of these fouled peasants this night. I am too weary and there is no more space. We shall wait until morning and then see how many more have died. It is not as if anyone will enquire after them. London cares not how the plague lingers in these forsaken places.'

'I shall have one of the men move him.'

'They are busy,' the senior monk snapped. 'He is not heavy; move him yourself.'

The younger monk nodded his head in a small bow of deference to his senior and turned reluctantly to lift the sodden child from the filthy floor. The bundle was indeed light and the monk easily carried the boy to the door, kicking it open and stepping out into the cool blue of the late summer evening. The clean air rushed at him and he felt dizzy as he breathed in and filled his lungs, trying to clear the stench of death from his nostrils. He had no desire to rush across the courtyard of the abbey to the huts which acted as a hospital for those who had a faint chance of survival.

His scrawny load did not burden him and so he walked first to the main gate to find the boy whose duty it was to watch it. Finding him asleep, he kicked the slumped figure hard to wake him before ordering the gates locked for the night. That done, he started back to the huts.

The air in here was worse than in the mortuary as the sisters refilled the censers all day, burning the sticky yellow incense to drive off the vapours believed to carry the pestilence. Incense had always made the monk sicken and, no matter how many years he spent surrounded by its choking grip, he always felt bile rise as the smoke leaked into his lungs, and this time was no exception.

'Sister Goodman, take this boy from me,' he called into the darkness.

From the shadows a figure emerged, robed in grey smoke from the golden ball swinging from the chain in her hands. As she drew closer, her pale, round face became visible and he could see how the last few years in this diseased place had taken its toll on her. She looked as though a great sorrow had pulled her features down until she had no muscles left in her face to fashion a smile. He understood this and wondered for a brief moment when he himself had last smiled, but in times of plague there was little to smile about.

This plague had stalked the land for too many years, tearing the country into random divisions, not of rich and poor but of healthy and afflicted. Here, in these shabby buildings, lay a constant stream of country folk in varying stages of the disease, most too ill to even groan in their suffering. Those who were still alive enough to call out in pain were dosed heavily with an opium tincture to quieten them and ease their suffering. A mattress was never empty for long as another unfortunate came to fill the one left by the dead; as soon as someone had recovered enough to walk, they were sent back to whatever flyblown village they had crawled in from.

But at least it was better in here than in the hut where the child's mother lay. That was a place of lost hope and final prayers. At least some left these gruesome buildings, if a miracle visited and the disease fled a body, as it sometimes did under the care of the sisters.

'How far is he gone?' the sister asked.

'He has no buboes yet, but he burns hard with fever,' he replied.

'Then there is still a faint chance for him.' Sister Goodman looked around for a space on the crowded floor. 'Over there.' She pointed to a small, clear patch against the far wall.

The monk carried the boy over and lowered him to the grey straw-stuffed mattress before brushing himself down and turning back to the sister.

'Alive or dead, Father Dominic will call for him,' he said.

'Does he have enough assistants to grieve for all of these?' She waved her hand through the foetid darkness at the bundled shapes just visible in the dim light.

'We still have a number of mothers who have lost all; they grieve for every child that passes,' he sighed. 'The deceased will be grieved for by friends and villagers; anyone left will be taken on by Father Dominic and his order.'

'What will happen if the king wishes to destroy the monasteries? I have heard he means to do so,' she asked.

'Father Dominic has a plan to deal with such a threat. He has not told us of the details yet, but I have heard it promises some hope.'

'Would that it works,' the sister added. 'Help is greatly needed here, and I have lost another sister today.'

'Plague?'

Sister Goodman snorted, a small noise which may once have passed for a laugh, but her face did not match it in expression.

'No, she fled through the orchards and over the rear walls. I came in this morn and found she had taken the dress from one of the dead and had left her habit in torn strips on the floor beside the body. She is a fool as she will succumb for sure now that she has left God's protection and will have no one to grieve for her as she is alone in the world – but she was young and listened to no argument anyway.' She breathed a deep and tired sigh.

'It must be near your time to leave, sister. When do you depart to care for the hidden texts?'

'In three days,' she said with relief. 'The first are already in place. I and the remaining sisters will all arrive before the end of the month.'

'You shall be sorely missed here.' He patted her sturdy arm.

'No.' She shrugged his hand away. 'There are others to care for these wretched souls. I have more than served the Lord here, and so it is time for a cleaner place. Are you finished, father? I must attend to my work before more die unnoticed.'

'No, that is all, sister.' He walked back towards the door. 'Do not forget about the boy – try to keep him alive through the fever; it will be one less to find grievers for.'

'I shall do my best, but his fate is now the will of the Lord.'

The monk made his way back across the courtyard and through the cloisters to the main building. Entering through the north door, he passed through the dark and silent chapel into the labyrinth of cells beyond. He knocked gently on Father Dominic's door.

'Enter,' a deep voice came from within.

Father Dominic was a big man, large in height, and weight, with fingers so darkened by inks that they resembled blood sausages. Before he had been called to take up holy orders he had worked with metal and his broad forearms carried many red scars from molten splashes. He surprised those who knew him by producing the most delicate and beautiful illuminated manuscripts. The atmosphere in his room was heavy with the oily smell of paint and a few flecks of gold leaf always decorated his thick beard from each time he licked his gilding brush.

'The hour is late, father. I was not expecting a visitor,' the big man said without looking up.

'I shall not interrupt you for long,' the monk replied. 'I have come to tell you of a boy who is in the huts. He has no family and will need three to pass him over should he die.'

Father Dominic nodded slowly and rested his huge hands in his lap. They were speckled with deep cobalt blue from the document lying on the oak desk next to him.

'I am busy.' He turned back to his work. 'The sisters would have told me of this in due time. Is there something else you would ask of me?'

The young monk looked at his feet nervously. 'I am curious about your plan, father,' he mumbled. 'Your plan to save us from the Dissolution; to save us from King Henry's destructive designs for the monasteries.'

Father Dominic laughed, a huge rolling chuckle that seemed to shake the room.

5

'I cannot deflect a king from his will, and so my plan will not save us from the Dissolution. King Henry's men will take this building just as they have taken so many others across the land; it is simply a matter of time. I can only do my best to prevent all our good work from being wasted.'

'Our good work,' repeated the monk. 'Will we be able to stay here?'

Father Dominic's face fell once more. 'Our work to pass these poor lost souls over is the most important duty we perform. Has this slipped from your mind?' the big man said.

'No, it is just … How shall we live if the abbey is taken from us?' the young monk stammered.

'That is not my worry. My primary concern is to deal with how they shall die –' he gestured towards the small window and the huts outside '– and what happens after, not how *you* shall live. There are matters of greater importance than food and drink for two dozen monks. Now I have much to do, if you will excuse me.'

Father Dominic reached across his work and picked up a small brown notebook before dismissing the young monk with a wave of his plate-sized hands.

Disturbed by his encounter with Father Dominic, the monk walked out of the sleeping abbey and, instead of following the footpath back to the cloisters, he passed on through the garden gates into the orchard. The air there was sweet and heavy with the fermenting smell of windfall apples. Too many were busy with the sick to pick all of the fruit this year and they fell from the boughs to rest in the uncut grass and turn brown in the sun. The day had already rolled over into night, but still the air hummed with the lazy buzz of a thousand well-fed wasps.

A sharp, silver half-moon lit his way through the trees as he followed a faint trail in the grass, crushed by the passing of the fleeing sister. Dew-soaked grass bled into his robe, making it swipe cold across his legs as he walked. Continuing all the way to the rear wall of the orchard, he stopped at a spot where he knew the latest runaway must have climbed over. The wall was not tall here, little more than shoulder-high to the monk; it had been built to keep out sheep, not keep people in.

Sliding his feet into a gap in the lower stones, he lifted himself up enough to rest his folded arms in the scuffed and torn moss on the top of the wall. He could just make out the zigzag path in the distance that the fleeing girl, unsure of which direction to take, must have made. He closed his eyes and pressed his palms close to each other, lacing his fingers together, and prayed so hard for the runaway girl that the bones in his hands cracked in protest.

Chapter Two – The Boy with No Name

Central London – Now

He woke in the ambulance; not that he realised where he was, just the cold white light and the noise, and all around him the terrible din of the sirens.

'Why am I tied down?' he asked, or at least he tried to, but the words seemed to stumble and fail as they reached his lips.

'It's OK,' a loud voice boomed above the noise. 'You're on your way to hospital. Don't pull at your safety belt, kid. You just lie still.'

He tried to focus on the voice, but the colours and sounds smudged and blurred and a massive and crushing pain in his chest suddenly erased the world.

Opening his eyes filled his head with an image he did not understand. Lights were flashing by over his head one by one. He was being pushed down a corridor, and remembered something about a hospital. People were talking all around, a cacophony of noise that crashed in around him.

'What's your name?' A voice was repeating the question over and over. 'Can you hear me, son? What is your name? Can you tell me your name?'

'No,' he mumbled. 'No name.'

There was no way he was going to tell these people his name. They had to take care of him – it was a hospital after all, he knew they had to take care of him – but there was no way he was going to tell them that. Telling people your name meant social services. Then it would all start over again. He slowly shook his head and closed his eyes.

'It's OK,' she said. 'We'll take care of you, but we still have to know your name.'

'No,' he repeated. 'No name.'

'It's no good,' the woman said. 'Admit him – we can't wait for permissions, we don't have time. Take him down.'

And again the darkness came …

When he woke, the room was full of people and voices tumbled over one another and he could not hear a distinct word. He was aware of something over his mouth and lifted his arm to pull it clear.

'He's awake!' someone shouted. 'Stand clear, give him some room. Thank God, he's hanging on. Don't pull at your mask, son; you still need it.'

This last comment was addressed to him and he could vaguely see that a face now hovered above his own.

'Can you hear me?' He nodded, or at least he thought he did.

'I'll take that as a yes.' The blurred face smiled. 'You're in hospital. Don't try to talk yet; you've been through a nasty time. You need your sleep, don't fight it. You're quite safe now.'

His eyes drifted open and closed, and the sounds receded as the pull of sleep dragged him down into darkness.

He knew that time was passing rapidly, slipping away from him, but had no idea how much. He opened his eyes to another ceiling, this time in darkness, and another empty room. He closed his eyes again and, when he found the strength to reopen them what felt like only seconds later, he was no longer alone.

'Can you see me?' the nurse asked.

'Yes,' he mumbled back.

'Do you have any family?'

'No,' he said truthfully. 'No family.'

'So there is absolutely no one to come for you?'

'No, no one's gonna come.'

'How do you feel?'

He found lucid thought almost impossible. His breathing came ragged and hard in his chest and his body felt impossibly heavy.

'I'm fine,' he lied. 'I want to leave.'

'I'm sorry, boy, but there is no way that you will be leaving here.' The nurse smiled coldly at him. 'No way at all. Is there anything you need? A priest?'

He almost laughed, but coughed instead and it tore his body up with pain.

'No priest then.' The nurse did not call for help as he coughed and clutched at his chest. 'So there is no one we can get for you at all? No social worker? No friends?'

He shook his head as the cough became a blinding white light of intense pain. His body convulsed and he became vaguely aware of an alarm going off. He could see the nurse standing at his bedside, watching him.

'Do not struggle,' she said. 'It is far too late for that.'

The door burst open and the room suddenly filled with people all talking at once and throwing back the covers from him and dragging equipment to his bedside. It was the last thing he saw.

'He's not going to make it; the damage to his heart is just too severe. That's why they brought him here from casualty.'

'Why?'

'Well, he's going to die, isn't he? Nothing they can do for him over there and it's upsetting for the whole hospital to have a kid lying around, waiting to die.'

'How old do you think he is?'

'About fourteen, I reckon, maybe less; he's probably older than he looks, think he was living rough for some time.'

'Damn shame. Where on earth are his family?'

'No sign of them, and he wouldn't tell them his name upstairs, must be a runaway. We've been calling him Adam for want of something better. He was found in Adam Street under the archways; paramedics said he was so filthy he must have been living rough for some time. Last few nights were just too cold for him; hypothermia combined with long-term malnutrition, irreversible organ damage. Then the coronary …'

The two hospice nurses fussed around the grey-faced, fair-haired boy who lay as still as death before them. His frail body barely made a lump in the crisp white sheets and his feet lay far short of the end of the bed. Machines sprouting tubes and wires decorated the bedside, trailing to the backs of his thin hands. The room's silence was punctuated only by the beep of the heart monitor as it registered the failing beat and the regular suck and blow of the ventilator. The nurses whispered as they spoke, although neither was sure if the boy could hear them.

'I just can't believe stuff like this can still happen in the twenty-first century,' the younger of the two whispered as she affectionately brushed his fair hair back from his narrow face. 'He would have been so handsome, but he'll never grow up. How can things like this happen?'

'When you've been here as long as I have, you'll understand we've not come as far from the Dark Ages as we like to think,' the older one commented scathingly.

'At least he's clean and warm now, even if he doesn't last long,' the first said wistfully. 'Did you see his eyes before he lost consciousness? Such a pale blue-grey, like ice, so beautiful but such terrible sadness in them …'

'Don't get involved.' The older woman gripped her colleague by the arm and tried to turn her away from the boy. 'You can't go getting upset over every body that comes in.'

'I know.' She finally tore her gaze from the boy's pallid face. 'But it's so difficult sometimes. There was something in his eyes; it was like he was older. I dunno, like he was …'

'Weary.'

'Yes, that's it, like he was tired of living.' She sighed. 'Shouldn't have that look at his age. He looked older than his years.'

The senior nurse ushered her junior out of the room and once more the boy was left in peace. The staff had given him a side room, more to spare the emotions of others in the wards than to benefit the boy. This was the first time for a long time that he had a room of his own and he was too far gone into his coma to even notice; instead his thoughts drifted to all that had gone before. His memory ran through the violent foster home from which he had fled as soon as he had been able, to the bitter cold of the London streets where all he had to keep him alive were the handouts from strangers. It was a stranger who had found him that morning and he had a fleeting moment of recollection as she had called for an ambulance while her dog licked his blue-tinged face; then there was the noise and the pulling around …

It was quieter now, but he had heard brief snatches of conversation as they tried in vain to stabilise his heart after the coronary. For a while he felt he was already dead as he drifted in and out of consciousness while the doctors worked on him. He could recall a few faces from that hectic room, but soon had no strength to resist the coma. Several people had rushed him through into the first room, the one with all of the machines and the constant noise and shouting, but only two nurses had wheeled him very slowly into this silent room and so he knew it would be his last. He didn't mind; it was warm in here and, though he only felt he had the tiniest grip on life, he felt safe for the first time in years.

'Sleep, young man; you need your rest now,' a nurse told him but, despite the warmth in her voice, cold had already begun to run in his veins.

He gave up trying to fight it and, feeling the overwhelming drag of sleep, he gave in and the beep that accompanied him gradually began to slow down …

Chapter Three – D'Scover

'I cannot send anyone until at least next week, possibly Thursday; that is my final word on the matter.'

The tall, thin man leaned across his desk and flipped the pages of a large desk diary lying in front of him. Loose black hair fell forward across his almost impossibly pale skin as he ran a lean finger down a list of diary entries. Using both hands, he pushed his hair back, frowned and adjusted his telephone earpiece as the voice on the other end of the line continued to speak.

'What do you mean?' he snapped. 'Why did you not say this before? This puts a very different light on the matter. You know full well that activity of this nature is dealt with by the lower departments.' He slammed the diary closed. 'You can call them yourself and arrange an agent; Section One does not deal with matters so trivial.'

He waited while the person on the other end responded.

'No!' he suddenly snapped. 'I care not which minor royal is involved. As a courtesy, I will put the alert through to Section Three myself, but there my involvement ends. Now, if you will excuse me, I have far more important work to attend to.'

He disconnected the caller and tossed the earpiece on to the desk. Leaning back in his chair, he expelled a long, slow breath while rubbing his eyes wearily. Pulling out the drawer by his knee, he removed a small black cube, which he clicked into place in a niche at the far right of his laptop keyboard. The screen turned black as he reached out and pressed the middle finger of his right hand into the cube. It now turned deep purple and a map of the world appeared upon it. This was liberally decorated with red patches clustering tightly round all of the major cities.

He touched the map over England and a more detailed one filled the screen; this he tapped again and raised a complicated mesh of lines representing London. The red patches split into hundreds of smaller points of light; these he watched for a moment before touching again and raising a detailed map of Gerrard Street and London's Chinatown. On this screen the dots were fewer, just four or five, and they moved slowly around in a gentle waltz of colour. He tapped the keyboard and a single dot became a vivid yellow. When this was touched, the screen changed and went blank, taking on the purple shade of a day-old bruise. A single yellow-coloured word blinked in the centre of the display – *Searching*.

'Come on, Marcus, I know you are there,' the man muttered to himself.

He laced his fingers together behind his head, rocking his chair impatiently while he waited. A moment or two passed and the yellow word on the screen fractured into a spiral as the screen appeared to spin before settling itself on an image of a red-brick wall. He reached out for the keyboard and pressed a combination of numbers before speaking.

'Marcus? I cannot see you. Point your CC the other way.'

'What?' a distant voice said.

'Your Communication Cube, point it the other way; you have it pointed at the wall,' he said through gritted teeth.

'Oh yeah, right,' the voice said again. 'Knew I forgot something.'

The view of the wall swam past and the image of a chubby man of about twenty suddenly jumped into the frame. He looked pale and grubby and his hair was an unruly mess; he looked as if he had woken up in a gutter.

'Hi, To— er, Mr D'Scover, sorry. How are you, sir?' he asked.

'Marcus, why are you in Gerrard Street?' D'Scover asked, getting straight to the point.

'Not sure exactly – think I had some drift last night after I Dispersed,' Marcus replied. 'I just Dispersed in South Kensington as usual and when I pulled back, I was here.'

'I do not see how you can have drifted such a long way, and I am not prepared to discuss it with you now – just get back where you belong and keep a lower profile.'

D'Scover pointed at his diary and it obediently slid across the desk towards him and fluttered open at the pages for the following week. Scanning down the cluttered pages, he found a small, empty line towards the bottom of the second page.

'I am calling you in next week,' he continued. 'We need to have a bit of a talk about your drift problem, do we not?'

'Yes, sir, anything you like, sir,' Marcus grovelled, but the face on the screen carried a flash of anger for a split second.

'The sixteenth – do you have date awareness?'

'Yes, sir, always know what day it is,' Marcus said.

'Very well, I shall be in touch on the morning of the sixteenth to Hotline you back. Until then, stay in South Kensington. You are no use to the Brotherhood if you lose stability before your due time.'

D'Scover touched the Communication Cube and the screen once more returned to the stark white map of the world. Reaching out, he flicked his hand in a small gesture and a large brown box file dutifully rose from its position on a shelf on the opposite side of the room and slid through the air towards his outstretched hand. Laying the box file on the desk, he opened it and pulled out a file marked 'Marcus Resnick'. Opening it, he added a note to a number of others on a page marked 'Unauthorised Movement'. Closing it up again, he placed it in the bottom drawer of the desk before flicking his fingers to gesture the box back into its place on the shelf. It was halfway across the room when the office door suddenly opened. D'Scover flicked his right hand up in a circular motion so quick that it almost defied perception and the file plunged to the floor, fanning out its remaining contents across the carpet.

'Oh!' The young woman who had just entered gave a start.

'Emma!' D'Scover said. 'You must knock; this office is not exactly always ready for visitors, as you well know.'

'I'm sorry, sir, it's just that you had an urgent call on seven and I couldn't get through as you've disconnected.'

'Could it not have waited?' He frowned at her. 'It has been a busy morning and I have held substance since four a.m. I am exhausted.'

'Sorry, sir, but I'm afraid it can't wait. There's been a fire in a homeless shelter in Birmingham, Zone Nine, terrible thing. The system's picking up at least five not passing through and at least one is showing some destructive tendencies. It may be the spirit that started the fire in the first place and the thought of a fire starter in a heavily residential area is not ...'

'Yes, yes, I understand.' He sighed. 'I will see who I have on for that region.'

'Yes, sir. Is there anything I can get for you before I go?' she asked.

'No thank you. Are you leaving soon?'

'I have about another forty minutes of good substance, but Julie's due here soon.'

'Julie?' D'Scover was surprised. 'Is she ready yet? I thought she was still in training?'

'She is, sir, but this is her final month. Section Four thought she could do with some experience in the field from a more observed viewpoint first,' Emma replied.

'Section Four? Training now think that they can meddle in my department,' D'Scover grumbled, 'so they send a fresh Shade with no experience in the field to work for me?'

'Not exactly, sir,' Emma said. 'They've sent her to work with *me* actually. With respect, I'm perhaps more senior than you care to remember.' She could see concern on his face. 'She was a secretary before; she already has office skills.'

'Well, I suppose that she will have to do. Pass the information about the fire on to her when she arrives, will you? I will inform agents in the area right away, but Julie will need to know too as I intend to Disperse as soon as possible after I have dealt with this matter.'

'Of course, sir,' she said and turned to leave his office.

'And Emma,' he continued without looking at her, 'can you please remember that the details need to be finalised for the movement of the Texts from America this week? This will mean liaising with the living members of staff in both libraries. I would like you to handle this aspect of the transfer.'

'Certainly, sir,' she said with confidence. 'I'll start right away.'

D'Scover looked over the edge of his desk at the spilled paper and gestured for it to refill the box, which it did with a rustle, before the file rose once more and slotted back into its place. He turned back to the map and repeated the process of isolating a region once more before selecting a single red dot. *Searching* blinked yellow on the screen. After a few brief moments a woman's face appeared before him and silently waited to be addressed.

'Carol?' D'Scover said, and the woman looked up. 'You are the senior agent in this area, have you felt the disruption yet?'

'Yes, sir, a bad one. How many?' she asked.

'At least five, with some possible poltergeist activity,' D'Scover replied. 'And I will need a Level One watch for a possible fire starter. Can you handle it?'

'Yes, I can handle it,' she confirmed. 'I may need a substance boost later to watch for the fire starter. I can't hold together for a whole night.'

'I shall arrange it right away,' he replied. 'Thank you for your efficiency. I will Hotline the details for you. Are you ready?'

She nodded and, with a few taps on the keyboard, he raised an overlapping grey screen of information. This he reached out to with his left hand and moved the information up so that it covered her image. Holding the fingertips of his left hand over the information, he once more placed the middle finger of his right hand over the cube and took a deep breath. The screen momentarily swam with a rainbow of colours like oil on water and then restored itself with the image of the agent. He breathed out and shook his head briefly as if to clear his vision.

'Did you get it, Carol?' he asked.

'Yes, sir. I'll be back in touch if there are any problems,' she replied, giving a brief nod as the screen faded to purple again.

The display returned to the map once more before D'Scover removed the CC and replaced it in the drawer. He stood and stretched before walking to the door, opening it and leaning round it into the reception area to find Emma. She was reaching into a filing cabinet, holding a large bundle of paperwork.

'Emma,' he called, 'I want no disturbances for at least two hours – and this is a Code Red instruction.'

'Absolutely, sir, I understand.'

She leaned over her desk and passed her hand over a small flat panel embedded in the surface. This flicked on and began to emit a pulsating red glow. As D'Scover closed his office door behind him, it gave off a slight hiss and a sucking noise as it sealed from the outside.

Walking back across his huge but sparsely furnished office to a blood-red couch standing against a vast expanse of window, he sat briefly. Drawing in a number of deep breaths, he closed his eyes and the room filled with a deep silence. When the silence seemed to begin to crush the air from the room, he stood and walked to the windows. One whole wall was made of glass, forming huge sliding doors leading out to a balcony, and it was towards this that he waved his hand. In silence the glass slid effortlessly open to reveal a wide and empty balcony overlooking the slate-grey mass of London in early February. This building was one of the tallest on the south bank of the Thames and from here he could see across the river and over the city and even out to the thin band of green where the countryside still tried in vain to resist the urban sprawl.

D'Scover walked out on to the damp stone slabs of the balcony and lifted his head as the wind forced itself around him, ruffling his hair and clothes. Closing his eyes, he raised his hands, palms skyward, in front of him. He held this stance for a number of minutes before moving his arms, still extended and palms upwards, out to his sides. Expelling a long breath, he raised his hands swiftly above his head, clapping them together. In an instant the city became dark, as though a gigantic shadow had fallen across it for just a fraction of a second. On the balcony a faint image of a man held its shape momentarily before it shattered into a million tiny glistening grey particles that swirled away with the wind.

Chapter Four – The Good Sister

D'Scover had returned to form hours later in a whirling mist that thickened until it took on the shape of a man, gradually becoming more recognisable until he lay re-formed on the couch in his room, regulating his breathing in a slow and steady rhythm. With each intake of air he became more solid until, after another ten minutes of steady control, he looked as alive as any person in the street. With a final deep sigh he sat up and smoothed his hair back and stretched. Standing, he walked over to his huge oak desk and flicked the intercom unit.

'Emma?' he said.

'Emma has Dispersed, sir,' a youthful female voice replied. 'It's me, Julie. Did you have a restful Dispersal?'

'Indeed I did. It has been a while since I was away for such a lengthy period. Are there any messages for me?'

'Yes, sir. I'll bring them straight in.'

D'Scover sat at his desk and looked down at his hands, idly fading them in and out of solidity while he thought. He looked close to forty, but as if it had been a lonely journey to get to that age. With his clean-shaven face framed by a thick gloss of collar-length black hair, his pale skin seemed to shine out from a halo of deepest night. His high cheekbones defined his lean face and his eyes were large and dark, and with no pupils they gave away none of his emotions. On the rare occasions that he smiled, it sat uncomfortably on his face like a party hat on a head teacher – an effort towards jollity that he did not really welcome. His work was everything to him and he made sure that all around him knew. Very few things – living or dead – meddled with Toby D'Scover.

Julie wafted through the door to bring D'Scover his messages. Arriving in the room, she looked down at her empty hands, remembering only then that the file could not pass through the wood as she could. It had tumbled to the office floor behind her.

'I … I'm s-s-sorry, sir,' she stammered, turning back towards the door and banging her face hard against it.

'Julie!' he said brusquely. 'I realise you have not yet finished your training, but what is the Prime Rule of the Brotherhood?'

She looked down at her feet as she answered. 'Concentrate,' she muttered.

'Concentrate,' he repeated. 'We rest our success on never being caught out. Those who are seen are not fit for the Brotherhood. Concentration ensures that we can move amongst the living without their knowledge. And what would one of our living agents say if they saw you marching through doors? You know it makes them uncomfortable to be reminded of their own mortality.'

'I'm truly sorry, sir,' she muttered through obviously gritted teeth. 'I'll try and concentrate harder.'

'Do so.' He stared hard at her as she stood in front of the closed door.

A moment's awkward silence flooded the room as she stared at her shoes.

'Messages?' D'Scover queried with his eyebrows raised.

'Oh!' she said. 'Yes, the messages!'

She opened the door and reached out to gather up her fallen file and the paperwork that had spewed from it on to the floor. D'Scover impatiently flicked his hand and the scattered paper shuffled itself into a neat pile and rose through the air towards his desk.

'Do not bother,' he said dismissively. 'I am in a hurry to get on with my work. Can you just get back to the desk and watch the incoming reports, please?'

Julie sniffed loudly and turned away from him before scuttling from the room and back to her desk. The door closed heavily behind her and D'Scover could hear her muffled sobbing through the wall.

'Amateurs,' he muttered to himself before looking at the folder of messages.

There were the usual reports of spectral sightings from around the globe, many of which he could recognise as familiar spirits that needed no further action. Some were spirits causing a fuss close to their Final Dispersal and could be left to pass on without any help – time would take care of those for him. Others were agents caught momentarily going about Brotherhood business: these would need a caution, but could wait until later

By far the most persistent reports were about fakers, charlatans. These were D'Scover's pet hate, so-called psychics who cashed in on the beliefs of the weak and needy. Many of these he dealt with personally and had done so for as long as Spiritualism had existed. Not all of these people were fakers; in fact some of his best living agents had been recruited from these meetings. Some people were genuinely sensitive and could maintain contact with the Spirit World, but most were just out to make money from the lonely and bereaved. This vile trade made him angry – and an angry D'Scover was a force to be reckoned with.

Often, all it took to expose the charlatans was to attend a seance or so-called 'spirit reading', find out their tricks and show the other clients. He would attend as a living person and, while attention was diverted by the charlatan, he would detach wires, or pull back curtains, to reveal the trickery. On rare occasions it took what D'Scover called 'a bit of a scare' to put them off. No one had ever continued with their deception after a 'scare' visit from D'Scover.

Flicking through the final messages, one caught his eye and he reached for his CC and slotted it into place in the keyboard. Isolating a particular location on his screen, he waited for the image to load. When it did, it was of a solid-looking woman wearing a nurse's uniform and with a broad smile across her face.

'Sister Goodman,' he said. 'It is good to see you after such a long time.'

'Hello, Toby, how are you?' The rotund nurse squinted at him. 'You look terrible. Are you getting enough rest?'

'Now you did not ask me to call you just for social reasons or to comment on the state of my apparent well-being, did you?' D'Scover evaded the question. 'What can I do for you?'

'Straight to the point, as usual.' Her smile faded. 'I have a boy here, very close to the end, and I think you should come and take a look at him.'

'If you say so. I trust your judgement,' he replied. 'Do you have a safe computer for me to Hotline?'

'I'm sending you the code now,' she replied.

A series of numbers scrolled across the monitor and an empty black square unfolded at the bottom of the purple screen.

'Good. I will be there immediately,' D'Scover said.

The image of the nurse faded and all that remained on the screen was the black square. D'Scover moved this to the middle of the display. He took a deep breath and straightened his back, shuffling his chair backwards a little so that he was exactly at arm's length from the monitor. Reaching out both hands, he placed his fingertips on the glass and closed his eyes.

'*Inter vivos*,' he whispered to himself. 'Once more amongst the living.'

Blue sparks crackled around his fingertips and gradually began to spread up his hands. A rolling blue haze boiled over his arms and, within seconds, covered his whole body, enveloping him in a cold light that drained the colour from the room. He looked down and expelled a noisy breath; as he did so, his shape flickered and began to destabilise. Then, with a *whoosh* of static that made the loose paper on the desk jostle and dance, he became a spiralling vortex of glistening grey particles dissolving into the screen.

In a locked office at St Mary's Benevolent Hospice a computer in standby mode began to flicker and automatically load a deep purple background. Another black square unfolded on it and the room fizzed with static electricity. The lights in the corridor pulsed as a blue spark showed on the screen, then another and another until a spike began to form. The spike extended and grew from the screen, becoming larger and larger and then expanding until a tall shape began to form in the room. A sudden rush and whirl of grey particles within the sparks and D'Scover stood in the dark room.

He brushed himself down and straightened his suit before walking towards the door. At the door he hesitated as he remembered something and reached his hand up into the air. He clicked his fingers and a security badge appeared in his hand bearing his photograph and the name DR T SMITH; he clipped this to his pocket. He touched the keyhole in the door, which sparked blue and clicked as it unlocked and swung open, allowing him out into the corridor.

Following the gentle beep of Sister Goodman's CC, he soon found the way. She was waiting for him outside the boy's room, quietly standing alone, looking through the window to where he lay deep in a coma. D'Scover could see the faint violet aura that she had created to shield her from the eyes of the living. She turned and smiled at D'Scover as he came towards her and stepped forward and hugged him, much to his obvious distaste. Pulling back, he held her gently at arm's length.

'It has been a long time,' D'Scover said blandly, his faint smile resting only on his mouth as though it did not have the strength to reach his eyes.

'Yes, Toby, it has, far too long. It is a shame you are always so busy with the troubles of the living; too busy to come and see an old friend?' she reprimanded.

'The dead are equally demanding,' he said by way of reply. 'Recently there has been a rise in incidents. I feel there may be too many disturbances to write them all off as a coincidence or another transitional phase.'

'Still caught up in your precious Vision?' Sister Goodman chortled. 'Honestly, Toby, I do despair at your affection for the living.'

'There are still many on both sides who have faith in the Vision, sister,' D'Scover said, 'despite the long wait.'

'Hmm, so it seems,' she smiled. 'You and I will never agree.'

'What do you have for me?' he said, changing the subject. 'It sounded urgent.'

'This boy.' She gestured at the bed on the other side of the glass. 'I think you might be interested in him.'

'He is still alive, sister; we do have rules.'

'Do not mock me, Toby, I know all the rules. This boy is different.'

'How long does he have?' D'Scover peered through the glass at the small heap under the bedclothes.

'He will not last the night; his heart is failing fast.' Her face fell into a frown for the first time. 'He was found in the street, no family, no one to grieve for him, a lost waif.'

'This sounds very familiar.' He stared through the glass. 'Are you sure that you are not just being sentimental?'

'I am possibly the least sentimental sister you will ever meet and you know that full well,' she snapped.

'So why is this one so different? Why does he need my special attention? You could easily have dealt with him without my help.'

'He is different,' she replied slowly, 'because he *saw* me.'

'What did you just say?' D'Scover turned quickly to face her.

'He woke briefly a couple of times, and he could *see* me.'

'Hmm.' D'Scover peered through the glass once more. 'How long has it been since anyone saw you?'

'Such an impertinent question! You know my experience: no one has *seen* me without my express desire for over two hundred years,' she replied.

'This is indeed interesting,' D'Scover agreed, 'and with the rise in disturbances, it could all become even more interesting.'

'I thought you should know,' Sister Goodman said. 'As I said, he does not have much time left.'

'Thank you, sister; if fate is running true to course, this boy could prove to be what we have been waiting for.'

Chapter Five – Death Day

'Am I dead?'

'Yes.'

'Simple as that? No softening the blow?'

'You are no longer a child; do you wish to still be treated as one?'

'I just thought … You an angel then?'

'I have been asked that so many times. No, I am not an angel and, before you ask, I am no devil either.'

'So who are you – or what are you?'

'I am D'Scover. I am here to help you.'

'Sounds dead creepy to me. Why do I need help?'

'Because you are dead and yet you are still here.'

'I had noticed, thought it was a bit odd, but I kinda thought I was dreaming and that none of this is real.'

'Real is a phrase with many definitions.'

'Bloody hell, what sort of answer is that?'

D'Scover walked down the corridor of the hospice, grateful to no longer hold full substance. In this fresh state of death, the world hung between the living and the dead. The living could not see him here because they did not believe it existed – and therefore to them it did not exist.

The boy looked through the window into the room where his

body lay. His skin sunk into his half-starved frame making him look more skeleton than boy. His body weighed very little and, though he was fourteen, he looked much younger. Two male nurses lifted his corpse carefully into a black bag, doing it slowly up and moving his wavy fair hair out of the way so it wouldn't catch in the zip. They placed it on to the lower level of a trolley and covered the whole thing with a clean sheet. Loaded up like leftover dinner, the boy thought, to be wheeled through the corridors without causing any upset. No one would even know the body lay there as the apparently empty trolley rolled through the wards to the mortuary. He watched with curiosity for a moment before realising his companion had walked on.

'Hey, wait up!' the boy called after him.

D'Scover turned and waved his hand. The walls rippled in a wave from his sides all the way to the boy and, before the boy could refocus, he was standing right in front of D'Scover.

'Wow, now that's cool. How d'you do that?' the boy asked, looking around.

'Practice,' D'Scover replied brusquely. 'Do you have a name?'

'I suppose so; I mean, I must have one.' He frowned. 'It's just … just I can't quite catch hold of it. It's like it's just out of reach; d'you know what I mean?'

'No one is here to remember your name, so it is not remembered. Do you have a name you wish to use instead?'

'I can't think of any.' The boy wrinkled his forehead as he tried to recall one. 'I'm not really bothered though. I mean, I don't seem to care.'

'Adam – will that do?' D'Scover suggested.

'OK – Adam, I like it – Adam will do.'

'It is what the nurses put on your admission papers and death certificate; they had to put a name and they chose to name you after where you were found, Adam Street. It is a good enough name and it carried you to death; it seems fitting that it should carry you past it,' D'Scover said.

He turned back to the corridor and began to walk once more. Adam followed at a brisk pace, half running alongside his tall and long-legged companion.

'So what happens now?' the boy continued to babble. 'Do I have to do something to get to? Do I have unresolved business – that's what they have in the scary movies – is that why I'm still around? Or is that just all rubbish? If it is, where will I live?'

'You will not live.' D'Scover strode on. 'You are dead; try to hold that thought.'

'No, I know I'm dead, well, I must be. I mean, I saw my body back there so I must be dead, unless someone really looks like me and this is all a set-up. Is it a set-up? No, can't be, why would anyone bother to set me up?' He continued to flood D'Scover with questions. 'I'm just a bit confused about why I'm here, why I'm not just dead and gone. Hold on, is this a dream? Am I imagining all this?' Adam stopped and looked around the corridor. 'I mean, this doesn't even look quite real, does it?'

He was right, it didn't look quite real: the colours were drained and everything had an almost two-dimensional quality as though they were watching it all on a TV screen.

'That is because it is not quite real; we are currently within the Memoria,' D'Scover explained. 'This is a place constructed entirely of your memories and life experiences. The corridors look solid enough until we go beyond that which you have seen. You have never entered any of the rooms off the corridors and so they do not exist because you have no memory of them. In fact, as you were wheeled through the hospital to your room, you only saw the ceiling and because of this the floor does not exist here.'

Adam looked down and the floor was not there. It was not that it was a hole, but it just simply did not exist. It was rather like trying to look at stars: the harder you stared, the fainter the image became. The effect made Adam feel slightly sick.

'Hey, how come I can still feel sick, even though I'm dead?' he asked. 'Shouldn't all that sort of thing stop?'

'You feel sick because you can still remember what feeling sick is like. You know what would have made you feel sick, you remember, and it *does* make you feel sick. You do not actually feel sick, you just think you do.'

'Easy for you to say,' Adam grimaced, 'but I feel like I could make a proper mess of your shoes, real or not. So, what now?'

'Now I have to take you through some of your memories so that you understand yourself and your life.'

'Really? God, that's a bit depressing, isn't it? Can't I just skip on to the next bit?'

'That is rather a rash request,' D'Scover said, 'considering you do not know what the next bit is.'

'Ah,' Adam nodded, 'now that's a fair point. OK, lead on, Mr Spooky. Let's get on with this.'

The corridor began to fade and was replaced with a large open green space surrounded by a blurry green wall. The green began slowly to pull itself into focus and showed itself to be a large park ringed with tall trees. A small brown dog appeared from nowhere and ran off into the trees, hotly pursued by a young girl calling for it to stop. Other details of the park smudged into existence – a set of swings, a slide, a paddling pool full of children – all fulfilled the illusion that the park was real. D'Scover looked around at the environment gradually forming about them both.

'What is this place?' D'Scover asked. 'It must be an important memory of yours.'

'It's the park where I lived last summer when I ran away from that bunch of nutjobs who called themselves my foster parents,' Adam replied incredulously. 'It's so real! Is it real?'

'That all depends on your definition of the word real,' D'Scover replied enigmatically.

'If I can touch it – it's real,' Adam grinned, pleased with his cocky answer.

'Ah, but if something is out of reach, too high up to touch, does it mean it is not real? A mountain top, the sky, are they not real?'

'Now you're just messing with my head,' Adam laughed. 'No, this place looks too real to be in my imagination, just like it did when I was here last summer. Everything's the same, the ice-cream van, the kids in the paddling pool, the park keeper telling off the kids for riding on the grass, it's all the same as it was back then.'

'We have not travelled in time, and so how do you suppose that we can be here last summer?' D'Scover quizzed.

'OK, let me think,' Adam said, walking round the grass in front of the paddling pool. 'Well … I suppose … this is my clearest memory of the park … and so that's how I've recreated it in my mind?'

'Excellent, a brilliant supposition and quite accurate.' D'Scover was relieved; the boy did indeed show promise.

'Why are we here?' Adam asked, bending to touch the grass beneath his feet and marvelling as it smudged like wet paint. He watched as it settled and once more became lush green turf.

'This is one of your good memories shown here in the Memoria, but you may have to let it go,' D'Scover answered. 'You must listen very carefully to me now. We should sit down; this may be a difficult stage for you.'

He looked around for a bench to sit down, but there were none visible.

'Hey, that's not right,' Adam grumbled. 'There were loads of benches in this park. I should know, I slept on most of them.'

He closed his eyes and screwed up his fists, concentrating hard, and a grey mist began to take shape beside them. The blur struggled in and out of focus for a few seconds before settling into the shape of a shabby bench. It was just about wide enough for two, but still much smaller than a normal park bench. D'Scover watched in amazement; no one had ever mastered such object control their first time in the Memoria – no one.

'What?' Adam was staring at D'Scover. 'You look like you've seen a ghost!'

'You like to joke, do you not, Adam?' D'Scover composed his sombre face once more.

'Suppose so,' Adam said, 'and I'm guessing you don't? So why aren't I freaked out? Why aren't I running around doing the whole spooky *oooooh* thing and clanking chains like other ghosts? Why aren't I scared stiff? I feel kind of … well … chilled.'

'I imagine that in life you had a somewhat pragmatic character, and that has traversed with you.'

Adam stared at D'Scover blankly for a moment. 'Nope,' he said. 'You've lost me, brainiac. What did all that mean? Prag what?'

'Pragmatic. It means that you were down-to-earth, practical, well grounded.'

'Oh yeah,' Adam grinned. 'I was that, I suppose. Not easily scared, seen a few things that should have scared me, but I always figured that as long as I could always be quick on my feet, I could outrun most things. Mind you, not much chance of me outrunning death!'

'More jokes?' D'Scover asked.

'Not that you'd notice!'

They both sat on Adam's bench and, for a number of quiet minutes, they did not talk and instead watched the park evolve around them. More people walked past and an ice-cream van jingled its noisy way along a narrow road dissecting the green field.

'The next issue is always a difficult one.' D'Scover broke the silence. 'I will not deceive you on this. These memories are here to ease you through this state into the Passing,' he told Adam in a serious tone. 'You must decide what you wish to see before you move on. Many of these memories will be lost to you forever once they have played out here. It is important you discard any deep woes you may be harbouring as these can trap your spirit in one place.'

'The Passing? What's that then? Is that the proper deadness kind of thing?' Adam asked.

'You could say that,' D'Scover replied coldly. 'Grossly simplified but, basically, yes.'

'And what if I don't want to go there? What if I just want to hang around the living and haunt someone?'

'Do you?' D'Scover asked.

Adam shook his head. 'Nah, not really. I suppose I just don't feel as though I had enough time to do anything, to really live. Like my life was over before it really got started and now I'm just going to fade away. D'you know what I mean?'

'I do.' D'Scover looked around at the verdant greens of the park and marvelled at the accuracy of this particular Memoria. 'There is another way.'

'Another way?' Adam gripped D'Scover's arm and was surprised that it was solid; somehow he had expected to pass through it. 'Don't mess me around here; if there's something else I should know or do to stop from just … well … ending and me being proper dead, why don't you just say it? I can handle it.'

'I will tell you, but you are not ready yet. The Memoria has not finished; you have more to explore.' D'Scover stood up and took a last look at the park. 'Show me more.'

Adam stood up too and shoved his hands deep into his pockets.

'I don't know what you want,' he shrugged. 'How am I supposed to give you what you want if you don't tell me? This is all way too much for my brain to cope with.'

'Just let your mind go, let the memories flow.' But as he spoke, the green of the park began to drift out of focus and was replaced with a dull red mass that wavered as though in a heat haze.

'I know where this is too!' Adam said as the image became clearer. 'It's the town centre, and that's the library building.'

As he said these words, the building snapped into sharp focus. Again D'Scover was impressed with the detail. The Memoria was as clear and vivid as if they were standing on the busy street looking at the building. People streamed past them in a hectic flow to and from their work. The road ran with car after car in a steady river of motorised metal. Adam stepped out into the road and walked briskly towards the library entrance. The cars coming towards him just passed around him, as though engaged in an effortless and well-choreographed dance.

D'Scover watched this, pleased again at this boy's seemingly natural ability to accept the Memoria and to understand its capabilities. He seemed to have no fear. D'Scover followed Adam into the entrance hall of the library and through its squeaky turnstile on to the main floor.

'I loved this place,' Adam said as he entered the building. 'Always warm and safe. No one could try and rob you or sell you drugs in here. The librarians liked me and I could just read all day or use the computer, even have a bit of a kip if I wanted. Best place in the world. Look,' he said, in an almost reverential tone, 'my favourite chair.'

He ran over and patted a low chrome-framed chair that stood tucked away deep in the maze of book-filled shelves.

'I'm gonna miss you, old friend,' he said solemnly to the piece of battered furniture.

'You will miss a chair?' D'Scover asked.

'I don't have anything else to miss, do I?'

The library faded and was replaced with another building, the homeless hostel where Adam had spent Christmas. After this came the Salvation Army soup kitchen and the smiling faces of the Army handing out food and blankets. Then images of cold alleys and rainy nights fading into the doorway where he had spent his last night and finally the hospice and its quiet, darkened corridors.

'I have to show you something,' D'Scover told him when the Memoria settled once more. 'I am afraid this may be painful for you.'

'Why do you have to show me?' Adam asked nervously. 'Don't show me if it's horrible.'

'I must show you because it is important and because you have not shown it to yourself. It is a condition of the Memoria that you expel all emotional dead weight,' he explained. 'I can sense that there is a memory long hidden deep in your psyche; you may not

34

know you even possess it, but it presses on your consciousness and so must be seen.'

'You can see inside my head?'

'No, but you are still here in this Memoria, and so there must be something stopping you from releasing these images. I shall attempt to unlock them, if I may?'

Adam nodded and D'Scover lifted his arms and spread them wide as though opening curtains. The hospice whirled from view, torn away to be replaced with a small room full of sunshine. Dust motes hung in the afternoon sun, slowly spiralling in a fluid pattern in the languid air. Sunlight cut through the shadows above a desk where a young woman, no more than a girl, sat opposite an ashen-faced middle-aged woman. The girl clutched tightly at a chubby baby that lay sleeping peacefully across her tiny lap. His thick pink legs hung down over the edge, occasionally twitching gently in his sleep, deep in his innocent dreams.

'He should go to someone who can take care of him,' she pleaded as slow tears rolled down her cheeks. 'You will make sure, won't you? I just can't look after him myself. He needs a proper family. I can't be a mother to him, and I never even wanted him. It was an accident and his father's no good. I can't be with him and I just can't have a baby – it's not right. He should be with someone who actually wants him. He'll be safe with someone else, someone who can feed him properly and give him everything he deserves, someone who'll actually love him because I don't. You will make sure of all that, won't you?'

The older woman walked to a tall grey filing cabinet and pulled a file out of the top drawer. Slapping it down on the table, she pulled out a number of sheets of paper and pushed them across the desk towards the girl.

'You must sign this release for the boy, and the other paperwork is all just standard.' She smiled a grim smile. 'And we'll take care of everything else. You mustn't worry; we have a number of families who are keen to take good care of such a bonny baby.'

The girl leaned forward and looked at the sheets of paper, scanning them through, but not reading them.

'It's all very standard, I can assure you,' the woman said.

'And you're sure I'll never have to see him again?' the girl asked, hesitating as she reached out for the pen. 'It'll be just as if I never had him, as if I'd never had a baby at all?'

The woman nodded and the girl took the pen from the desk and signed a childish and unpractised signature at the bottom of the page. A button was pressed on the desk, a sharp buzz could be heard through the wall and a gangly woman in a nurse's uniform entered.

'She'll take good care of him, won't she?' the girl pleaded.

The older woman nodded and the girl stood up with the still sleeping baby lying oblivious to his impending abandonment in her arms. She kissed him on the forehead and held him tight.

'I'll always remember you,' she whispered. 'You might not believe me, but one day you'll know I did this for you, for the best.'

She handed the baby to the nurse, and he did not even stir from his slumber. The nurse walked from the room, letting the door swing shut heavily behind her. The noise it created ran like a gunshot through the room, and the girl crumpled into the chair, torn apart by great sobs that she could barely breathe through.

'STOP!' Adam screamed and the Memoria froze.

D'Scover had never seen it do this; it faded out but never stopped with such a clear image like this. He swung his arm out and the room looked as though a thick veil had been pulled across it. Adam turned his face away.

'I did warn you it would be emotionally painful,' D'Scover said. 'But you needed to see it.'

'That was my mother,' Adam said blankly. 'My real mother, that was her, wasn't it?'

'Her image lay deep in your memory from when you were a baby.'

36

'I want to see her now. I want to see her and … and tell her … and just say that …' He slid down and sat on the floor, or rather on the grey smudge that currently represented the floor. 'Who am I kidding? I don't know what I want.'

D'Scover walked over and sat down next to him.

'She thought she was doing the best for you,' he said gently. 'It may not mean a lot to you now, but she did do it for what she thought were the right reasons, you have to understand that.'

'NO!' Adam stood quickly and turned his tear-stained face away from D'Scover. 'I have to know for myself why she gave me away. Please, I have to know. I want to see her NOW.'

Adam looked back to the veiled Memoria and curled his small fists at his sides; turning his face upwards, he began to scream. Above the two of them a swirling black mass began to descend and envelop them both. Adam's scream became the noise of the wind and in the middle of the black cyclone he stood with his eyes closed and his hair whipped around by the rush of air. D'Scover grabbed him by the shoulders and shook him hard, trying to snap him out of the hurt rage that possessed him.

'ADAM!' D'Scover yelled. 'THIS WILL NOT WORK. YOU CANNOT FORCE THIS!'

Adam opened his eyes and looked hard at D'Scover and the wind fell like a stone. D'Scover stared at Adam through the stillness and realised the boy was looking past him at something behind. He let go of the boy's thin shoulders and turned slowly. Behind him there was another green space, a garden this time with a smaller swing set and slide and a tiny weedy pond. Next to the pond sat a young woman in a deckchair, a discarded book in her lap. Time had passed, but there was no mistaking the face of the young girl who had given up her baby over fourteen years earlier. She carried a thin but content smile as she stared down the garden, watching something. A child of about three years old played in a sandpit a few metres away, driving a bright red truck backwards and forwards, scattering sand over the edges into the grass.

'Adam,' D'Scover said softly, 'you cannot stay here; we have to move on.'

Adam crouched down by the child and looked into his face. The child remained unaware of Adam's presence and carried on playing his simple digging game.

'This should be me.' Adam looked over his shoulder at D'Scover. 'If I'd not been born when I was, if I'd not been an accident, I could've been *this* kid.'

'No,' D'Scover said gently, 'that is not the way it works. *You* were *you*. This child has a different spirit and will live out *his* life. Your life is over and however tragic, brutal and short your existence was, it was still *your* existence. You have had your time; this is his time,' D'Scover explained. 'We have to leave now.'

Adam ignored him, and instead walked over to where the woman sat.

'My mother.' He said the words carefully, experimentally. 'I don't think I've ever said that out loud before. I've cried it in my sleep, and wished it in my dreams, but never said it out loud. It sounds strange.' He looked closely into her face. 'Mother.'

Leaning forward, he kissed her cheek lightly. He reeled back as she shuddered and her hand flew to the spot where his lips had briefly rested. Staggering back a few more steps, he reached D'Scover.

'She felt it!' he gasped, turning to stare into D'Scover's face. 'How the bloody hell did she feel it? This isn't real, is it?'

'This is *not* real; you are imagining what she would do and have constructed this to suit what you imagine will happen,' D'Scover said, but he sounded unconvinced. 'We have to leave this place.'

His voice was cold as he once more reached into the air and pulled across the veil and they were standing in another dark room.

'Where are we now?' Adam asked.

'Where we always were,' D'Scover replied. 'The place in which you died.'

Adam looked around and realised that they were in the hospice. The room was still empty and the bed had been stripped, but Adam recognised it and, inexplicably, he felt safe here.

'I have to leave you here for now,' D'Scover said. 'I have some work to do at my offices, but I will return shortly.'

'Leave? But what am I going to do while you're gone?'

'I will place you in Dispersal so that you do not disturb anyone here.'

'Dispersal? You make me sound like weedkiller,' Adam said sullenly. 'What's Dispersal?'

'We can only hold our substance for a few hours at a time. After that our solid appearance is affected and we start to look too, well, faint and ghostly,' D'Scover explained. 'We need to Disperse, to scatter ourselves into the ether, allow ourselves time to build our substance again. You will not be able to control your own substance yet and so I will have to put you into Dispersal.'

'I thought it was over. I thought I could do that Passing thing now and be done with it?'

'Not quite yet. I need to confirm some details first. You will not be aware of the passage of time whilst in Dispersal,' D'Scover explained. 'Sister Goodman will watch out for you whilst you are here.'

'Whatever.' Adam shrugged and turned away, his face wracked with sadness.

D'Scover watched the boy's thin shape in the darkness and decided against trying to talk to him about what had happened in his Memoria. Instead he stood behind him and held his hands out, palms facing towards the boy. He took a deep breath and the boy began to break up into angry red pellets that swirled in the room like scattered blood before they exploded into nothingness, absorbed by the black shadows of the room.

Chapter Six – Old Friends

'Impressive.'

'I am glad that you agree. I have never known *any* spirit with enough strength to change the Memoria on the first attempt.'

'No, I meant the view.'

Sister Goodman turned from the glass wall to look back towards D'Scover, a broad grin on her round face.

'Sister, I did not Hotline you here just to see the view from my office,' D'Scover remonstrated.

'No, but it is impressive all the same. This new office of yours is a little modern for me, but you have good taste when it comes to artwork.' She walked around, looking at the many works of art that decorated the room. 'Of course you have had plenty of time to assemble such an impressive collection, have you not?'

The large square room was indeed like a small and very exclusive private art gallery. A dozen paintings filled two walls, and represented most of the history of art of the western world. From the Renaissance period there was a large icon of the Virgin Mary that was a perfect example of the then new art of Perspective. She gazed tragically out of her frame, resting one of her pale hands on an exquisite necklace, a rosary of beads carrying a single piece of curved metal, a crescent moon. A landscape of hills, a Calvary of crucifixes reeled back behind her demonstrating perfect depth. Around Mary, on the other walls of the office, hung paintings from every century since, each one a perfect example of the very best work of its time.

The display on the walls ended with a canvas of only two colours – slate grey below vibrant orange. The top colour bled into the bottom, creating a canvas that gave D'Scover a lot of pleasure. His long red couch stood opposite this painting and he spent a great deal of time sitting on it, deep in thought. Dotted around the office there stood a number of small but impressively ornate tables and these carried pieces of exquisite porcelain and glass. All of them were bowls and the collection stretched from the sixteenth century to the modern day; each piece was a one-off – no others existed like them anywhere in the world. D'Scover had seen to it that the moulds and designs were destroyed so no other bowl could be made; each was unique. Every piece of art in this private collection was worth a small fortune – not that money meant anything to D'Scover.

'I am pleased by things of beauty,' he offered as an explanation, running a vaporous finger round the rim of a cobalt-blue glass bowl.

'You were fortunate that the powers that be decided to build so close to your former home. How did you claim these offices for the Brotherhood?' the Sister asked.

'We still have considerable influence in high places,' he said. 'The Brotherhood carried out a number of clearance cases for a certain royal personage and these two upper floors were gifted to us by the Crown. Below us is a television company and film studios; the technology they utilise has been most useful to us.' He frowned at her. 'You are not addressing the issue. What is your opinion of this boy?'

Sister Goodman turned and walked back towards the desk and lowered her sturdy frame into his blood-red leather desk chair.

'I think he could possibly be what you have waited for, but it is still too early to tell,' she said. 'You know as well as I do that a Trial is the only thing that can prove his will and strength.'

'But what Trial? It has been centuries since anyone was strong enough to even consider one and he is just a boy. Admittedly he has life experience beyond his years, but he is still just a child,' D'Scover said, pacing around the office.

'They all were,' she reminded him. 'Granted, they had more time to settle in, but the Vision dictated that they were all children.'

'In any case, the old Trials are not even possible now, not in these days of dense population. How could we consider a full Demon Trial with the possible loss of life that might entail? The last one of those was over two hundred years ago and, if my memory serves me, on the Russian Steppes. With modern satellite imaging, that kind of heat would be lit up like a flare. The military would be on it before we could do anything,' D'Scover said in an anguished tone as he paced the floor. 'I am at a loss. It is the boy's right to have a Trial, but how can we use such antiquated methods today?'

'Calm yourself, Toby,' Sister Goodman told him as she swivelled the chair to face him. 'Your affection for the living has always baffled me. For heaven's sake, we could manipulate them however we desired and simply erase all memory of the event. There has been no need for a Trial for two centuries, that much is true, but why should it be antiquated? There must be one that is appropriate for today. Have you consulted the Texts?'

'No, it has been a long time since there has been need to.' He stared down at the city below through the rain-streaked windows.

She rose and walked to his side. The wind whipped around the balcony, carrying the few remaining leaves up from the trees far below and whirling them around the damp concrete surface. She placed her hand on his arm and forced him to turn and face her.

'This is not a weakness, Toby. The Texts are there for a reason, and it is time you consulted them,' she said in a firm but gentle voice. 'This is not about you, it is about the boy. Have you considered looking for an aide?'

'No!' D'Scover snapped and shook his arm from her grip. 'I will consult the Texts, but it is not time to call for an aide, not yet. I am not ready to give him over and, from your time on the Council, you know that will happen if I have to summon assistance. They will step in and assert an authority that I will not be allowed to resist.'

'As you wish,' she replied coldly, 'but promise me that you will consider every option should the answer not arise from the Texts.'

'I will,' he assured her, 'but I will not consider raising an aide yet or reaching out to the past. The portents are not yet right.'

'I understand that there has been quite an increase in spirit activity already, even the reactivation of dormant spirits,' Sister Goodman said carefully. 'Maybe even a fire starter?'

'How did you know that?' D'Scover rounded angrily on her. 'Did one of my agents tell you? That is a breach of …'

'Calm yourself,' she interrupted, 'You forget that I am still an Attendant to the Senior Council.'

'Of course.' D'Scover relaxed. 'I apologise for snapping at you, but I insist on total confidentiality from my agents. I will not deny that there is an increase in unauthorised activity, but it does not worry me yet.'

'So where is the boy now?'

'I have placed him in Dispersal back at the hospice; he is safe there for a while.'

'Promise me that you will consider every option?' She repeated her earlier question. 'Do you keep the Texts close to you – are they close at hand?'

'Yes, I will consider every option, and you can be assured that the Texts are safely guarded,' he replied. 'They have been safe with me for centuries, and you know that I cannot discuss their whereabouts, even with you.'

'Of course.' She patted his arm reassuringly. 'What was I thinking?' She wrinkled her nose as she looked around.

'You know, Toby, this room may look impressive, but it does not smell very good,' she said, deftly changing the subject. 'You should get some air in here. I suppose that you are too important for anyone to point out the obvious.'

'I have very few visitors.'

'The presence of the boy may be a good reason to get a bit of fresh air in here once in a while, just in case the place gets too stuffy,' she said maternally. 'Leave the window open whilst you Disperse, there's a good fellow.'

He leaned forward and hugged her awkwardly, and she looked totally shocked.

'Well!' she said, stepping back. 'What was that for?'

'Just for never changing,' he replied. 'Thank you, I always know I can trust you.'

'Well, if you cannot trust me, who can you trust?' she said. 'Toby, I had better get back. It has been wonderful visiting you, but if you want to expend such a lot of energy and Hotline me, could it be somewhere hot and sunny and with significantly less members of the living?'

'Anywhere you wish,' he said, and managed one of his weak smiles.

'And it would not do you any harm to work on that smile either,' she playfully chided.

She stood next to the desk and took her CC from her pocket. She rested it in her right hand and waited while D'Scover isolated the location of the hospice and called up the remote terminal details. When they were fully logged in, he nodded in her direction and she rested her finger on her CC.

'Goodbye, Toby. Keep me informed, won't you?' she asked.

'I will,' D'Scover said, 'and thank you.'

He placed his fingertips on the screen and almost immediately Sister Goodman began to destabilise. Blue sparks danced around

D'Scover's fingertips as the Hotline began to take hold. Where Sister Goodman had once stood there now lingered a fading image, gradually breaking apart into millions of vivid violet fragments. They whirled in a bright mist that sparkled and glittered as it spiralled next to the desk. Then, with a fierce final crackle from D'Scover's fingertips, the mist rushed into the screen and was gone.

D'Scover leaned back and rubbed his hands together, staring at the plan of the hospice until he saw the yellow dot that represented Sister Goodman once more walk the corridors.

A light tap on his door broke his concentration. 'Come!' he called out. Emma opened the door and leaned into the room.

'I have Marcus Resnick on line four, sir. Do you want to talk to him?'

'Marcus?' D'Scover waved his diary open to the current date. 'Blast, it is the sixteenth. I said that I was going to call him in today. Yes, thank you, Emma, you can put him through.'

A moment later the computer screen faded out to be replaced with an image. With his sallow skin, short and dirty black hair and, as always, looking as if he could use a good wash, Marcus looked nervous, but his already pale complexion seemed even more ghostly than usual.

'Are you ready to come in?' D'Scover asked abruptly.

'Yes, sir, but it won't be a full Hotline, will it? Those things make me weak for days and, to be honest, I'm having a bit of trouble with my substance lately,' he whined.

'Very well, I shall just boost you via your CC so that we can talk without interruption. Could you Disperse, please, and I will pull you in?' D'Scover said.

Marcus nodded and closed his eyes, still holding his CC parallel with his face. The CC had taken over a century to develop, but it had been worth the wait. It allowed two-way communication over huge distances and could only be used by the spirit registered to do so. It Dispersed with its user and, if it came into the possession of a living person, just crumbled to dust in seconds

45

and gave off a restriction charm so that the strange box was forgotten moments after it vanished. It was a device that had revolutionised the Brotherhood, and D'Scover regarded it as one of his finest works.

A flickering shape began to form in the room, and as D'Scover tapped a few more keys on the keyboard, it became clearer. Eventually a hologrammatic image of Marcus Resnick stood before D'Scover in the office.

'Hello, sir,' he said when his outline became clear enough.

'I shall get straight to the point.' D'Scover removed a file from the desk drawer and opened it in front of him. 'I have had a number of complaints from other agents that they have seen you in their zones. Can you explain that to me?'

'I've had a bit of a drift problem. When I Disperse, I …'

'Do not give me that nonsense,' D'Scover interrupted. 'Drift is never a problem on the scale you are claiming here. I am giving you the opportunity to explain; do not waste it.'

Marcus looked at his feet and thought for a while, plainly weighing up whether to tell the truth or not.

'I'm not happy where I am and I've been kind of looking for somewhere else to settle,' he muttered.

'Marcus, Marcus,' D'Scover sighed, 'you know that reallocations are only done with the full consent of the Senior Council. You simply cannot just decide to go off somewhere else. What would happen to the Brotherhood if we all decided to drift off to wherever we pleased whenever we felt like it?'

'I don't know,' Marcus mumbled.

'Chaos, that is what would happen, Marcus!' D'Scover flicked through the pages of Marcus's file. 'Why are you unhappy? South Kensington is one of the better locations in London, after all. Plenty of older buildings, a large concentration of Brotherhood agents, you are hardly lonely.'

'I was an RTA, a road traffic accident. My location is literally in the middle of the road. I hate it. It was tolerable here thirty years ago, but today the road is just so crowded and the noise is overwhelming and keeping out of sight is virtually impossible,' Marcus explained. 'I just wanted to save the Brotherhood some work and figured if I could find a suitable location then I could apply for a reallocation with all the details complete.'

'Hmmm.' D'Scover did not look up, instead jotting some notes down as he spoke. 'So you do not wish to leave the Brotherhood and take the Final Dispersal?'

'No, sir, I certainly don't. I feel strongly about the Brotherhood and very much want to remain a part of it. I'm very loyal,' Marcus insisted.

'Hmmm, that is as maybe.' D'Scover looked up. 'I have considered your case and am able to offer you a reallocation.'

'Really?' Marcus gasped. 'That easy?'

'I guessed you were angling for one and so I submitted a request on your behalf last week and it has been approved. You have done some good work for the Brotherhood in the past and you have been a useful agent, if a little erratic, and that warrants some flexibility,' he replied.

'Great, I have a location in mind, over in Russell Square; it'd be just perfect for ...' Marcus blurted.

'It is not up to you to choose the location, Marcus,' D'Scover interrupted. 'You will be reallocated to the Natural History Museum. Not a great distance, but your new location will, however, be inside and that should please you somewhat. The building is of a suitable age and size to house multiple spirits. You will share the location with two other agents, one of whom is very senior, and two spirits who are tied to the building.

'The spirits who are tied to the building are *not* agents and are *not* Brotherhood aware; see that it remains so,' D'Scover warned. 'I will contact the senior agent in the museum and she will arrange a residential area for you within the building. She is very influential and has a connection with the Senior Council and so I suggest you listen very carefully to her advice and do nothing to antagonise her. All work conditions will remain the same; discretion is your watchword.'

'Yes, sir, absolutely,' Marcus answered, but he did not sound happy. 'Sir, could I not just …'

'That will be all, Marcus,' D'Scover interrupted. 'Your reallocation is immediate. I will be in touch.' He tapped the ESC key and Marcus was gone.

He added all of Marcus's comments to his file and, folding all of the notes back into the folder, picked it up once more. He leaned out into the reception area where Emma sat at her desk as usual, flicking her gaze over the four active screens in front of her. These screens held details of agents the world over and needed constant monitoring as reports of spirit violation came in. Most spirits needed no assistance in passing over: three to mourn and they slipped into their Passing without a struggle. The unloved and ungrieved-for needed the Brotherhood to aid their passage and it was Emma – his ever-efficient secretary – who assigned agents to do just that.

Some spirits were destined to be trapped forever in the place where they had died, regardless of how many people had grieved for them. These were the tragic spirits with unfinished business in the realm of the living. The Brotherhood usually left these alone to Disperse over time – unless they became problematical. On rare occasions, a trapped spirit caused trouble for the living and D'Scover, or a select few agents that he trusted, dealt with these cases. These reports had become fewer and fewer each decade, until recently.

Emma still prioritised any report of spirit disturbance, no matter how minor it appeared, as occasionally a spirit showed a particular sign of compatibility and could be recruited into the Brotherhood. Such sensitive spirits were rare, none had been found now for nearly a decade, but the search still went on. Recently Emma's time had been taken up logging reports of disturbances and unauthorised hauntings.

'Emma,' D'Scover called. 'I have given Marcus Resnick a real-location to the Natural History Museum. Will you contact one of the agents inside and sort the details for me?'

'Certainly, sir,' she replied. 'Will you be Dispersing now … or will Sister Goodman be visiting again? I just wondered …'

'I will be Dispersing very soon,' he interrupted, 'but I would like a Code Red placed on my office to lock it down for at least six hours. I have some papers to work on and I do not want any interruptions. I will Disperse afterwards.'

'Yes, sir, not a problem.'

He turned back towards his office and Emma's hand hovered over the panel in the desk that would apply the Code Red. Before he closed the door he turned back to face her.

'Emma, would you give me an honest answer about something?' he asked.

'If I can, sir, yes,' she replied.

'Do you trust her?' he asked. 'Julie, I mean, the new secretary.'

'Well.' She shuffled uncomfortably in her seat. 'I really don't know her very well yet, but she was in a position of great trust before she died and the Senior Council feel that that trust should not have been damaged by her Passing,' Emma said. 'She died a natural death of cancer after a short illness. There's nothing in her file to suggest that she shouldn't be trusted.'

'So you have read her complete file?' he queried. 'I am not sure it is appropriate for you to read such documents. Do you read all files of this nature?'

'I've only read the files of all the people who have close access to you,' she reassured him. 'It's part of my job description to be aware of anything that may affect you or this department. Is there any specific concern that you have about Julie?'

'No, at least not yet,' D'Scover replied enigmatically and walked back into his office, allowing the Code Red to seal the door closed behind him.

Alone in the huge room again, he strode towards the icon of the

Virgin Mary. He gazed at the gilt-framed image for a few minutes as if awaiting approval from the serene face on the blue-cloaked young woman. Breaking concentration, he raised his hands, palms facing upwards, and began to murmur in a low, indistinct voice. A steady hum began to fill the room and the air prickled with static electricity. Silver sparks began to appear around his hands, running over them in a seething, almost living, pattern – like tiny, dazzling insects. He turned his hands towards each other and pinched his fingertips closed, then, with a movement that looked as though he was trying to tear the air itself, he pulled them apart.

The silver mass collected in the space between his fingertips and started to form a shape in the air. D'Scover lowered his hands to his sides and waited for the shape to settle. Gradually the rain of sparks calmed into a silver haze that hung like a mirage in front of him. In the centre of the wavering light there lay a key. It was the silver crescent that had been hanging round the neck of the Madonna in the painting and now it shimmered in the air in front of him. D'Scover held his hand under it and it dropped, ice-cold, into his palm. The key was so thin that it could only be seen straight on. From the edge it was still as two-dimensional as it had been in the painting and it looked as though it was no more than a brief wobble in the air..

He closed his hand round it and, with his empty one, gestured for the balcony doors to open. Obediently they slid back and out he walked on to the windswept balcony.

The weather had changed and the breeze that had once toyed with the leaves now ripped around the building like an angry beast. D'Scover shifted his substance to allow the sharp wind to pass through him as he walked the length of the balcony to the end where the blank wall looked out over the sprawling city. He turned to face the wall, opened his hand carefully and looked at the key that lay in his hand, stuck fast under a lustrous silver haze. Lifting the key hand, he placed it against the wall, palm first, and the silver haze bled out from underneath, forming a liquid that coursed over the brickwork and ran along the mortar cracks like mercury through a maze. The silver liquid soon crept across a large rectangle area on the wall in front of him and then, abruptly, it stopped and sank in. Gradually the bricks and mortar began to blur and fade away until they were replaced instead with a smooth black stone surface shot through with silver veins. D'Scover stood back and waited for it to finish taking shape and, with the hollow sound of stone scraping against stone, a door appeared.

Chapter Seven – The Keeper of the Texts

The huge dark room had only a weak square of light at its centre. This trickled down from a glass pyramid that rose from the ceiling, cutting into the churning winter sky. D'Scover looked up to see the bruise-coloured clouds tear across above him, pushed rapidly by a vicious and aggressive wind.

He walked across the dark room with the confidence of someone who knew every square centimetre of this cavernous space. At the circular table in the middle of the large square room, he reached out and waved his hands over it and a green glass lamp standing in its centre gradually illuminated much of the room, forcing the shadows into reluctant retreat. The conjured light oozed slowly like glowing treacle into all four corners of the room and showed the walls to be entirely covered with books. Tall mahogany shelves climbed to the ceiling and towered over D'Scover, groaning under the weight of countless tomes. Volumes of all description were crammed into this library and each looked older than the last with the oldest of all high up on the soaring shelves.

Walking towards one of the bookcases, D'Scover counted his way along, looking for just the right one. Stepping backwards into the thin pall of natural light, he cast his eye to the very top where the cobwebs hung like gossamer bunting in a macabre parody of decoration. Still staring upwards, he gestured towards the remaining shadows in the darkest area furthest from the light and a narrow wooden ladder, supported by a rail on one of the uppermost shelves, rolled towards him, stopping just a few centimetres away. He climbed up and, as he reached the upper level, brushed away the cobwebs to reveal the ancient texts beneath.

As he pulled one from the shelf, it sent a cloud of spiralling dust into the room, which caught the thin light and danced around him. Ignoring the dust, he opened the book and scanned down a few pages quickly before replacing it. The ladder moved steadily along from shelf to shelf and D'Scover continued to pull out book after book, each time searching the pages carefully for the correct content. Occasionally something would catch his attention and he would place a text carefully in the air behind him and gradually it would descend to rest on the table below, drifting slowly like a leaf dropped by the wind.

Time passed and the pile grew; soon nothing could be seen of the table except the brass stem of the lamp and its glowing green shade. D'Scover looked at the table and grudgingly descended from his lofty perch and returned to the desk. Pulling an imposing oak chair towards him, he sat and gave a beckoning gesture to the lamp. The light from it dutifully crawled back towards him and arranged itself in a thick golden puddle, concentrating its greatest strength over the chosen volumes. D'Scover opened the first one and began to read.

The paper was brittle with age and only D'Scover's carefully diminished substance allowed him to turn the pages without them shattering in his hands. The Texts had been in the possession of the Brotherhood since its founding, but many were much older. Father Dominic had collected manuscripts from all over the world, from the small works of fables by twelfth–century scholars and the human-skin-covered grimoire of the fourteenth century, to the sixteenth-century works in his own hand.

The history of civilisation was laid out between these faded covers on countless elaborately decorated pages. Here fabulous animals and flowers of all description wound their way round the words of teachers from many centuries. Across this parchment landscape marched the armies of Kublai Khan, hunting for now extinct animals, and unicorns pranced among a twisting maze of vines. Armies fought long-forgotten battles on a world that was most assuredly as flat as a plate, and kings brutally seized blood-stained land they believed was by right of God theirs, only to have another god instruct his minions to seize it back a century later. Each manuscript appeared to glitter in the half-light as the heavily applied gold leaf curled up, flaking from flowers and borders.

D'Scover read on, carefully transposing some key phrases into a small brown leather-bound notebook. Once an entry caught his eye, his finger hovered above the section and, as he moved his finger from line to line, the words formed on the open pages of the notebook as though soaking through from inside the paper itself. The pages filled and the weak winter daylight began to fade as the clouds above the Text Chamber split to reveal a sky dotted with sharp white points of starlight. After many hours, and with his substance beginning to weaken, he pushed the books away across the table and laid his hands flat on the patinated surface. Taking a long inbreath, he pursed his lips and blew a sigh across the table, ruffling the pages of the books and making them jitter.

'It must be here,' he muttered to the empty room.

He cupped his hands together, curving one hand round the other to form a bowl, and breathed into it. A cascade of blue sparks rolled into his hands, whirling and twisting until he could hold no more. Squeezing his hands together, he crushed the blue light, causing sparks to pop out and skitter across the table. When he opened his hands again, a small blue sphere lay in his white blood-less palm. Holding it up, allowing the moonlight to fall through it, he could see the indigo clouds roll around inside. After a few moments the outline of a human head started to form within the clouds. As the image cleared, it triggered a memory within D'Scover and he dropped the ball. It rolled along the table, tumbling from the edge and disappearing in a glittering blue shower before it hit the floor.

D'Scover pulled one of the books out from the bottom of the pile and briskly flicked through the pages until he found the one he was looking for. A treatise on witchcraft from the seventeenth century lay open in front of him with its pages bearing many later additions in an inky scrawl. On one of these pages was a detailed drawing of the trial of a young witch in Hertfordshire. In this drawing the young girl sat, with a defiant expression, tightly tied to a post in the middle of a village green. The crowd around her looked angry and many of them raised farm tools above their heads. The account of the trial listed her supposed crimes, the crimes that damned her to a public burning. The book told how, among other acts of witchcraft, she had cured a child of deafness, pulled back a tree that had been blown over on to a house and diverted a flood that threatened a family's crop. The picture of the so-called trial was small, but even so D'Scover could see that this witch was the same girl he had seen form in the ball.

'Another piece of the puzzle,' he said to himself.

D'Scover stretched out his arms and looked over the piles of manuscripts on the table. He became aware that his substance was so weak that he was only barely managing to hold his shape. His arms had become a thin grey shadow of his usual form and his hands were almost transparent. One by one he gestured for the books to return to their places on the shelves and they rose slowly and gracefully to slot themselves into their niches once more. When the table was cleared, all that remained upon it was his full notebook and the book containing the witch trial. Standing up, he gestured for the table to move to one side, and this it obediently did.

Once the floor space was clear, D'Scover took his place beneath the glass pyramid and turned his face towards it. He stretched his hands aloft and the great glass sheets of the pyramid opened to expose the cold night sky. D'Scover began to softly chant his Ritual of Dispersal and, after his grey vortex scattered into the darkness, the pyramid silently closed behind him.

'How do you feel?'

'Hard to explain really. I don't feel dead, I actually feel kind of … alive.'

'Adam,' D'Scover turned the boy to face him, 'you must let that feeling go. You are dead and nothing will change that. There is nothing in the known universe that can make you alive again. You have had your time.'

'You really do love a speech, don't you?' Adam sighed. 'You asked, I answered. This is all new to me and I don't know what answers you want so I just tell you the truth.'

The hospice was in darkness and, as the offices were empty, D'Scover had managed to Hotline into one unseen. Adam had been a little tricky to find as a first Dispersal into a building of that size often caused drift. D'Scover eventually tracked him down to the mortuary and pulled him back into the empty office he had just used. Adam's old room was now occupied and so restabilising in there was no longer an option.

'What was your Dispersal like?' D'Scover asked.

'D'you actually want to know or is that another question that I should give a dumbed-down answer to?' Adam said.

'Adam, I know that you are angry, but it will pass. It is quite natural at this stage to …'

'Look, I'm sorry, I'm not really angry. I don't mean to seem angry. I'm finding it hard to understand all of this, I think I want it all to end. Please, just tell me what you want from me and let me go,' he pleaded. 'I'm sure I'm not cut out for all this. If I'm dead and I've dealt with all that memory stuff, then why am I still here?' He waved his hands at the blank walls of the cramped space. 'Am I always going to be here, haunting this place?'

D'Scover sighed and walked over to the computer, removing his CC from his pocket and placing it back on the blank screen.

'I think that it is time we had a proper talk,' he said. 'We will go to my offices and I will explain as best as I can.'

'At last!' Adam said, walking over to where D'Scover was holding his hand against the screen. 'Hey, you have to use the keyboard on that and not the screen, you know – or do you ghosts not have technology yet?'

The screen began to ripple and turn purple and the familiar blue sparks crackled across the matt surface, gathering pace as they started to swirl.

'Oh, we have technology,' D'Scover said to a stunned Adam. 'We have plenty of technology.'

The sparks spread out and Adam stumbled backwards in the darkness, trying to move out of their reach, but D'Scover grabbed for his arm and pulled him into the enveloping neon light. Adam twisted around in panic as the sparks grasped at him and began to swarm over his arm. Once the first lick of sparks had touched his arm, he became rapidly absorbed in a swift wave of blue crackling light, and then was gone … All that remained was a red spiral that shimmered in the darkness for a second and vanished.

'Whoa, now that was amazing!' Adam gasped. 'How did we do that? Where the hell are we?'

He now stood in a darkened office high up, looking down on the blinking lights of the city.

'Just a tweak on your friend technology, and we are in my offices,' D'Scover answered. 'When we Disperse, we can take advantage of the Internet, telephone lines, wireless connections, all manner of electronic systems; it is just a question of opening the right pathway and sliding in.'

'Can anyone do it? I mean, can anyone dead do it?'

'No,' D'Scover explained, busying himself at his desk. 'It is a difficult procedure and one that is exclusively managed by the Brotherhood.'

'The Brotherhood?'

'Take a seat,' D'Scover gestured towards the couch, 'I have a lot to explain.'

Adam turned, taking in D'Scover's private collection. 'Is this some kind of art gallery?'

'No, as I said, this is my office.'

'Tasteful,' Adam grinned. 'You must earn a mint.'

'I earn no money for what I do,' D'Scover replied.

'Still, looks like you don't exactly go without though, do you?'

'There is nothing I require, no.'

Adam flopped down on the couch and leaned back into a softly yielding corner of the large piece of furniture.

'Very classy, comfy. None of your superstore rubbish here, eh?'

'Adam,' D'Scover's voice had taken on an even more sombre tone, 'I am prepared to give you the answers that you need.'

'That's all very well, Mr Mysterious,' replied Adam, 'but I don't know what the questions are, do I? Can I have a clue?'

D'Scover sighed. 'Maybe if I explained more about the Brotherhood, you would have a greater understanding.'

'Worth a shot.' Adam swivelled round to put his feet up on the couch and rested his hands behind his head. 'Let's give it a go.'

'I will not be explaining this in the conventional fashion; it is a little more complicated than I have time for. I will use a technique I developed for the Brotherhood.'

'You're the boss,' Adam quipped. 'Bring it on.'

'Adam, please try to take this seriously.'

'I am.' Adam sat up again. 'Honest, I'll be serious.'

D'Scover turned from him and made a gesture in the air with his fingers. The chair from his desk swivelled round and slid across the room towards him and he sat down, facing Adam.

'You have to show me how to do that stuff.' Adam pointed at the chair. 'That is too cool.'

'Close your eyes and listen carefully to my voice.' D'Scover ignored Adam's comment and carried on. 'Let the images come into your mind and do not resist anything that happens.'

'Well, that all sounds totally creepy, but if you say so.' Adam closed his eyes and rested his head on the cushions of the couch.

'*In the sixteenth century,*' D'Scover began, '*Europe was ruled then as now by kings and politics, but disease and poverty were its real masters and had been so for centuries. Plague still marched across the civilised world and poverty was both companion and assistant to this horror.*'

D'Scover's voice had fallen to a soft tone that lulled Adam into listening closely, and as he did so, he realised that the edges of the room had begun to blur. He could no longer make out every word that D'Scover was saying, and felt he must be falling asleep. Shadows walked at the edges of his vision and dark shapes loomed around them. The shadows gradually began to take a stronger shape and he could see that they were people in simple, ragged clothes moving between dirty, rustic buildings. Soon the office had faded completely to be replaced by a perfect tableau that looked as if it had fallen from the pages of a history book.

Adam turned about himself with a start and looked upon a scene that was apparently solid and real; he marvelled at the detail of his dream. He jumped back in fear as a cart rumbled past him along a muddy road, throwing up a shower of earth and water, and realised this was more than just a vision. He looked down at his legs and saw that the filthy water had passed straight through him. The people around him were not the illusion here – he was.

Around him everyone carried on with their daily grind of work, but to Adam it looked as though food was not part of this equation. The people were thinner than anyone he had ever seen. Even in the homeless hostels and crowded doorways of London no one had looked as near to death as the gathering he saw before him. Children carried baskets of wood past him and Adam could see nothing but the spectre of a young death in their grey faces. He walked on, turning away as the pathetic wretches came close to him. He knew how it must have been for those who had once passed him by in the streets towards the end of his own life. It was not that they didn't care, just that they didn't know what to do to make it better.

Forcing himself to watch, he continued through the village, stepping over rivers of human waste as he went, despite the fact that he knew it could not touch him. Some of the villagers staggered from house to house with dirty bandages flapping from their diseased limbs. Others recoiled in horror as they passed and clutched their filthy sleeves to their faces in a pathetic attempt to prevent infection. Adam knew from the rough plague crosses daubed on many doors that in these shabby houses lay the sick and dying.

D'Scover's words hung in the air, a gentle rhythm of sound that throbbed and built up this world of pestilence further.

'*Villages … struggled … poverty … plague … feudal lords … controlled … population … iron grip …*' D'Scover continued with his speech and as Adam listened to the soft, intermittent music of his voice around him, there unfolded a world as vivid and real as the one Adam had once lived in.

'*Plague … stronghold … weakened population … no resistance. Travelling … Europe … rats … decimated … cities … too few alive to bury … dead … superstition … ghosts stalked … living … demons … assumed … control … damned … village. Time passed … spectre of disease … rose from the darkness … slaughter more and more people … religious houses … met … discuss … solution.*'

Adam could see this world unfolding around him as real as if he had been born into it. D'Scover stood – a weak shadow by his side – explaining. The scene changed and began to fade from the foul horror of the villages to the towering mass of a great cathedral that now grew up around him. Its creamy walls climbed high above and brilliant light streamed in through a tall plain-paned glass window. Around him sat a large body of men, all dressed in elaborate, highly coloured robes.

Adam realised that these were the heads of religious houses, monks and priests, cardinals – men from all aspects of the religious world and from all over Europe gathered together. He saw and understood deeply that they could no longer cope with caring for those who were suffering. These realisations came to him in a rush that made his head spin. It was the most intensive history lesson imaginable as D'Scover laid out the monastic world and high-church life in front of Adam's stunned eyes.

The congregation shuffled uneasily in the dark wood high-backed chairs and a solemn murmur ran around the gathered men. An elderly abbot in a dark purple robe slowly and stiffly rose to his feet and cleared his throat. A hush descended on the gathering and he began to speak.

'Brothers,' he said in a voice heavy with age, 'this is the darkest time we have ever known.' A rumble of agreement rippled around him.

'The king moves closer to breaking down our great houses, closer than he has ever done before. If we do not take this threat seriously, then all of our efforts have been for nothing.'

The congregation clearly supported this man. Spurred on, he continued.

'Here we have gathered time after time, talking our throats raw, and still we have come no closer to an accord. All of you have made arrangements for your greatest texts and many have taken to moving silver and monies to places of safety.'

A hearty laugh burst from several of the older men who knew which of the priests the speaker was referring to.

'We have all taken steps to protect that which we hold dear, but it is not enough. We have an obligation to others. Try as we might to ignore the truth of this, we can no longer afford to do so. We must take the warnings of Father Dominic of the Benedictines seriously.'

With this statement, the crowd suddenly split angrily and faces began to grow red with the shouting. Some of the men stood and tried to shout down the abbot.

'HEAR ME!' he bellowed above the mêlée and they listened once more. 'Plague has irrevocably damaged the beliefs of our world. As more were taken by the pestilence, belief was diminished and the strength of our world is weakened. With less people to believe, more and more spirits have become trapped in the world of the living instead of passing on. Father Dominic's theories have been borne out. How many of you can say that you have not had reports from your diocese about spirits walking amongst the living? We must hear what Father Dominic has to say, and this threat must be dealt with. It is our solemn duty. That we can no longer question.'

He raised a fat hand and beckoned to a figure hidden in the shadows at the back of the nave. The sturdy form of Father Dominic walked into the light. Dogging his footsteps was a thin servant boy with an unruly mop of black hair. He stumbled as he attempted to keep up, trying not to drop the large bundle of papers and books in his arms. The congregation growled with dissent, but remained seated as the father walked into their midst and took his place in front of them. He waited a moment for the rumble to die down before he spoke.

'You are aware of my workings and of the Dissolution that comes upon us.' His soft voice made everyone lean forward to listen. 'It is my solemn belief that we must take action to prevent the world of the living from becoming overrun.' He looked around, waiting for a response; none came and so he continued. 'These papers,' he grabbed a large parchment scroll from his servant and held it aloft, 'list hundreds of reports from around the country. Spirits are not resting and the nation is in danger of being overrun with the dead. In the Augustinian priory of Lanercost in the north there is the bare start of a new Brotherhood, a Brotherhood that can cope with the demands laid upon us by the coming Dissolution.'

The abbey filled with sharp intakes of breath and more murmurs.

'This new Brotherhood will, with your agreement, remain a clandestine order. They must never be identified and must never be attached to one of our great houses as they must be able to act independently. This is why we have chosen the small priory at Lanercost to gather the necessary texts; these will be moved to a safe place should the Dissolution reach that far north. If necessary, we will continue to move them to keep them protected.'

'But how can this new order be any different?' a thin man with grey hair and long white robes called out from the midst of the crowd. 'What is the purpose of this? This new order will surely be broken apart, just as our orders will.'

'No, that will not happen,' Father Dominic responded. 'It will not be broken apart because it will not move within the world that we know. This will be an order of spirits – a Brotherhood of Shades.'

With that, the congregation stood and many shouted and even hurled prayer books across the floor to land inches from where Father Dominic stood. He gave a small bow to the angry crowd and spoke over them, but his words were lost to the chaos of noise.

'Fools!' a shrill voice came from the back of the congregation.

Everyone turned as a hooded figure stepped out of the shadows and walked on into the aisle. In one swift moment the hood was thrown back to reveal a thin, scruffy-looking girl with long and knotted brown hair. Outrage once more rippled through the gathered men.

'I said you are all fools!' she shouted. 'And, as sure as day follows night, you will all perish in your ignorance. This man,' she pointed at Father Dominic, 'brings you a way of preventing the inevitable creep of the dead into the world of the living and you shout him down. What vexes you here? Are you too afraid that he is right and that you will all be overcome?'

'Who let this girl child in here?' the white-robed monk bellowed. 'Servants, take her from here; this is a closed assembly.'

'I know of her!' another monk shouted. 'She is from a village close to my abbey. Seize her quickly; this meeting must not become common knowledge.' He spun on his heels and pointed at her, his face purple with rage. 'Her interest lies in our destruction,' he spat. 'She is a witch. She must not be allowed to live and tell of what she has seen.'

Several servants ran up the aisle, armed with swords, and surrounded the girl before one of them grabbed her arms and held her tight; another pointed a sword at her stomach.

'You will see,' the girl cried out. 'You fear my kind, but I will last longer than any of you. One day superstition and ignorance will be overcome and on that day you will all need the help of such as I.'

The guards grabbed her hard and bundled her from the nave. Chaos ensued as some of the monks used the interruption to leave while others shouted to Father Dominic to explain. The father thrust the scroll back into his servant's hands and, ignoring everyone's pleas, he turned away from the gathering.

'I will take my leave!' Father Dominic shouted. 'I will not be party to such murderous deeds.' At the door he turned back and bellowed once more.

'Think on!' he shouted. 'You will come to me before the year is out and ask for the help of the Brotherhood – that much I can promise you.'

Turning, he walked back into the shadows and was gone through the transept doors.

Adam looked around at the scarlet and angry faces of the men as, one by one, they began to filter out of the building into the night. He suddenly became aware that D'Scover was standing by his side in the empty abbey.

'What happened next?' Adam asked him.

'Father Dominic was correct. Within one year, the heads of the great houses sent representatives to talk to him and let him explain how his new Brotherhood would function. The good father had discovered a text that could manifest a spirit indefinitely. These spirits could then maintain the Brotherhood and continue to assist those passing ungrieved-for long after the monasteries had been forgotten. The father had also had visions, visions that he described as images of angels, including the Archangel Uriel, who explained the Ritual of Sustainment to him. This he recorded and adapted to suit the needs of his new Brotherhood. He believed that if the Brotherhood was formed entirely of spirits – Shades – then King Henry and his Dissolution of the Monasteries could not affect them. The plans were put into motion and five monks were chosen from five different holy orders to assist with the new Brotherhood. Franciscan, Benedictine, Carthusian, Augustinian and Dominican monks all represented the views of their houses and brought ancient texts to form a central library. They arrived with their servants to meet in one of the last abbeys to resist the Dissolution, a Benedictine abbey in Hertfordshire.'

The walls around Adam changed again and flaking-plaster pillars painted with vivid depictions of the crucifixion replaced the creamy stone of the previous abbey. He stood in a nave once more, but this one seemed much longer, and the wooden roof rose higher above him. The building was busy with the movement of monks in black habits bustling around, filling crates with everything that was not nailed down. Pews were pushed back and stacked one upon another in a messy heap of wood that cleared the aisle, allowing the men to rush backwards and forwards in their work.

Ahead of Adam, right at the end of the nave, stood four monks, two in robes of brown, one in white and one in black. The man in black was Father Dominic and he clutched a small, cream-coloured book close to his body. The other men stood by a long table draped in burgundy velvet that rested in front of the high altar. They pored over the many books that lay scattered across its surface. Overlooking them, the high altar screen rose almost to the roof. This simple wooden panelling bore no decoration save for a plain shelf carrying a large crystal crucifix that caught occasional beams of light and cast them in prismatic colours on to the illuminated texts.

'We shall never complete this,' one of the men complained. 'This is a fool's errand. We will all die in this task. Even as we speak, the king's men grow ever closer. They were expected in Wycombe only this morning. It is not a day's ride from here. It will be our legacy that we threw our final moments away on such a waste of time.'

'No,' Father Dominic insisted in his soft but forceful tone, 'it shall be done. We are closer than we have ever been. We just need a little more time, a few hours, and a suitable candidate. I have kept the Sisters of Southwark informed of our progress and all is in readiness for the first full trial of our methods. We must be patient as we do not know how much time ...'

A deafening pounding interrupted them as the great west door was hammered on. The men all looked to the monk who had rushed to the small spyhole in the door.

He called out to them. 'The king's men!'

'Our time is lost,' the white-robed monk said in an urgent tone, grabbing the books from the table. 'We must hasten from this place with these books; they must not fall into the hands of the king's men else it will give him all the evidence he needs to raze every monastery and convent to the ground.'

'Quickly!' Father Dominic shouted to the other Benedictines who had gathered near the door. 'Bar it well; it will give us a little time. The other doors are already sealed as I anticipated this. Where is my servant?'

'Here, father.' A young boy ran to his side.

'Boy, come with me. I have to add a little more to this text and then you must take it and the Master Text to the Sisters, as we have planned. You know what you must do?'

'Yes, father,' the boy replied. 'On my life, I shall see it done.'

'Good lad,' the father said and ruffled the boy's mop of black hair.

The monks rushed to make sure that all was copied into one great volume. The hammering on the door grew greater and the other monks began to drag all that they could move to the door to create a barricade. Pews were piled in front of the door and the stem of the tall brass lectern jammed through the oak handles.

Father Dominic hastily filled the final pages, ink spilling over his fingers as he dipped his quill with haste. A few last notes and, with the young servant hot on his heels, he ran into the recesses of the abbey to hide the texts from the king's men just as they burst into the building.

With a final crash, the oak door gave and with a splintering of wood, the soldiers smashed through and rode their great horses down the nave, swinging out their broadswords, cutting down all who stood in their way. Adam screamed at the scene played out right in front of him. The soldiers' swords cleaved into the walls, sparking wildly as they struck stone and leaving deep cuts in the paintings that adorned the pillars. The hooves of the enormous horses in heavy armour ground deep scars into the tombs on the floor, crushing hoof-prints into the soft brass that decorated them.

Father Dominic wrenched open a cupboard and drew out an ornate sword that lay hidden within, before fleeing deep into the shadows of the abbey. As the remaining monks and their servants scattered, the father gave two of the books to the boy.

The boy nodded and, holding the books close to his chest, he crouched low and crept along the walls behind the high altar, slipping under the embroidered cloth to hide. Adam ran towards him and crouched alongside the table to watch what the boy would do next. He waited, listening to the scrape of metal against stone and the chilling sound of those around him crying out as they fell to the soldiers' swords.

The boy lifted a corner of the cloth and he could see the impatient hooves of a stamping horse just in front of the altar. It was facing away from them. There was a shout from the shadows in the nave and Father Dominic stepped from his hiding place, drawing the soldier's attention. Raising the sword above his head, he called out to the leading soldier. The horse stepped slowly forward, and the abbey filled with the cold laugh of the soldier as he raised his sword and cut the Father down in cold blood and rode on up the aisle. The slain monk crumpled to the floor with his black robe lying like a dark pool around him. The sword slipped from his hand as he fell, and slid across the floor, singing against the cold stone, and coming to rest at the far end of the altar.

The boy crept out from his hiding place and made his way to the end of the altar, moving stealthily from shadow to shadow. Reaching the sword, he wound his fingers round the still warm hilt and thrust it into his belt. Worming his way along in the darkness, he prepared to make a dash for the transept door, aiming for the cloisters and a way through to reach the fields beyond. He took a chance and bolted from his hiding place, and a cry went up. The soldier pulled his horse hard about to face him – swinging his heavy sword in a great arc round his body. But he was too slow, and his weapon caught the great crystal crucifix that glistened on the altar.

All stopped to watch as the cross fell, seemingly caught in a pocket of slowed time, and crashed to the floor, shattering into countless pieces. The shards flew in all directions and a piece from the heart of the cross buried itself deep in the boy's leg. Gasping from the pain of it, he dragged his bloody leg, and managed to flee in the chaos that ensued as the remaining monks rushed the soldiers. With a final heave of his shoulder against a small door low in the wall of the north transept, he made it through and out into the fields.

Adam ran through the wall after him without thinking, and rushed straight through several stones in the graveyard. Using the sword as a support, the boy limped through the teeming rain, managing to stagger across the cloister towards the outbuildings and the barn. Reaching the barn unseen, he took a moment and leaned against the wall, gasping for air. Adam could see the blood seeping down the boy's thigh, leaving a large, darkening patch on his breeches. The boy shook the rain from his head and, still using the sword for support, he stumbled to a small stall at the back of the barn.

'Hello, girl,' he cooed to the fat grey mule that waited patiently in the darkness. 'Father Dominic, God rest his soul, was right.

They took the horses, but did not bother with you all the way back here. Come, we have a job to do.'

Throwing a blanket over the mule's back and another round his shoulders, he braced himself against the wall and managed to heave himself on to her back. Pulling hard on the rough rope bridle she wore, he kicked her on deeper into the building. Adam followed as the boy carefully steered the mule across the floor to where a thick rope hung. The boy reached out and pulled it and a door, just big enough for him and his mount, creaked open. The door led on to the sodden fields that stretched out behind the monastery, and freedom.

'*The journey was arduous, but the boy did not stop, despite the fever that rose in him.*' Adam jumped as D'Scover spoke again and his words rang clear as a bell in his head. He looked around him and the image was fading fast; he could barely see the boy as he rode off across the fields, still clutching the books and with the sword bumping clumsily at his hip.

'*His leg began to throb with infection round the scale of crystal, and after three days on the road he reached London. Following the father's instructions, he made his way to the convent in Southwark to hand over his precious burden to the nuns who protected the texts of the Brotherhood that Father Dominic had already placed there in the care of Sister Goodman. And so the Brotherhood was formed, and for nearly five hundred years the Ritual has been performed for a select few. We who have been Sustained have kept the peace between the living and the dead.*'

Adam turned round and about, trying to make out the final faint images around him. He could see another building, smaller and darker, with nuns fussing around over something on the floor. One of them shook her head and gestured to a servant to come forward. The man stepped out and leaned over to pick up a dirty bundle from the floor.

'The boy,' Adam asked, 'what happened to him?'

'I have not shown you this,' D'Scover said. 'It is not relevant; do not force this image.'

'I want to know.' He clutched D'Scover's arm. 'Please?'

'Very well.'

D'Scover sighed deeply and the images strengthened again, enough for Adam to fully focus on them. The servant held the limp body of the boy in his arms and the blanket fell away. The blanket was now as covered in mud as he was, but the stain on his leg lay on a huge swelling and the blood reached to his ragged shoe.

'The boy collapsed as he entered the convent,' D'Scover said, and again Adam felt the words rather than heard them. 'The infection in his leg was too advanced by the time he arrived and the fever overtook him. There was nothing they could do. He died of his wounds a day later. Now we must end this.'

Adam took a last look at the sweat-stained body of the boy lying in the servant's arms and watched until everyone had faded and disappeared. D'Scover's office and its stylish decor once more took hold around him and Adam was again sitting on the blood-red couch, looking at the man who had guided him through this extraordinary experience.

'Adam?' D'Scover asked quietly. 'Are you with me again?'

Adam swallowed and shook his head to clear his thoughts as the last smudgy shadows retreated from the edges of his field of vision.

'I think so,' he said. 'I saw it; It was so real! I can't believe it, I was right there. What was that? It can't have been another Memoria – that wasn't my life, but I was there. I could even smell it. The stink of the villages, the sweat and fever on the boy – how can that be possible? And why do I feel so cold?'

'The cold is an after-effect, you are imagining it; do not worry, it will pass quickly. What you experienced is a technique called Hypnagogia. I developed it many decades ago to explain things quickly and in a way that causes most impact,' D'Scover answered. 'Only Senior Council members can apply it and few can manipulate it in such detail. It is my procedure, and an illusion that I have engineered can be vivid and quite disorientating. Are you more clear-headed now?'

70

'Not really. It's like waking up from a really vivid dream; my brain doesn't quite accept that what it's seen isn't real – does that make sense?' Adam was clearly confused.

'Actually you are closer to the truth than you realise,' D'Scover said. 'The technique uses a subtle manipulation of the Hypnagogic state. This is a realm between waking and dreaming when the brain is at its most suggestible and reality is a little easier to influence. The right tone of voice and the right atmosphere, and the subject can actually live through whatever we suggest to them.' D'Scover lifted his hand and the room became a little brighter. 'How do you feel now?'

'Better, thanks. It's passing,' Adam replied, blinking in the brightness. 'Who was the angry girl in the abbey?'

'Which girl?'

'Yeah, that's her,' Adam said. 'The witch girl.'

'I am not sure who you mean.' D'Scover frowned. 'I am not conscious of placing a witch in my reconstruction, but I was reading about their craft shortly before your Hypnagogia. I may have inadvertently placed her within the images.'

'I don't know how these things work, but she seemed, well …' Adam hesitated while he searched for the right word, 'impressive, important, you know? Like I should pay attention to her.'

'Interesting.' D'Scover picked up his notebook and jotted something in it. 'As you come to know me better, you will understand that I do not believe in coincidence. All things happen for a reason, whether we like it or not. So,' he changed the subject, 'you have learned more about the Brotherhood. What do you think?'

'Amazing,' Adam yawned, 'and exhausting. Sorry, but I'm wiped out and I don't even know if I sleep any more! I'm still confused though, still not sure why you've shown me all of this. Is it important to me doing the Passing thing?'

'It is nothing to do with the Passing.' D'Scover's expression became deadly serious. 'Far from it, in fact. Adam, I have shown you this because I would like you to join us.'

71

Chapter Eight – Two Boys

'Did he accept?'

'He did not want to answer straight away.'

'What do you mean?'

'He wanted time to think, and so I have placed him in Dispersal again to give him some. He is a challenging youth. He is intelligent and forthright, if a little prone to unnecessary bouts of humour. I am hoping that he will make the right decision, but did not wish to rush him.'

D'Scover walked the darkened corridors of the hospice with Sister Goodman, pausing occasionally to peer in through the glass panes into rooms where their occupants slept, watched over by slowly wilting flowers.

'Is he here?' she asked.

D'Scover shook his head. 'I have reallocated him; he is linked to my office now.'

Sister Goodman looked worried. 'Is that wise?' she asked. 'He hasn't yet agreed and it may not be possible to reallocate again. He could be tied to your office indefinitely. If he does not agree, then there is a chance …'

'Please do not presume to tell me what it could mean. I am well aware of the possible long-term problems,' D'Scover interrupted. 'He *will* join, that much I know for sure.'

'Toby D'Scover!' the sister snapped, visibly crackling with violet sparks. 'If you continue to treat me as though I am some fresh spirit still warm from her deathbed, I shall consider our friendship to be over,' she scolded. 'I am not sure that you are thinking objectively here. Are you honestly able to say that you are treating this boy just as you would treat any new spirit?'

D'Scover sighed and looked down into the stern face of the short stocky woman.

'No,' he answered, 'I cannot honestly say that I have dealt with him as I have treated others. But with the rise of spirit activity and disturbances, I fear that our time may be short.'

'I can understand that, but to leap to an assumption that he is the child of the Vision could be disastrous,' she warned. 'If you are wrong again, the consequences could be dire, for both you and the Brotherhood.'

'I am aware of this, but I cannot let this boy slip through our fingers,' he replied. 'If the time is right, so be it, but if not, then I alone shall bear the consequences.'

'Indeed,' Sister Goodman said. 'I strongly advise you to take it to the Senior Council; after all, they should not discover this from a third party.'

D'Scover rounded on her. 'You will inform them?'

'I am still an Attendant,' she reminded him. 'I may not have a choice.'

He turned away and began to walk away up the corridor. 'You have made your intentions clear,' he muttered. 'I am returning to my office.'

'Do not dare walk away from me, D'Scover!' she snapped. 'Do not make me pull rank on you, Toby.' Her voice dropped to a softer tone that hung heavy with a faintly veiled threat.

He stopped and turned back towards her. 'I am sorry,' he said. 'On occasion I forget your senior status.'

'Easily done, and no offence is taken.' She smiled at him as he walked back towards her. She slipped her arm through his and guided him back along the corridor.

'Now,' she said cheerfully, 'you have not told me if you consulted the Texts. I trust you did as I asked?'

He nodded.

'And?'

'As I suspected, there is no precedent for a non-aggressive Trial. The last Demon Trial was in 1812 on the battlefields of Russia during the war with France – easy to hide a body amongst so many and those were more superstitious times anyway. Nothing was thought of sightings of the unusual; angels and demons were commonplace on the battlefield,' he answered.

'Who undertook the Trial?'

'A girl, Elizabeth Rossingdale. She took on Barbatos,' he said, looking away from her and sadly shaking his head. 'I put her forward; it was a mistake.'

'Ah, the Duke, he does love a battlefield, if I recall. Did he seize a legion or bring one of his own?'

'He took one. A major died in battle and he seized command of the men, driving them on against hopeless odds. It was a French legion and they were outnumbered ten to one, but still he forced them on. The carnage was terrible and this alerted the Brotherhood and Rossingdale was sent.'

'I remember the event, it was a tragedy,' Sister Goodman said, patting his arm.

'She was destroyed,' D'Scover said sadly, 'and the Brotherhood had to step in; all of the soldiers were lost too. All that could be done was to contain the threat and wait until Barbatos lost interest and retreated. There were nearly two hundred lives lost because of that Trial. I will initiate the boy into the Brotherhood, but I will not rush to put him through. I am not prepared to take that chance again. I need more time,' D'Scover said firmly.

'What of the Vision; does it describe him clearly?' she asked.

'I appreciate your concern, but I cannot tell you any more than you already know about the Vision,' he replied. 'And you know that.'

'Very well.' She frowned. 'I only wanted to help. Have any other parts of it been fulfilled?'

'Not specifically,' D'Scover said, 'but there are other signs attached that have taken place, the rise in spirit activity being the most obvious one. There is also another child.'

'Which other child?' Sister Goodman asked. 'Are you dismissing this boy now?'

'No. This other child seems to be connected with the Brotherhood, although she may not be aware of this. I have seen her in the Texts, and had never noticed her before, but it has been over a decade since I consulted them. It is too great a coincidence, and she appeared in Adam's Hypnagogia.'

'It is an unlikely coincidence, but it could still be one,' Sister Goodman said, 'or your influence placed her in what he saw. In any case she must be long dead and, if so, it would be virtually impossible to find her spirit.'

'It could be that her fate is to be linked to the Brotherhood,' D'Scover explained. 'The information in the Texts and the Hypnagogia represented distinctly different periods of time. It is possible that her spirit is not affected by death.'

'I do not understand,' she frowned. 'What are you saying?'

'Her spirit may still be carried by a living person.'

'That is hardly likely,' the sister said. 'And even if it was true, it could take forever to find her.'

'Not if it is my purpose to find her,' D'Scover said.

'Oh, Toby.' Sister Goodman sighed. 'Such an old-fashioned idea! Nobody still believes that surely?'

'It does not require your belief to ensure that it is true,' he said. 'If it is meant to happen, it will happen. In the mean time, I will continue to train the boy in case a Trial is deemed necessary.'

'And we shall all pray that it does not turn out like Rossingdale's, or indeed like a certain Trial of 1666.'

'Thank you for reminding me of my previous errors,' D'Scover said with some disdain. 'Was there anything else?'

'Yes.' She smiled again and flicked a hand towards the large windows, which slid open a crack. 'Fresh air, that is better. I shall leave you to your work. I cannot force you to inform the Senior Council, but it will have to be soon.'

'We shall see,' he replied.

'In the long run that decision may not be yours to make, Toby,' she said ominously.

'How was your Dispersal?'

'Relaxing, and you were right, I had time to think,' Adam replied. 'It's a strange feeling this Dispersal thing. Bit like being awake and still asleep at the same time – kind of alert but drifting around; it's hard to explain.'

'That is because you have never known anything like it and so you have nothing to compare it to,' D'Scover replied. 'I am sure that you have had time to think of some questions that you would like to ask. Shall we sit?'

Adam nodded and walked past D'Scover to take a seat on the couch once more.

'As long as you don't do that zombie-hypno thing again,' he said. 'Still can't shake the image of all that death after the last time; it was like being in the most intense computer game.'

'Straight questions, straight answers, I assure you,' D'Scover replied, taking his seat too.

'OK – right.' Adam leaned forward and stared at D'Scover. 'Why me?'

'Sorry?' D'Scover was taken aback. He had not expected this question; most who were offered a place in the Brotherhood just assumed that it was a natural progression for spirits in this situation, but it had been a long time since there had been a new recruit.

'Why are you asking me to join the Brotherhood?' Adam pursued the answer. 'I mean, thousands of people, millions even, die all the time. So why me?'

D'Scover took a deep breath before continuing, not that it

helped as it had been a very long time since he had actually needed air, but old habits die hard.

'Few spirits are suitable for recruitment. Most pass straight on, others have no skills that would be useful for the Brotherhood and still more are in a permanent state of confusion. You showed signs of sensitivity before you passed over and you have maintained a clear consciousness throughout; these are classic traits of an agent of the Brotherhood.'

'Sensitivity? What do you mean by that?'

'Have you ever seen a ghost?' D'Scover asked.

'You mean apart from you?'

'Please try not to be sarcastic,' he chided.

Adam thought for a while before shaking his head. 'Nope,' he said. 'I'm sure I haven't seen anything weird before all this madness.'

'On the contrary,' D'Scover explained, 'I am convinced you have seen dozens of spirits. Your sensitivity is so strong that you see them and you are not even aware of it. Do you remember an older female nurse at the hospital?'

Adam wrinkled his forehead as he cast his mind back. 'I think I remember her,' he said. 'Don't tell me she was one of your agents?'

'In a manner of speaking,' D'Scover said blandly.

'OK, so I suppose I could've seen more and not realised they were ghosts and you might want me because I can see them like you. Right – next question. How many agents are there?'

D'Scover swivelled his chair round to face the screen and called up the world map and then brought up the agents' locations over it. A mass of glittering yellow instantly covered the world in a startling rash of colour.

'Over two thousand,' he said. 'The number remains fairly static as some choose to take the Final Dispersal whilst others are recruited. We try not to accumulate too many, and so most Shades serve for a set period of time. We do not recruit lightly; for example, we have not recruited anyone in London for nearly thirty years.'

77

'Final Dispersal!' Adam shuddered. 'Is that as bad as it sounds?'

'Its meaning is clear,' D'Scover said. 'Shades Disperse for the final time and do not re-form.'

'Yeah, bad as it sounds then.' Adam was fascinated by the seething yellow dots on the screen. 'How long do agents serve?'

'That depends on the circumstances, but most serve for around a hundred years,' D'Scover said.

'So some stay longer?'

'Some, yes.'

'How long have you been in the Brotherhood?' Adam asked.

D'Scover flicked the screen back off and stood up, striding towards a cabinet in the corner.

'It is not considered polite to ask a Shade how long they have served,' he said, opening the cabinet and removing one of the small black boxes.

Turning back to Adam, he tossed the CC across the room and Adam deftly caught it.

'What's this?'

'It is a device that we call a CC – a Communication Cube. You can use it to contact the Brotherhood.'

'I haven't decided to join yet.' He slipped the cube into his pocket.

'Yes, you have,' D'Scover said softly.

'Smart alec.' Adam grinned. 'I have kind of decided. I mean, what's the alternative?'

'Is that a genuine question?' D'Scover asked.

'Yeah, I suppose it is actually. What would happen if I chose not to join? What comes after this?' He gestured around the room.

D'Scover turned back to the screen before answering.

'It is not our place to question what comes after; we are simply here to assist those who have difficulty in achieving the Passing.' His reply was eerily enigmatic.

'That's a really bad answer, and way too creepy; you really should work on that,' Adam said. 'What happens after this? Where do we go when we pass over?'

D'Scover stood up and pushed his chair neatly back into place behind the desk. He walked slowly to the windows and looked out over the dark city, avoiding eye contact with the boy.

'That depends on what you believe in.'

Adam shifted on the couch so that he could see D'Scover's back; his suit made a blank canvas of deep blue in front of the windows.

'Hold on,' he said, 'so you're saying that you go wherever you *believed* you'd go?'

'That is the assumption of the Brotherhood,' D'Scover said. 'I have little time for the fashions of organised religions, the complexity of faiths. They shift and change over the centuries to suit worshippers. Mankind has created many gods to suit itself. I am interested only in the strength and power of belief, regardless of the empty doctrines in which it hides.'

'What if you don't believe in anything?' Adam asked.

'Everyone believes in something, even if they do not consciously acknowledge it. Most people simply cease to be. They die and that is it – over.'

'That's harsh,' Adam mused. 'Hold on, what if you were so evil that you knew for sure that you were going to hell, or whatever your religion believes is hell? Wouldn't some people want to resist going at all and just fight the whole thing?'

'This is another reason for the existence of the Brotherhood,' D'Scover replied softly. 'To deal with those who may be … unwilling to let go.'

Adam shivered at the idea, and then characteristically shrugged it off, looking around the room.

'Do you work here alone?' he asked. 'Is this where everything is done?'

D'Scover relaxed at the change of subject. 'No. There are a number of offices like this around the world and ultimately I report to the Senior Council. But this is the most established office – it was the first. It has moved only a short distance since it was first created. I have been on the banks of the river for longer than I care to recount. This is Section One.'

D'Scover waved his hand and the lighting level rose in the room. 'The Brotherhood has clear and established rules for how we should operate; these form our Articles and you will have to learn them. All Shades are under the control of the Senior Council. The Council rests in stasis, a kind of semi-permanent Dispersal, but are aware of everything that happens that would concern the Brotherhood. On rare occasions they are summoned but, as far as I am aware, it has not happened for over twenty years. Usually *they* summon whomsoever they wish to speak to. The Council is kept well informed by its Attendants.'

'Are you an Attendant?'

'No,' D'Scover answered curtly and he looked uncomfortable. 'Attendants are all former Council members. There are not a great number of them; in fact there are only two in the whole of London. All Attendants are attached to cities where there were once pre-Dissolution monastic houses or physical links to them. The great cathedral cities around the country all have Attendants bound to them.'

'They get kicked out of the Council? That means the Council changes members too?'

'They are not kicked out as you put it; they retire. The Council has undergone necessary changes since it was first established as some members have resigned to take their places as Shades once more, and others have been asked to leave for various reasons, but the current assembly has been in place for almost two centuries. I have been assured that it is not an easy job being on the Council.'

'Don't you want to do it? Isn't it like a promotion?' Adam queried.

'I have never been asked … I …' D'Scover faltered and turned away. 'There are complicated reasons for me not being called to service.'

Adam looked down at his hands and wiggled his fingers, feeling awkward at the change in mood that had swept through the room; a change of subject was needed.

'Why do I look so solid if I'm a ghost?'

'You do not,' D'Scover replied briskly, the atmosphere lifting. 'You only look solid at this moment because this room is bolstered by my presence. Until you have perfected your own Ritual of Sustainment you need a full agent to assist you. I am boosting your substance so that you can remain this cohesive. If I removed my influence, you would see how little substance you actually have.'

'Really, can I see?'

D'Scover turned towards Adam and, holding his hands outstretched with the palms upwards, he made a beckoning movement and the light in the room momentarily dipped. Adam gasped and reeled back in his seat, grabbing at the cushions, as the room seemed to fade from view.

'I can't see properly anymore,' Adam gasped. 'Everything has faded … hey, I've faded too!'

'I have allowed us to slip into the World Between,' D'Scover said. 'This is the realm between life and death. This is where you would remain without the Brotherhood, and this is what happens to those who cannot pass over successfully. This is not a safe place.'

Adam stood up and staggered as a great weakness overtook him. Abject terror gripped him as he looked down at his hands, curling his fingers into his palms as each one crumbled to a fine grey powder peppered with blood-red fragments. He lifted them in front of his face and the dust trailed in the air. Around him the office walls had become colourless and they shifted shape as he watched; they appeared to bend and flex, enveloped in a bleached vapour. All that remained of the room that he remembered were the paintings and porcelain bowls that still seemed to hold their vibrant colours in this veiled new world.

Adam spun round in the bloodied mist to face D'Scover and he could see the terror in the boy's eyes. He had seen this look many times in new recruits. He knew that he could offer no comfort, only explanation.

'This office has been constructed to remain outside the linear passage of time and so I can just as easily see the tenth century as the twenty-first. This site was the first official office of the Brotherhood, but it goes back much further than that. There has been a growth in this place for over a thousand years. The Romans built here, close to the river, and every group of inhabitants since has carried on adding to the city.

'Due to the great age of this place, and the number of people who have entered the Passing here, buildings have trouble holding shape in this realm. It is why the walls do not seem firm anymore. They are brick and glass just as any other building, but the spirits here have a greater influence than any modern building materials. I have maintained the floor for you, as it can be too disconcerting to suddenly be twenty floors up in the air. Here, with practice, we can slip between the leaves of time and look at the city as it once was and, so the ancient Texts say, even as it will be.'

Adam walked to the faint illusion of the window and looked down on the city. Pale memories of towering office blocks drifted in and out of focus over a tumbling mass of buildings from all of the ages of the city. Wooden structures spanned the slithering river for fractions of seconds and, as he watched, he saw a ripple of fire lick the heart of the city and vanish.

'I would advise you not to look for too long,' D'Scover said. 'It takes a lot more practice to handle the city in this state. Any city that has a long and bloodstained history heaves in and out of this state of flux. London is in constant struggle to stay out of this realm. Occasionally a sensitive person can see the rift in ancient places like this and they see a pocket of, say, the sixteenth century in somewhere like Versailles or Rome. Roman cities often hold troubled times, memories of conquest and siege, which is why soldiers are often seen there.'

'Who controls this world?'

'An excellent question,' D'Scover replied. 'Here no one is master, and the Senior Council would have us believe that this realm is beyond control as the past has already been played out. It is rather like a filmed image: you cannot change what has already happened. However, there is a theory that the right spirit could influence the past and change the future and so this realm is occasionally patrolled by agents to check that nothing is changing. Another reason for our existence – this place is riddled with malevolence and danger.'

'I can't see any danger … Are you …' Adam trailed off, dreading asking the question.

'I am holding it back.' D'Scover's voice was chilling. 'You are not ready to see the chaos of this place. You may never be.'

'Whoa,' Adam shivered. 'That's way too scary.'

'You wanted straight answers.'

'So it's really full of crazy ghosts and stuff?' Adam could not take his eyes from the misty world around him. 'And no one has full control? Kind of like the Wild West, lawless, out of control?'

'A fair comparison,' D'Scover said. 'We should leave. Too much time here can be potentially damaging to a new Shade.'

Adam turned back towards the room and shook his head in confusion at his frail surroundings. He looked around at the drifting illusion of faint walls and to stabilise himself he focused only on the bright colours of the paintings and the solid forms of the bowls.

'What about the …' Adam began, but his voice sounded distant and faint and this surprised him enough to trail off before he could finish the sentence.

'My collection?' D'Scover anticipated the question. He walked to the nearest bowl and picked it up. The vibrant blues of the delicate yet complex geometric decoration on its flawless surface rested uneasily in the faint hand that held it.

'There is such passion in these works,' D'Scover said, still looking at the bowl and running his fingers round the rim. 'All of these have been fervently believed in, and that in turn leaves a trace on their substance. They survive here in their solid form because their creators knew they were different and would last throughout time. Not all art lasts like this, only rare pieces.'

Adam looked with fresh eyes at the extraordinary colours that bled out from these works of art into the now bland room.

'You mean people died making this stuff?'

'I mean that people died *for* it, either creating it or protecting it. Items that have evoked such emotion leave a trace that time cannot diminish. It is why I collect them. I feel that the love left here is worthy of protection.' D'Scover spoke with genuine emotion.

'I'm cold,' Adam said, still getting to grips with a voice that sounded as though it was speaking from another room. 'but I'm probably remembering what cold is like and imagining it. Is that right?'

'You are beginning to understand,' D'Scover replied. 'Would you like me to return substance to the room?'

'I think I can do it,' Adam answered. 'Now I know it's not really here, I think I can …'

He closed his eyes and screwed up his face and fists, and the room flickered in and out of focus with sharp red sparks. Adam began to shake and the red sparks crept from his feet and crackled out across the floor like fiery drops of blood. After a few moments he gasped and slumped down into the shadow of what was once the couch.

'I can't do it,' he sighed. 'It looked so easy when you did it.'

D'Scover placed his hands, palms outwards, once more and moved them to his sides as though pushing through a curtain and the colour whisked through the room, returning it to the land of the living.

'Adam, all of this takes time.' He sat next to the boy. 'You have a natural gift; it is why you have been chosen. I have already seen you do things which should not be possible. You changed the Memoria. I have never seen anyone do that; I was not able to do it when I first died. You could be great, but it will take time.'

'Time? I've got loads of that. It's all I've got now, isn't it?' He slumped forward and dropped his head in his hands. 'I don't think I can do this. Maybe I should just take that Passing deal and be done with it.'

'The choice is yours, but I have great hopes for you within the Brotherhood,' D'Scover reassured him. 'I have confidence in you.'

'I can't get to grips with the whole dead thing,' Adam muttered. 'I can't do this.'

'I understand.'

'NO, no, you don't,' Adam snapped, standing quickly and striding forcefully around the room to where the bowl stood that D'Scover had previously held. 'You see, I died without anyone loving me; there's nothing to keep me in your world.'

He grabbed the bowl with one hand and held it up. 'You see this bowl?' he asked. 'Even this lousy bit of china has been loved more than me. It will stay perfect and whole forever because someone loved it, but I'll always be a damned shadow of a person. How can you know what that's like? You're an old man; you must've been at least forty when you died. You probably had a family and a nice warm life and love. How can you understand what it was like to be me?'

Adam held the bowl out and, as he lost concentration on his substance, it slipped through his blurred fingers. They both watched as the bowl fell to the floor and shattered into hundreds of thin blue and white slivers that cascaded round Adam's feet like jagged confetti. The boy slumped back to sit down on the couch and began to sob, a deep, shaking grief, and buried his face deep in his hands. D'Scover stood and walked to the couch to sit next to Adam; he rested his ice-white hand upon the boy's shoulder.

'I'm so sorry.' Adam lifted his red-eyed face. 'I didn't mean to; my fingers just weren't there. I'm sorry I shouted, but how could you know what it's like to be me?'

'I do understand, Adam,' D'Scover said. 'Far better than you could ever imagine.'

He walked away from the boy and passed his hands over the shattered fragments of the bowl causing them to gather into a neat pile at his feet.

'The reason I understand,' he continued, 'is because I too was fourteen years old when I died.'

Chapter Nine – Reallocation

'I don't see how it can be possible.'

'I am afraid I do not understand.'

'I mean, this place is big, but not big enough, surely?'

'I can assure you, Mr Resnick, that it is perfectly possible. The museum is more than sufficiently large to incorporate all of us, and our non-agent counterparts, with plenty of room for all.'

Marcus walked alongside a female Shade through the vast main hall of the Natural History Museum. The building had long since closed for the day and the hordes of staff and visitors had left, giving the place a curious echo despite its many exhibits. The dinosaur bones rose above them in various realistic poses or peered out from plinths tucked away in the recesses to each side.

'The main hall is not usually occupied as it is a thorough-fare and. the risk of detection is much greater.' She talked as she walked, forcefully and with a curt snap. 'Only non-agents are allowed to drift along the corridors and through the main hall. We do our very best to stay out of the way of the true ghosts and avoid interfering in any business they may have. You shall be placed in a wing on the first floor. This is not open to discussion and any drift from this wing will be treated as a disciplinary matter. As you are aware, I have close connections to the Senior Council and so will not tolerate any transgressions.'

'That's OK.' Marcus trotted alongside her to catch up. 'I promise I'll be good. I'm just happy to be here. I always liked this place when I was a kid; this all kind of takes me back.'

They reached the foot of the main staircase, which curved away to both sides and up to the floor above them. The grey stone, polished by countless footsteps, glistened in the dim light from the windows above. Marcus and his new controller did not need the light; one of the benefits of the Ritual of Dispersal was that it enabled all Shades to see in the dark.

She stopped and turned back to him and her thin face looked even pointier in the weak light.

'Naturally you may use levitation and transportation, if you have these skills, but only when the building is locked for the night. All substantial movements – changes of floor etcetera – are to be cleared through me first.' She certainly meant business. 'My offices are on the first floor, the gem rooms.'

'Nice,' Marcus said. 'They must be very pretty.'

'Pretty?' She looked almost puzzled. 'Well, yes, I suppose they are; however, I see them merely as specimens. It was my field of study before I joined the Brotherhood.'

'You died here?' he asked.

She turned and walked up the stairs away from him, her spectral heels still clicking on the smooth steps. For a moment Marcus thought she had not heard him and he was about to repeat himself when she turned back and spoke again.

'Yes, Mr Resnick, I died here. As you are so interested, I suffered a heart attack whilst at work. I came in one winter with a case of chronic influenza, as I felt compelled to finish cataloguing some stones. The heating was very poor and my temperature rose throughout the day and eventually my heart could not sustain me and stopped.' She paused and stared at him. 'I was bound to this place as I had not finished my work. I was deeply honoured to be invited to join the Brotherhood as, I am sure, were you.'

She turned away from him and began once more to ascend the stairs.

'I was run over outside,' Marcus babbled, rushing after her. 'Didn't look where I was going and – *blam* – a black cab hit me. It was really …'

'I know all about your death, Mr Resnick,' she interrupted. 'It was all in your file and so it is unnecessary to explain.'

'Oh.' He felt embarrassed. 'I'll just shut up then.'

'Thank you,' she said icily. 'I still have a lot of work to do before I can Disperse and I would appreciate it if you would not waste my time. Follow me to your new location.'

He followed her through the corridors of cased animals peering out from behind the glass, stuffed and frozen in time. They stood in various assumed, permanently aggressive poses as if caught by the camera eye in the middle of an attack. Marcus attempted to maintain the brisk pace set by his new controller, but the distractions were too great. He trotted along behind her, stopping and turning as he walked to take in displays that had changed very little since he had last seen them as a child. Thin beams of ice-white moonlight fell through him to the floor, gathering no shadow and giving the building a magical appearance. Marcus loved every bit of it.

'This place is beautiful,' he gushed, although it was clear that his companion was no longer listening. 'Much better than being in the middle of the road.'

'Here!' she barked at him as they reached a huge pair of oak doors. 'This is your department. You are allocated to share with another agent. His name is William Lawton. He is very talkative; I believe you two will get along just fine.'

'Thank you,' Marcus replied. 'You've been very helpful.'

'I was merely following instructions.' She turned and began to walk away down the corridor. 'I shall be in contact soon to see how you are settling in.' She threw the words over her shoulder and, with a whiff of burning coal and a momentary glitter of white light, she was gone.

Marcus stood for a minute or two at the door, still enjoying the silence and space of the huge building. He had spent so long in the noise and stench of the main road that this peace washed over him like sunshine, warming him to his core. He felt truly happy at last and, for the first time in many decades, he did not regret his decision to enter the Brotherhood.

He had led a less than blameless life, as he had been a con man who specialised in wheedling money out of the weak-minded and lonely. When he was killed on the road, he knew no one would grieve for him and he instinctively feared what would come next. He was not a religious man, crediting neither heaven nor hell, and so was more than surprised to find himself wafting about after death.

Offered the chance to join the Brotherhood, he had jumped at it without much thought and, fearing what could come beyond this state, he had stayed. At first eager to please, and keen to cast off the wicked acts of his life, he had been an excellent agent, aiding in the passing on of countless spirits, of which there were many, thanks to London's busy roads. But recently he had been consumed with the idea of reallocation – and now he had it. Not quite what he had planned, but now he could make a difference again, with a fresh start.

'Well, are you bally well coming in or not?' a terribly posh voice said from apparently nowhere.

Marcus looked back at the doors which now had the addition of a head sticking through them. The head sported a large moustache and floppy fair hair that seemed to govern itself – badly. The face that carried it all must only have been about thirty, but it looked as though it had endured a hard life.

'Sorry,' Marcus replied. 'You must be Mister Lawton.'

'Good God, man, nobody calls me mister anything – call me Bill, please.' He grinned and his teeth glistened from underneath their blond whiskery curtain. 'And you still haven't answered my question, old boy.'

'Sorry?'

'Coming in, or not coming in? Pretty darn simple.'

'Oh, y-yes,' Marcus stammered, 'coming in.'

'Righto,' Bill said, and his head slipped back through the door.

Marcus took a deep breath to prepare. It had been a long time since he had transported through solid matter, as being in the middle of the road did not often call for it. Cars automatically passed through him without any effort on his part. He was desperately out of practice. He closed his eyes and concentrated, forcing himself to picture his substance thinning out until it was so weak it could pass through the molecules of the wood in the door and reassemble on the other side. He felt the wood break down and his own particles jostle for position among the grain as he began to pass through. Then it was done and he gradually pulled his shape back together.

'You might want to nip back for that arm, old man,' Bill said, nodding towards the empty space in Marcus's sleeve. 'Unless you're planning to do without it? You are pretty 'armless.' He guffawed heartily at his own joke.

'Blast,' Marcus swore. 'I knew I was out of practice, but that's embarrassing.'

'Don't give it a second thought, old man; used to do it all the time,' Bill chuckled. 'I'll get the evasive wibbly thing for you.'

He strode to the door and reached into the wood, pulling out a shifting grey mass of loose particles, which he carried carefully back to Marcus.

'I believe this is yours?' he joked, and shoved the squirming bundle of particles back into Marcus's chest.

Marcus concentrated for a moment and the particles gradually reassembled into their given shape as his arm.

'Welcome to your new home, old chap. The Ice Maiden told me all about you so we won't waste time with dull explanations,' Bill blustered. 'Pretty good place this, been with these slimy things in jars for over a hundred and ninety years myself, don't mind saying

90

so either. I know that some are not keen on saying how long they've been hanging around, but it's not easy to embarrass Bill Lawton.'

'Ice Maiden?'

'Miss Diamonds, the queen of this here establishment, the snooty cow who brought you down here? Secretive thing, that one; always snooping around the corridors. Watch out for her. Did she tell you her name?' Bill asked.

Marcus thought about it for a moment. 'No, now you come to mention it, she didn't.'

Bill shook his head. 'Didn't think so. I reckon she's forgotten it herself, just like she forgot to have a personality. She has to be one the deadest people I've met. Not me though, never forgot my name, although it should have been easy as not many people actually knew the whole lot anyway,' he babbled.

'I'm sorry, I don't understand,' Marcus said.

Bill stood up very straight and brushed himself down with his white-gloved hands before raising his head in a regal pose. In the thin light he looked like a ghost from an old-fashioned children's storybook. His white-blond hair and moustache were just the beginning of a stunning ensemble which incorporated a perfect crimson uniform with crisp white trousers, gleaming breastplate, shiny black boots and a sheathed sword hanging from his waist on a belt fastened with an ornate buckle.

'Sir William Charles Chapel Lawton, fifth Earl of Scarford and Commander of the second regiment, King's Light Horse … at your service.' He reached up to a tall red hat, crested with a tuft of white horsehair that had just appeared on his head. He clasped it by the sharp black peak at the front and swept if off with a low bow.

'Very impressive!' Marcus acknowledged the bow with a nod. 'So how come you're here? Was it a war or something?'

'Ah.' Bill straightened up and it was his turn to look embarrassed. 'Bit awkward that one actually. Not during a war, I'm afraid – although seen a good few skirmishes, I can tell you. Back when

91

old Napoleon was giving us a bit of a hard time, my boys and I had to send him packing, but no, that's not actually why I'm here.'

He turned back to the many cabinets that flanked the room like glass coffins on legs.

'It's actually the fault of one of these fellows here.' Bill gestured to the cases. 'Truth be told, old man, never could resist a wager. When I came home after the war, about 1816 I think, I was knocking around with some chums and we dropped into Montagu House to pick up a lady friend before heading off for the evening. She was there helping her father label some dusty stuff, bones and the like, lovely gel, very pretty and dashed clever too. There we were, all dressed up in best bib and tucker, and well, we were larking around a bit whilst we waited for her, as you do, and one of the chaps, Bertie Cauldwell, wagered that I wouldn't eat a beastie or bottled-up thing of some kind.' He bristled at the memory. 'Well, you can't turn down a wager, d'you see? So I took him up on it. Blasted fellow slipped me a poisonous creature of some sort and after I drank it down he scarpered quick fast without paying up. I popped off under this very cabinet here.' He tapped a beautifully polished glass and mahogany display case. 'Blighter never did pay up either, so, you know the way the Brotherhood works, unfinished business, none to grieve, and here I am.'

'Well, what about your girl? Didn't she grieve?'

'Tragic fact is, old man, she'd been carrying on with Bertie behind my back anyway and was glad to see the back of me. Relief is not grief, d'you see? I've often wondered if the whole thing was planned just to do away with me. Ah well, there you go. It's done now and he was killed in a shooting accident two years later anyway and here I am whilst he's long gone and forgotten.'

'Did you say Montagu House? Wasn't that the old British Museum? You didn't die here then?' Marcus asked.

'No, this place wasn't even built when I died, but the collection was moved here in 1883 and I seem to have become attached to this cabinet. I can't say that I miss Montagu though; that building was simply heaving with addled old spirits and musty books. What do you think of this place?'

Marcus looked around at the oak-panelled room surrounding them and the rows of splendid displays.

'I think it's amazing,' he replied. 'I've spent so long in the middle of the road, dealing with people who've been run over – this is a real step up for me. I had no idea a place could look so good.'

'That's the spirit, if you'll pardon the pun!' Bill laughed, and slapped Marcus heartily on the back. 'Now it can get a bit dull in here at times; the chaps at the Brotherhood tend to leave us alone unless something special comes along. Far too many of us in this area to get regular work in passing people over, so the nights can be a bit long unless you want to spend it all in Dispersal. Do you like to gamble?'

'Why?' Marcus replied nervously. 'What did you have in mind?'

'Who is she?' Marcus whispered.

'Name's Daisy something-or-other; she was a cleaner here about sixty years ago until she fell off a ladder under the big fella over there.' Bill gestured to the dusty blue whale that hung from the ceiling in the hall of mammals. 'Broke her bally neck, *crickkkk*.' He made an exaggerated cracking noise and tipped his head at a crooked angle to demonstrate his point.

They were both crouched behind a woolly rhino and watched as the girl vaporously moved from exhibit to exhibit, passing a cloth gently over each one.

'What's she doing?' Marcus whispered.

'Cleaning of course. What else would she be doing? She's a cleaner.' Bill's hoarse croak of a whisper suppressed his usual bellowing voice. 'Come on, it's nearly time.'

Bill slipped out from their hiding place and, looking upwards at the gantry above their heads, he began to lose his substance until he had disappeared from the ground floor and reappeared on the upper level looking down on the main display space. He beckoned for Marcus to follow and follow he did after a first failed attempt that left him halfway through the floor.

'Here's a good place. Better be quiet though; the Ice Maiden hates it if you wander around without asking her first.' Bill crouched back down, this time behind a stuffed lion that was so shabby it looked as if it had died of extreme old age. 'Not long to wait for the main event.'

'What do you mean by that?' Marcus shuffled around to avoid Bill's sword poking right through him.

'Each night, this poor gel dies again, and it is about time … So, what species do you think she will cark it under tonight?' Bill was grinning broadly.

'What?' Marcus was shocked.

'Oh, come on, old man. It's not as if she's never done it before,' Bill chuckled. 'She's no more real than fairies and goblins, just an echo of the girl who died here, like a stuck record. She's not an agent after all, so she doesn't know what she's doing. She never falls in the same place two nights running; it's like she can't remember. This hall has been rearranged dozens of times since she died. No harm in having a bit of a wager if she's going to pop off anyway. Just think of this as a big old game of treasure hunt, you know, like at the village fair with the little flags to mark the spot? We have no money to wager, but it doesn't mean we can't do it just for the fun of it.'

He looked over the gantry and down to where the luminescent outline of the girl wafted from mammal to mammal, flicking specks of dust from their backs as she went.

'Right.' Bill rubbed his hands together, the movement causing his sword to clink against the buckle. 'I'm going to have the bears tonight I think – how about you?'

'Well.' Marcus hesitated. 'Oh, all right, I'll have the … big cats.'

'That's my boy.' Bill slapped him heartily on the back. 'More fun with two. Not long now, just another couple of minutes.'

They watched in silence, but Marcus could see the excitement in Bill's face as the girl drifted first towards the bears. Her white form cast an eerie glow over the dark fur of the animals as she drew close to them, and then past them. She wafted on round the room for a few more minutes until she looked upwards.

Marcus pulled back rapidly, fearing she had seen their hiding place.

'Damn,' Bill muttered.

'Has she seen us?' Marcus whispered.

'No, she's looking for her ladder; looks like she's gypped us both tonight, old man,' he replied.

'What?'

'Watch.'

Marcus leaned back over and could see that the girl had ascended a little as if she was climbing steps where there were none. She got to a height of about two metres, began to sway a little, stretched out her hands and fell. Marcus stood up instinctively and reached out to her, but he was too far away to help her even if it was possible. She seemed to fall in slow motion and, as she hit the ground, her head twisted at a grotesque angle. She crumpled down into a tangle of limbs and her cold eyes stared into nothingness. As they watched, her body began to blur until all that remained was a smooth puddle of light that faded and was gone.

'Awful.' Marcus stared at the spot where she had vanished. 'Just too awful,' he muttered.

'Bally right, old man.' Bill stood up and straightened his uniform. 'Underneath the rhinos this time, no bloody use for either of us.'

Chapter Ten – Lessons for Life after Death

'How's it possible?' Adam gasped. 'How could you possibly be the same age as me?'

'This is merely an assumed form.'

'Assumed?' Adam was stunned to think that the apparently grown man standing in front of him was actually his own age. 'But why?'

'In your experience, how many people trust and afford authority to a fourteen-year-old boy?' D'Scover asked.

Adam gulped a deep breath and slumped down hard on the couch. 'But I … I don't understand,' he blurted. 'You're old, you must be, the way you talk and everything.'

'I have been here for a very long time, but when I died, I assure you I was no older than you. I too had no family; my mother died of plague and I was taken to a monastery hospice. I almost died, but for some reason the disease passed through me and I survived. I was given to one of the monks and was raised by him and the kitchen staff,' he explained. 'I spent my short life surrounded by the monks and remember no other existence, or other children. After my death I did not stop growing mentally, I simply stopped growing physically, and I have been here a very long time. Time has taught me many things, death has not stopped me learning and I have had a great deal of time in which to learn.'

D'Scover turned back to the piled fragments of the shattered bowl on the floor and looked sadly at it. He knelt down and began to pick up the pieces and gather them in his hand. The fragile broken sections began to form a sharp-edged pile.

'I'm so sorry,' Adam repeated. 'Can't you fix it?'

'When something like this is broken, it is broken forever,' D'Scover replied. 'I can no more restore it than restore life to you.'

He walked to the desk and tipped the remains of the bowl into the rubbish bin before returning to his seat and waiting for Adam to speak again.

'I didn't mean to …' Adam apologised. 'I can't explain. I feel so hurt about it all. I didn't even die with a name. I mean, how bad is that?'

'I too died without a name,' D'Scover said as he dusted off his hands.

'But you've got a name.'

'No, I have a name that was given to me when I recovered enough to be put to work,' he said softly. 'My mother died without speaking and the sisters wrote upon my blanket, "Name to be discovered". Do you see? To be discovered – Toby D'Scover. It amused Father Dominic to call me Toby afterwards and it is the name I died with.'

'But the monks, they must've been like a family?'

'Monastic life is very hard, Adam, and not for a young boy. I slept on a cold floor and ate only table scraps; what extra I had I stole. Like you, I spent my time in the safety of the library and I taught myself to read to try and find a way of escape. We have much in common – but I died in the heat of a fever and you died in the grip of cold.'

'How are you like this? How did *you* join the Brotherhood?' Adam asked.

'Do you remember the images I showed you of the foundation of the Brotherhood, the Hypnagogic visions?'

'How could I forget?' Adam shuddered at the memory.

'And you recall the boy who fled the abbey with the texts stuffed into his cloak?'

'That was you!' Adam gasped. 'You were the first, the first to use the Ritual; they tested it on you as you died of your fever.'

'Excellent guess,' D'Scover said, nodding.

'Why aren't you the boss then?' Adam asked. 'Shouldn't you be in charge of the Brotherhood if you were the first agent, the first Shade?'

'I think that you already know the answer to that question.'

'Not because of your age?'

'Exactly that. I was not considered to be of a suitable age to lead the Brotherhood; that honour was given to others some years later. The Brotherhood was led by the living, the monks, for just under a century until more suitable candidates were found. That is why there remains an agreement for living agents within the Brotherhood. I am considered an authority on certain historical matters, and I am afforded a certain respect for the time I have spent within the Brotherhood,' D'Scover continued. 'This department was given to me just over three hundred years ago to suit my skills.'

'Even though you know everything about the Brotherhood, they still think you're a kid?' Adam marvelled.

'I am no longer conscious of what the Senior Council think of me; it has been some time since they let me know,' D'Scover said. 'I am afforded a great deal of respect within this department and I have perfected a good deal of the technology that the Brotherhood now uses and so I have my niche. I have grown to feel more comfortable with my position over the centuries.'

'Can I see what you look like, for real? I mean as a kid,' Adam pleaded.

'I would rather not,' D'Scover told him. 'I have spent many centuries in this form and would rather stay this way. The image you saw in your Hypnagogic state was my death form, so in a way you've already seen what I was like in the beginning.'

D'Scover looked upset by the path this conversation was taking and so Adam searched for a subject to lighten the atmosphere.

'What do you do here?' He clutched at the first question that popped into his head. 'I mean, I have a vague idea, passing people over and all that, but you said that this place suited your skills. What are they?' he asked.

'Adam, I have something else to show you,' D'Scover said enigmatically.

He stood and walked to the centre of the room, lifting his hands palm upwards as if he was carrying an invisible tray. He began to murmur a low, repetitive chant and the room darkened as though night had begun to fall. Adam turned to look out of the window and watched thick clouds boil around the building, erasing the view. Turning back, he now realised that D'Scover was immersed in a cloud of his own that started to spiral.

As it whirled before him, Adam could make out shapes in the vortex. Letters first, single letters in an elegant brush script, then whole words in a language that he did not recognise. They began to gather in front of D'Scover and, with a scratching of quill on paper, they rolled themselves out on to the book, taking shape in D'Scover's arms.

The book began to gain substance until it was the most solid thing in the whole spiralling mass. Shimmering with gold leaf that caught the dying light of the day, ornate illuminated text spread out to fill each page as though the vines that decorated the pages grew like a living plant. Gradually the pages ceased their fluttering and the book lay wide open like a tamed bird in D'Scover's outstretched hands. The clouds split apart outside the building and a last yellow shard of winter sun filled the room, bouncing from the gold on the pages.

'The Master Text,' D'Scover said solemnly. 'The original, the first.'

'It's beautiful.' Adam breathed the words in a whisper. 'So beautiful, and they gave it to you?'

'I look after it. I am the Keeper of the Texts, this is my calling. I have protected them since I fled with the Master Text as a child. This book contains the Ritual of Sustainment. It has been duplicated successfully since it was written and now each department around the world can use it. This is the Master.'

'So you keep this book; what else?' Adam stared at the book as he spoke.

'I am responsible for most of the practical developments of the techniques outlined in the Master Text. As I was the first, I have had more time to practise Sustainment and I have to admit that I am the most proficient at it. I can sustain my form for a great length of time, longer than any other agent. I have exceptional Hotline skills. I could leave this place and Hotline anywhere in the world and appear as solid and real as a living person. It has been most useful in keeping track of certain psychics and charlatans and for tracing trapped spirits who may need help.'

'Cool,' Adam said. 'D'you get a lot of that?'

D'Scover carried the book to the table where the bowl had once rested and laid it reverentially down, smoothing the pages with a stroking motion as though he was calming a pet.

'Not as much as in the past,' he replied without turning back.

'Why not?'

'There is one thing you must understand about the Brotherhood before you decide whether or not to join.' D'Scover joined him on the couch. 'This,' he gestured to the room, 'is all a question of belief. If enough determined people believe in something, then it is true, simple as that. If enough strong minds believe in heaven and hell, then they exist. *Our* existence is based on strength of belief, faith, which is what keeps us here. The Texts are a statement of faith; so many have died for them that they are now as real and solid as the stones of St Paul's. Whilst people believe in an afterlife, we are needed.'

'What if someone doesn't believe?' Adam ventured.

'Then they die and that is that. They know no different and

do not need us,' D'Scover replied. 'As time passes and religions diminish, the need for us becomes reduced.'

'Which god do you work for?' Adam asked.

D'Scover smiled a weak and uncomfortable smile. 'I have told you before, I am not an angel. How many religions are there, Adam?'

'Loads, hundreds, maybe thousands.'

'And how many gods are there?'

'Must be thousands too.'

'Exactly,' D'Scover replied. 'There are as many gods as people *believe* that there are, and whilst they believe in an afterlife, there is one and some may need help getting there.'

'What about fairies and elves and stuff like that?' Adam asked.

'Once again, it is a question of belief,' he explained. 'It is a bit like this book.' He waved his hand and the book rose from its resting place and drifted towards them. 'This is a link between the living and the dead, the real and the unreal, if you will. The same can be said of other beliefs: they need a link. Once in a while, someone believes in something so strongly that they can *become* the link between the solid world that everyone knows and the fragile, intangible world of that which we imagine to be true. A link between here and the World Between.'

'I'm really confused now,' Adam frowned.

'It is like this,' D'Scover continued. 'Have you ever heard of the story of the Cottingley Fairies?'

'I think so, read about it in the library.'

'Two young girls living in the English countryside towards the end of the First World War saw fairies dancing by a river at the end of their garden. Those innocent girls believed in the fairies so much that they could actually see them and know them to be real. The country was in the final grip of a brutal war and young men were being killed overseas at an alarming rate. Everyone needed something wonderful to believe in and so the rumour of these fairies began to grow. Belief in them increased and soon they began to take substance, to become real to everyone and not just the girls. A charming story fed the hopes and childhood dreams of a whole country and people so wanted them to be real that they were.'

'I know the story; even that writer believed them, the Sherlock Holmes one, Conan Doyle? But the pictures looked so phoney, how could anyone believe them?'

'The pictures look faked now,' D'Scover said, 'but it took a lot of work to do that.'

'You did it?'

'It was a tragic thing to have to do, but the world needed protection from itself. I had to make people believe the children had faked the pictures as a prank. It worked after a while, but in their hearts the girls never really stopped believing.'

'Does it matter?' Adam asked. 'Why can't people just believe what they want to believe? You said yourself it took almost a whole country to make a few fairies, so what difference would it have made if you'd just left it alone?'

'Human history is littered with powerful people who have convinced the masses that their way of thinking was the right one. Imagine if those people could conjure real and solid demons and monsters to do their bidding. What would it do to the world?' D'Scover said darkly. 'Hitler came close when he began to search for holy relics. He knew about the Texts and came looking for them. It became a war. The world cannot risk another confrontation on that scale.'

'You expect me to believe that the Second World War was started because Hitler knew about you lot?' Adam said sarcastically.

'There is that word believe again,' D'Scover said. 'That war started essentially because he invaded Poland and engineered genocide, but he was also searching for the Texts to form an indestructible army – or so he *believed* – and that became a war within a war.'

'It's crazy, all that death and destruction for a book and a bunch of beliefs?'

'Faith, Adam, is the most powerful force on Earth.' D'Scover called the book to his lap and closed it. 'It can destroy nations and cast brother against brother. Religious hatred has killed millions around the world throughout history, more than any disease. Our job is to act as gatekeepers and make sure nothing slips between the real and the accepted unreal. We do not take sides, we just prevent – how can I put it – leakage.'

'Hold on, I don't have a god or believe in any of that stuff, so why did I come here and not just die and be gone?' Adam demanded.

D'Scover took a deep breath before speaking again. 'Within the Brotherhood we also have our own beliefs; they are recorded in this book.' He stroked the black leather cover as he spoke and Adam could have sworn that its pages ruffled with pleasure.

'You haven't answered my question, what are these beliefs? What's all this got to do with me?' Adam asked.

'Some you already know and they have formed the bare bones of the Brotherhood. That it takes at least three to grieve to pass someone over, that we are here as gatekeepers, that we do not interfere unless the Text allows it, amongst other elements. But some of this book is the recording and retelling of a Vision.'

D'Scover lifted his hand from the cover and the pages breathed out. The cover opened and pages flicked past, searching for a specific section. Colours streamed before Adam's eyes as he tried to focus on the fleeting images of flowers and birds and twisted animals seething over each page. Gradually they began to slow down and, with a flourish of dust, settled at a section that was inscribed in thick black ink. Unlike the rest of the book this section was not bordered with gold and green in a vibrant frame, but carried a border of twisted thorns and dead leaves. Between the gaps peered evil-looking faces carrying expressions of such torment that Adam wanted to look away.

'A good amount of it Father Dominic wrote after a series of visions in which he said he talked with an Archangel,' D'Scover continued. 'Here the pages tell of how someone will know of the

Brotherhood and will use the Texts against us to take control of the living world.'

'Hasn't that happened? Didn't Hitler do that?'

'No, Hitler was not the one, although for a time the Senior Council did think that he was. There have been other times too, when demons have walked the Earth and others have been sent out against them, but they are not the cataclysm that the Text speaks of.'

'How can you be sure?'

'Because the Text is very specific and no other cases have quite matched the Vision – here, do you see?'

D'Scover skittered through a few more pages and pointed to a section of the page where the ink seemed to be a deep dark brown, like dried blood instead of ink.

'I can't read that, is it Latin?' Adam squinted at the pages.

'It is partly constructed in Latin and partly in a code of Father Dominic's creation. The Vision is quite fragmented as we have not broken all of the code, but it goes something like this.' He found the relevant section and began to read aloud.

'In times of chaos, a great weakness – or possibly disaster – will fall upon the Brotherhood. Faith shall weaken – or possibly be destroyed – and many shall be lost forever to the void. In this confusion of spirits, darkness shall rise silently and take upon a form known to many. This force shall command – we believe this section says demons or possibly a force of evil. This evil one will take hold whilst others look away, but some shall see all and one shall be triumphant.

'The next part is clearer. There shall be three who take on the enemy. The one who overthrows shall have known nothing of the wickedness of the living world and shall have died unsullied by the mire of the living. This innocent shall raise the pure weapon – and then there is another undeciphered part – then it says "cast out the demons that rise to overthrow the living world." This will be the Sentinel; "their shape will be true and it will be that of a child."'

D'Scover looked up from the book, which slowly closed in his lap, and stared into Adam's stunned expression.

'It has been a very long time since I have heard these words,' D'Scover told Adam. 'The Senior Council have restricted knowledge of the wording of the Vision to prevent anyone from using it to gain control of the Brotherhood. If the wording was common knowledge, someone could fake the portents of the events contained within it. Even the Senior Council have not seen the Master Text for over two centuries and they do not know of the exact location of my library. All of the Texts must be protected from opportunists; if anyone knew where they are, it could be catastrophic to the Brotherhood.'

'Why tell *me*?' Adam asked. 'I mean, I don't know where you keep the books, but I've seen this Vision thing now. How do you know you can trust me?'

'Adam …' D'Scover's voice wavered slightly as he spoke. 'I have reason to think that you may be the Sentinel.'

Chapter Eleven – The Senior Council

'Sister Goodman, why have you pulled me from my Dispersal?'

D'Scover stood in the middle of his office, unnaturally summoned from his rest and visibly shaken by the event. Daylight had fled and the sister was barely visible in the gloom as she stood before the painting of the Madonna.

'Sorry, Toby, it was unavoidable. The Senior Council have called an extraordinary gathering to discuss the boy and his future.' She spoke flatly and without expression. 'You are summoned.'

D'Scover ran his long fingers through his hair to smooth it into place as he spoke. 'You told them?' He was stunned. 'Why?'

'As an Attendant, it was my duty,' she explained. 'But there was more to it than that. The Council members have been aware of a problem, a disturbance in the spirit activity around the world; they have received information they wish to have confirmed. They wish to talk about the boy, and this girl that you have seen.'

'I have seen an increase in reports lately,' D'Scover said, 'and yes, each day at least one new report from the living agents, but, as I have said before, it is probably a transient phase and may still settle down.'

'Is that what you truly believe?'

'No.' He sighed. 'In all honesty, I believe it is the opening phase of the Vision. The old and once rested spirits are possibly disturbed by sensing the arrival of the Sentinel.'

'The Senior Council do not share your thoughts on this matter,' she said. 'They do not feel that the time is right.'

'When is the convergence of the Council to be?' D'Scover asked.

Without warning, a jagged silver bolt of lightning cut through the clear sky outside and illuminated the room with a cold white light that did not fade and, despite its luminescence, cast no shadow. A thick broil of clouds burst into the sky and enveloped the building.

'They are here.'

The walls seemed to flux and pulse as the clouds thickened around the building until the upper floors were entirely concealed by the thick mass. Inside the office the air prickled with static electricity that bounced from all surfaces, and a slow haze of it ran over the two occupants. Slowly twelve shapes began to form round D'Scover in a circle: dark outlines seething with the various colours that represented the memory of the life force of their host. Deep purples and blues that were so dark as to be barely visible forced the dark shapes to take on the forms of people robed in black and heavily hooded.

D'Scover felt the weight of a sword at his side and realised that he was clothed once more in the simple, rough hessian outfit he had died in. He was a child and his cloak felt heavy with rain just as it had when he died. He flinched in pain as he took a step forward and, glancing down at his leg, could see the dark stain of fresh blood. Drawing his sword from his belt and flicking his heavy cloak behind him, he dropped to his one good knee, resting his forehead on the weapon's icy hilt as the sharp point dug into the floor.

'My lords,' he offered without raising his gaze, as the Council members took solid form around him.

'STAND, KEEPER OF THE TEXTS.' A deep and sombre voice echoed in D'Scover's head. As the Council addressed him, the sound seemed to come from within all of the members, as though they spoke with one and many voices at the same time. Each word was rich with a layer of voices twelve deep, a dark, resonating harmony. 'AND YOU, HOLY SISTER, MAY LEAVE US.'

'But my lords,' she protested, 'I may be able to offer some insight. If I could ...'

'BEGONE!' The chilling order of the Senior Council boomed through the room.

Sister Goodman, now clad in the simple black habit of the holy order she had served in life, bowed to the Senior Council and Dispersed with a crackle of bright violet sparks.

D'Scover stood and slid his sword into his belt, but kept his eyes lowered in deference.

'WHAT OF THE BOY?'

'He is not yet fully integrated into the Brotherhood, but he will make a most excellent Shade.' D'Scover still kept his gaze to the floor.

'DO YOU BELIEVE THAT HE IS THE CHILD OF THE VISION?'

'I am not yet sure; he meets many of the requirements, but it is too early to say.'

'WE HAVE DECIDED HE IS TO TAKE A TRIAL.'

'No, he is not ready; you cannot ...' D'Scover looked up at the assembled Council.

'KEEPER.' The voice cut through his thoughts and D'Scover flinched from the intense pressure of it inside his head and dropped at once to his knees.

'WE HAVE AFFORDED YOU MANY PRIVILEGES BY VIRTUE OF YOUR SKILLS AND YOUR DEVOTION TO THE BROTHERHOOD, BUT THIS IS NOT YOUR CHOICE TO MAKE. THE COUNCIL FEEL A GREAT CHANGE IS COMING AND WHILST *OUR* TIME IS ENDLESS, WE CANNOT RISK HUMANITY BY WAITING UNNECESSARILY. IF THIS BOY IS THE SENTINEL, HE WILL PROVE TRIUMPHANT IN A TRIAL. IF NOT, HE WILL PERISH AND THE SEARCH WILL CONTINUE. SUCH IS OUR JUDGEMENT.'

'Bound by our rules, I will, as always, obey, my lords,' D'Scover said in a voice loaded with resentment. 'How much time do I have?'

'THE TRIAL IS TO BE HELD WITHIN ONE CYCLE OF THE MOON.'

'One month! It is too soon,' D'Scover protested. 'He will not be ready for any kind of fight, and how will he know what to prepare for? What form is the Trial to take?'

'THE VISION CALLS FOR COMBAT, BUT THE FULL FORM IS AS YET UNDECIDED. THAT ISSUE MAY NOT EVEN BE IN *OUR* CONTROL AS HE MAY BE CALLED TO TRIAL WITHOUT OUR INVOLVEMENT.'

'What does that mean?' D'Scover asked.

'WHAT OF THIS GIRL?' the Senior Council asked, ignoring D'Scover's question.

In the centre of the circle a dark ball of cloud formed and parted with a sliver of white light. Within the cloud stood a frozen image of the girl D'Scover had seen in the Text and Adam had seen in his Hypnagogia.

'IS SHE LINKED TO THE BROTHERHOOD?'

'It is possible, yes,' D'Scover answered. 'Finding her present living form may be difficult and it may take time, more time than I …'

'IF IT IS THE RIGHT TIME, YOU WILL FIND HER,' the booming chorus interrupted. 'SEEK HER.'

The image of the girl suddenly vanished.

'WE ARE AWARE OF YOUR PRESENCE, SISTER. WE ORDER YOU TO APPEAR.'

A violet spiral whirled in the corner of the room and Sister Goodman walked out of the shadows.

'My lords, forgive me,' she grovelled, bowing low to the assembled Council. 'I feel somewhat responsible for these events, as it was I who alerted Toby to the presence of the boy.'

'WE ARE AWARE OF THE BACKGROUND OF THIS CASE,' the Council boomed. 'WE CONSIDER YOUR INVOLVEMENT TO NOW BE AT AN END.'

She stepped backwards into the darkness, avoiding eye contact with D'Scover.

'WE ARE FINISHED HERE, KEEPER,' the Council said. 'BE READY WITHIN ONE LUNAR CYCLE.'

The room heaved again with a silent pulse of energy and the static sparkle of muted colours began to darken to a light-absorbing blackness rising up through the ceiling. The fading outlines of the Council members joined to form one vast mass of black particles that became a maelstrom and, just as suddenly as they came, they dissipated in a crack of thunder that shook the building. The clouds parted to reveal a sky studded with the cold decoration of stars.

'You know I like you with a sword, but I am not sure about the tights, although I suppose they are hose, not tights, really.'

D'Scover stood and remembered that he was still wearing the changed clothes and Sister Goodman was still there. He smoothed his hands through the air just over the surface of his body and his clothes became the perfectly fitted charcoal-grey suit he had previously worn and his body stretched to adulthood again. Walking to the window, he looked down upon the acrid yellow lights of the city below.

'As an Attendant, you had the ears of the Council, sister. What is it that they mean when they say the issue may not be within their control?' he asked.

'Toby, I do not know what they think, only what they wish me to know.' She moved to his side and looked up at him. 'I do know they feel something is coming, something that may change the Brotherhood for the remains of time, but I do not know what that is. There has been talk of disturbances in other countries – tales of malevolent spirits and once quiet souls suddenly taken to violent acts. The Senior Council are unsure why this is, but it may have something to do with the Vision.'

'You were with me when I died, sister; you nursed me in my fever and helped me into my Ritual long before you followed me yourself. You are all I can think of as a friend and I must trust you and your opinions accordingly.' He looked into her round face. 'Do *you* think this boy is the Sentinel?'

She sighed and raised her gaze upwards. He watched the stars reflected in the dark pupils of her eyes. Silence filled the empty spaces in the room and she did not reply for the longest time. When she finally spoke, her words hung like weights around him.

'I just do not know, Toby. But I do know that, Sentinel or not, you must prepare the boy for his Trial.'

'Your training must begin in earnest,' D'Scover told Adam when he had pulled him back from his Dispersal. 'And the first thing that you must learn is to control your own Dispersal and to perform your own Ritual of Sustainment. This is most important as it will enable you to maintain your substance and pass amongst the living.'

'Hang on, I've only just decided to join. Can't we have some fun before the work starts?' Adam pleaded.

'Sadly we no longer have time; we have wasted enough already. Your first task is the Ritual and for that we need to consult the Texts.'

D'Scover moved back to the Madonna key painting and raised his palms in offering to her – murmuring the low chant as he did so. Tearing the air through the silver accumulation, he pulled out the crescent key and laid it in his palm. Turning back to the balcony doors, he waved them open and turned back to Adam.

'Follow me.'

'Where are we going?' Adam trotted after him and out on to the balcony.

'To the library,' D'Scover replied.

'I thought no one knew where your library was?'

'That situation is about to change. Follow me.'

Adam caught up. 'Should I close the windows?'

'No,' D'Scover said, 'leave them; the office could do with some fresh air and these windows are well protected from infiltration.'

'By height, I imagine,' Adam said, peering over the balcony's edge.

Morning had found the city sleeping fitfully under a thick, frosty mist that pushed an unnatural silence through the streets. This now crept up the building and wound its way round them as they walked the length of the balcony. Through gaps in the mist Adam could just make out the grey-green slick of the Thames worming its way past the base of the building. D'Scover reached the end of the balcony first and pressed his palm against the brickwork allowing the sinuous trickle of silver to seep out across the bricks. The door slowly took its black shape and the hollow scrape allowed Adam to eventually see that it was an entrance.

'Sweet,' he said. 'You've got a real flair for the dramatic, don't you? Why can't you just have a normal door?'

'The Texts must be protected at all costs; remember what I said before about the power they contain? There are other texts in here that could bring about the ruin of the living world, or open the way to the World Between,' he replied as he gestured for the slab of a door to open.

D'Scover signalled for Adam to follow him into the darkness and the tall wooden steps trundled towards them while the light on the table rolled out its thin illumination. Climbing the shelves, he began to search for a manuscript among the many in the upper levels. As he did, Adam kept himself busy by wandering along the crammed shelves, tipping his head this way and that to read the gold blocked words on the spines.

'Is this it?' He pulled out a massive ox-blood-coloured tome heavily decorated with gold leaf. 'It looks impressive.'

'No,' D'Scover replied, looking down from his perch. 'That one refers to methods of dealing with animal deaths.'

'Animals, you're kidding, right?'

'In your admittedly limited experience of me, do you think that I joke much?'

'Ha!' Adam scoffed. 'Good point. But animals? Don't tell me places get haunted by animals?'

'Not for long thanks to that book,' D'Scover muttered over his shoulder, returning to his search.

'How do you find stuff in here?' Adam gestured up to the rising shelves. 'I mean, do you have a catalogue or something?'

'No, disorder is protection,' D'Scover replied. 'If, by some extraordinary chance, someone did get in here, they would not have long before the room's defences came into operation. I hope that they would not have enough time to find the correct book. I am also hopeful that the correct book will find me today if it is meant to be, and I believe it is.'

'Defences, you said defences, you mean like booby traps?' Adam asked.

'In a manner of speaking. The Texts will defend themselves if threatened or if they feel concerned about their well-being.'

'You expect me to believe they have feelings?' Adam laughed.

'Not exactly, they only have those which their author has given them. The feelings a book holds are passed on to the original text only if the author has been very passionate in his or her beliefs.' D'Scover looked down at Adam. 'And I think the one that you hold is passionate about being returned to its shelf.'

Adam looked down at the book that he had forgotten he still cradled and gasped as an angry green cat's eye stared back at him from the cover. Jumping back, he dropped the book which fell a short distance from his hands before stopping in mid-air as though it had fallen on to an invisible cushion. Resting for the briefest moment, it rose in front of the boy, its eye keeping a close watch on him. It drifted to head height and slotted itself neatly back on the shelves.

'WHOA!' Adam was stunned. 'All this stuff you do, is it like magic or something?'

'How many people believe in magic?' D'Scover said from his perch high up among the shelves.

'Loads, millions, I suppose. I mean, there are people in places like Haiti with the whole Vodou thing, and the Native Americans with shamans and Goths and Wiccans and all the crazy stuff they believe ...' Adam answered. 'Ah ... I get it, it's a belief thing again? That means that magic actually works?'

'On occasion some magic does, yes,' D'Scover confirmed. 'But it is not as simple as conjuring things up with a snap of the fingers; it takes practice and the right words and objects.'

'Can anyone do it?'

'No.' D'Scover's tone showed he was not keen on continuing this line of conversation. 'Now, if you have quite finished badgering me, I do have some work to do.'

'I think I'll just have a quiet sit-down over here for a bit.' Adam pulled a chair out. 'This is making my head ache.'

Adam leaned back and looked up at the glass above his head, watching the sky clear and the morning sun make a weak effort to burn through the cold atmosphere. Dust motes caught the last fragments of light and revolved gently around the room as D'Scover lifted book after book from the shelves in his search, creating curling eddies in the still room. Time ticked slowly past and Adam allowed his eyes to drift closed as he breathed in the dusty smell. He relaxed into the warm and secure atmosphere of this most exclusive of libraries.

'Ah, here it is,' D'Scover called out at last, and descended from the shelves.

Adam opened his eyes and was surprised to see that D'Scover held only a small book, no bigger than a modern paperback, bound in a dirty grey cloth.

'What's that manky-looking thing?' Adam asked.

'This is the Addendum,' D'Scover replied as he placed it reverentially on the table.

'Isn't that one of the books I saw you with in the Hypnagogia, in the monastery?'

'It is. This book contains all of the additional notes that Father Dominic made after the Master Text was written. It allows us to adjust the Ritual to suit individual needs. It is not often needed as the basic Ritual suits everyone, but we need something different in your case. It had hidden itself well, a slight frustration.'

'Oh yeah, because I'm the Sentinel, right?' Adam said in mock deference.

D'Scover cast him a look that chilled him as completely as if a bullet of ice had run clear through his body.

'This is no time for humour,' he said. 'If you are not willing to enter into this fully, you must say so now.'

'Sorry,' Adam smiled. 'I'm serious really, but it's difficult to get my head round.'

'You will need to be able to do that before this is finished.' D'Scover picked up the book and walked to the door. 'Come, you must perform your own Ritual.'

He strode from the room with Adam in brisk pursuit once more. Back in the office he lifted the Master Text from where it still rested on the small table and carried it back to the couch. It opened in his lap as if obediently trained and lay showing a page bordered by silver instead of the usual gold. This page looked cold among the heat of the other pages and even the paper seemed to shiver with the ice of it.

'Here is the Ritual of Sustainment. You must say this, with all your heart and with true commitment, or it will not work,' D'Scover said and offered the book to Adam.

'I can't read that out. I haven't got a clue what it says.' Adam looked down at the pages as he took the book from D'Scover.

The words on the pages were a jumble of Latin and code that seemed to defy translation. Adam felt the cold breath of the book in his face and shivered.

'It blew at me!'

'Indeed,' D'Scover replied, unimpressed. 'You must extend your arms with your palms upwards during the first section and when you reach here,' he pointed at the second section, 'you move them out to the side, then up into the air. Clap your hands hard together on the final words, like this …'

He showed Adam how to perform the final movements before Dispersal.

'Where do I put the book while I do all this hand-waving?' Adam asked.

'Eventually you will know the Ritual as well as you once knew how to breathe and it will become as natural to you too; you will not need the book then,' D'Scover explained. 'But for now it can remain in front of you. Let it go and it will stay wherever you place it.'

Adam laid the book open in the air and it loyally remained where he could clearly see the pages.

'I still can't read it – this is crazy,' he complained.

'Look at the words, Adam, *really* look at them,' D'Scover insisted. 'You know these words; you can see past the language and into the meaning. It is all there inside your mind. Trust yourself and look deep into the pages.'

Adam shook his head in disbelief, but looked back at the pages once more and took a deep breath. He stared hard at the text for what felt like a lifetime and his eyes began to prick with exhaustion. He kept staring as his frustration and anger grew. Suddenly the words moved about the page, sliding into each other in a slow-flowing silver mass that shifted around the creamy paper. As he watched, the ink began to separate from the liquid silver and form words he could now recognise. Soon the page filled with a legible script in a smooth and clear hand that Adam had no trouble reading. He took a deep breath and spoke the words out loud.

'Though I may be caught in this time and place I shall not lament and shall choose instead to give myself to the Brotherhood. I will allow myself to remain in the place of neither death nor life to do the bidding of the Brotherhood. I shall do my utmost to ensure the safety and protection of the living world. I have given up the trappings of the material world and instead I offer myself to this new purpose. I shall aid those trapped where they do not belong and provide assistance to those that require it. The Brotherhood shall be my master and I shall look to it for guidance until my Final Dispersal. By the powers of my belief and the belief of those about me I shall prevail over all adversity. These are my words alone and in performing this rite I shall be strengthened by the Dispersal and prove my commitment to the Brotherhood.'

The words moved again and a new section appeared below the first. Adam moved his hands slowly out to the side as D'Scover had shown him while he spoke this final section. 'In this place I now belong and I shall move amongst the living and the dead with equal fluidity and control. I am the master of the Texts and I alone have access to the gateway that links all that their creators have known and will know. This much I accept to be true and this always shall be mine own destiny.'

The room was gone, and with it D'Scover and the book. Adam realised he was in Dispersal around the room and the familiar feeling of comfort and relaxation filled him. Without the restriction of the walls around him, he spread out his essence and flowed out over the waking city. He recognised the feeling of Dispersal, but this time it was different. He felt as though he was the strongest he had ever been and yet he had no body or even a distinguishable shape. This was not like the Dispersals he had felt before; this time he felt as if he could tear the stars from the sky and cast them down to the earth. All seemed insignificant beneath him, tiny and fragile people moving pathetically through their short lives.

This was like nothing he had ever felt before. Here there was a level of control that filled him with the desire to influence the living Earth. He felt he could go anywhere, at any time, and make things the way he wanted. It was as if the world had been spread out beneath his feet. Suddenly he understood the terrible allure of power and it filled him with a cold sense of dread. Gathering his thoughts, he turned his scattered substance back to the building and soared towards it, stopping dead at the faint illusion of the balcony and forcing himself back into human shape once more. He walked into the office to find D'Scover sitting at his desk, waiting for him.

'True Dispersal is quite a different sensation to the one that you have previously experienced, is it not?' he asked Adam.

'You're telling me!' Adam gasped. 'I could get really carried away with a feeling like that.'

'That is why it is a gift that is not given lightly,' D'Scover said. 'It could be easily abused by the wrong spirit. The Brotherhood is here to carefully monitor any abuse.'

'I felt as if I could've torn the world apart,' enthused Adam. 'I could've done anything, anything at all.'

'I performed the Addendum so that your Ritual would be specific to you and it may have been stronger than the one you usually experience, but you will get used to it. The first time is always the strongest.'

'It was amazing!' Adam gasped. 'I could've taken on the world and won. I felt like I could have kicked some serious butt. I can't really explain. It was like a blade in my mind cutting through all the mess in my life and setting me free. My head feels totally clear. I feel … freed.'

'I cannot explain your feelings. I did not grasp your words as you performed the final section. To you it may have seemed as if you read and spoke them in English, but you actually spoke the code of Father Dominic.' D'Scover sounded confused. 'I did not understand your words, as they were not for me to hear in their base form, but that is the section influenced by the Addendum. Possibly something you said then caused the strength that you speak of.'

'I can't remember exactly; there was something about destiny and the Texts and a gateway and moving amongst the living and the dead,' Adam babbled. 'It's like I knew the words and they were a part of me, more than just something I'd read. It all rushed away from me, like it just poured out. But now I can't remember the exact words. I think I could probably say them again, but that's crazy if I don't actually know what they are. I do know I was so strong and had so much control over, well, everything.'

D'Scover looked down at his hands and laced his fingers together, all the while avoiding eye contact with Adam.

'What?' Adam asked. 'You're acting weird now – what's wrong?'

'Your success in the Dispersal Ritual has confirmed a few things for me. I think that the time has come,' D'Scover said quietly without looking up, 'for me to tell you of the plans the Senior Council have for you.'

Chapter Twelve – Demon

'Does he suspect?'

'The man is a fool and would barely notice the passage of time, let alone anything else.'

Two half-formed shapes drifted on the edge of the physical world in the darkened corridors of the Natural History Museum. Thin moonlight from the small windows in the ceiling barely offered enough light to see those that cared to be seen – and was certainly not enough for those whose main desire was to remain hidden. Both held themselves in a state of weakened substance, ready to Disperse at a second's notice. Two voices hoarsely whispering seemed to gather like the memory of a conversation in the air.

'Nevertheless you must be more cautious. This reallocation may prove problematical for us,' one rasped at the other.

'Stop fretting, nothing has changed. I will still do my duty as I have sworn to you many times. Do you doubt my devotion?'

'I do not, but the time draws near and we cannot allow the natural evolution of the Brotherhood to be hindered.'

'We are not alone in our mission, are we? Your servants are ready and waiting for the beginning of the end. It cannot be stopped now, surely?'

'It does not matter how many of us there are; the facts still remain the same. If we do not have the tools for the job, we cannot prevent a successful Trial. And if the Sentinel is found, then our time is lost. That ridiculous Vision could prevent us from achieving our aims. It seems that he has found another who may fit the Vision, and that would make two of the three.'

'But the Vision is a farce; surely no one still takes it seriously?'

'Many on the Council do; belief is still strong and that could cause us some problems.'

'Not when we have the artefacts. When we have them, even the Council will not have the power to stand in our way. Are you sure you can get them?'

'I told you last night, I know where the artefacts are and I know where the Text will be moved to. You have to get me into the building and then leave the rest to me.'

'I will get you in; have no fear on that count.'

'To the future?'

'To the future.'

A slight breeze created a disturbance in the corridor and the shapes were gone round the corner and Dispersed out of sight, leaving only the indigo darkness to fill the space where they had been. Marcus, making a careful note of all he had overheard, slipped further back into the shadows and Dispersed in total silence.

'I'm sorry, did you say demon?' Adam gulped. 'Now wait just a minute, let me get this straight. You want me to do some kind of trial and fight a demon so that I can save the living people of the Earth – is that right?'

'Basically,' D'Scover replied.

'And are we talking a total horns, flames, hooves and foul stink and long pronged fork kind of demon – the real deal?' Adam paced the room nervously as he talked.

'Possibly. It is not known exactly which demon will manifest; that is why you must be prepared.'

'Whoa, just hold on. Why the hell didn't you mention this *tiny* detail about a demon before?'

'The time was not right.'

'And now it is?' Adam slumped down on the couch.

'You must start to prepare so, yes, the time is now right.'

'And what if I don't go along with this mad idea?'

'If you *are* the Sentinel, the world will be lost for the living and the dead shall walk the Earth.'

'Man, you sure know how to put a chill up a spirit,' Adam sighed. 'But that's insane, it can't be right. What if I'm *not* the Sentinel?'

'You will fail and the time is not right and I will once more wait patiently for the Vision to be fulfilled.'

'Oh well, that's just fine for you, isn't it?' Adam said angrily, pacing the room. 'Your Brotherhood has nothing to lose from this, do they? If I fail, I'm not the right one, and if I succeed, then everything is cool and everyone can get on with being dead and stuff and wait for the next idiot to come along.'

'A crude summary but accurate,' D'Scover said.

'What'll happen to *me* if I'm not the Sentinel and I take this Trial?'

D'Scover turned away from Adam towards the picture of the Virgin on the wall. 'That is uncertain,' he replied, 'but this is bigger than your personal safety.'

'Will I die?'

'You are already dead.'

'You know what I mean; will I just Disperse forever? Will I go to heaven or hell or, well, anywhere?'

D'Scover sighed and remained silent for a moment before answering. 'I cannot lie to you, Adam; those who have taken the Trial before have not fared well. They have been forcibly Dispersed by the event and we do not know of their fate. Only one has remained afterwards to tell of it.'

'ONE! And just how many Trials have there been?'

'Twenty-two,' D'Scover said. 'Fourteen in fairly quick succession in the sixteenth and early seventeenth century.'

'*Riiiight,*' Adam responded with a calm but sarcastic tone, 'twenty-two have tried and only one has made it through? The odds aren't good, are they? Can I at least talk to the person who made it and hear what they've got to say about it?'

D'Scover turned back to face him. 'You already have. *I* survived a Demon Trial. I was the first,' he said.

'You?' Adam gasped.

'It was thought that I fulfilled some of the more obvious elements of the Vision; after all I was a child when I died, and so I was sent for the Trial. I failed but the demon was weakened and thankfully did not have the strength to pursue its aims,' D'Scover explained. 'Now I realise that my continuation after the Trial was important. I am convinced it is no coincidence that your death was close to me. I think I am here to help you.'

'What was it like – your Trial, I mean? What happened? What was the demon? How the hell do you fight a demon anyway?' Adam's head was spinning.

'I can explain, but for detail and full understanding, I will have to show you. Do you feel you can handle the Hypnagogia once more?'

'Oh no! Isn't there another way?' Adam groaned. 'I still haven't quite got the last time out of my mind. Can't you just tell me?'

'I am afraid not. To grasp the details fully you must see it for yourself.'

Adam looked out at the heavy February clouds and thought hard before answering. 'OK,' he said reluctantly. 'Knock me out, I can take it. I mean, if I'm going to face a real demon, I'd better be able to handle a dream one.'

'Very well, lean back and relax. This will need to be a more complex illusion than the previous one you experienced and so I am afraid that I cannot pull you out of this deeper state once we have started. This Hynpogogia will need to run to its conclusion, but rest assured you cannot be physically harmed in the Hypnagogic state. As you may recall, no one could see you and you could not interact with people; you are just a spectator.'

D'Scover wheeled the desk chair up and sat next to the couch – as though he was a doctor about to talk to his patient – and began.

'*The summer of 1666 dragged on for far longer than it should have. The city had been baked by months of relentless sun and even disease seemed to begin to slow down under the relentless temperatures. From my viewpoint, high in Southwark Cathedral, I could watch the busiest section of the city over the river suffer in its steaming mire of death and filth.*'

D'Scover's soft voice slowed and began to fill Adam's head as he felt his body grow heavy with the suffocating initial effect of the Hypnagogia. He became aware that the temperature was rising and that he was having difficulty in breathing as the air became thin and full of the stench of overcrowded living. Looking down, he watched the raw sewage drift past his feet before jumping to one side to avoid it. A few people had appeared around him and they wandered past as if in a drugged state and, as no one could see him, Adam did nothing to hide his revulsion. Grey faces pocked with the marks of old disease rested upon bodies so frail that Adam was amazed they could walk at all.

The streets closed in around him and the buildings seemed stacked upon each other in perilous piles of wood and flaking plaster. The air was full of the groans of the sick and dying and the heat seemed to drag the sound out. He knew that D'Scover must be here somewhere, but as he could not see him, he started to walk. After walking for what seemed like an eternity he reached the city gates and watched the crowds of people there waiting to get out of the city and into the fields beyond.

Adam stood back, realising he had no idea where he was going, and turned around, hoping for a clue as to what to do next. He slumped down by a bare section of wall to catch his breath, trying to convince himself that he was not tired and this was all an illusion. While he attempted to force the sweltering atmosphere from his mind, he thought he saw a familiar face making its way through the heaving crowds, but he lost it. Jumping to his feet once more, he wove through the throng and tried to see if he was correct. He dodged people and jumped over the filthy ditch that ran like a brown vein through the streets and was brought up short as he ran straight through someone standing stock-still in the moving mass of bodies.

'Sorry,' Adam offered instinctively. He stood back and looked up at the man he had just run into – and stared into D'Scover's eyes. Facially D'Scover looked the same as the man Adam knew, tall and thin with the same unkempt tousle of glossy black hair, but his clothes were different. He was dressed from head to foot in soft shades of brown as if he had tried his best not to be noticed. From his waist hung the sword Adam had seen him carry from the abbey.

In this confusion of a crowd D'Scover stood, looking around, apparently unaware of the chaos that spread about him. Adam did his best to follow as D'Scover wove his way through the masses and out on to the bridge over the Thames. The bridge was as crowded as the streets and Adam had trouble staying with him. He paused for a moment and looked ahead as D'Scover disappeared into the tightly packed streets.

'I can do this,' he told himself. 'None of these people are real. I can just walk through them. Just gotta concentrate.'

He closed his eyes, took a deep breath and ran forward. After a few seconds at this pace he opened his eyes and the blur of the streets around him made his stomach turn upside down. Shaking his head, he again careened through someone who had stopped directly in front of him – it was D'Scover. He walked towards a large building that looked like a church. Adam followed him inside.

Here it was cooler and the noise of the city seemed to suddenly dissipate within the thick walls. D'Scover nodded a greeting to the nuns who were wandering the huge main hall, and continued through into a small door at the far end, his soft shoes making no sound on the elaborate gravestones that flagged the floor. Adam followed and trotted up the narrow winding staircase behind

D'Scover. The stairs wound a tortuous path upwards on steps worn smooth by time, until they reached another even smaller door, low and dark brown in the brick. This door opened to a small square room at the top of a tower with windows in each wall overlooking the city, the Thames on one side and the streets of Southwark and the countryside beyond on the other three. The windows had no glass, but D'Scover had no need for warmth – and no need for a bed either.

Adam looked from the windows and puzzled over the fact that the view looked almost familiar and he realised why. This building must have been practically on the site of the new one, certainly less than a mile away from the office D'Scover used today. He had said the site had been reused many times, and that his office had been here for over three hundred years. The view was certainly lower than from D'Scover's modern office, and London had changed considerably, but it was familiar enough.

Adam stared hard at it, trying to put his finger on the main differences, while D'Scover busied himself at a table, rifling through sheaves of creamy paper covered with the black scrawl of hand-writing. St Paul's Cathedral was changed; it was there all right but a different shape – no dome just a square tower not unlike the one he stood in but much larger. Many of the buildings further out of the city seemed recognisable, but the crowded area they had just left looked totally unfamiliar. The bridge was nothing like the modern bridge Adam was used to; this one was as cluttered with houses as the streets were and the river that crawled underneath it was black and fouled with sewage.

A thick cloud began to gather round the tower room and after less than a minute Adam's eyes could no longer see to the ground below. Turning back towards D'Scover, he realised that the cloud was now inside the room too, eddies of it reaching into every corner. He stumbled back towards the desk as it spiralled round D'Scover who now rested on one knee in the middle of the room with his forehead on the hilt of his sword.

The spiralling cloud began to settle into human shapes, twelve of them. D'Scover waited in his supplicant stance until the shapes were fully formed and surrounded him.

'RISE, KEEPER OF THE TEXTS.' A deep voice boomed around them. It seemed to come from no one and everyone at the same time, a cold intonation that echoed inside Adam's skull.

D'Scover stood up, sheathed his sword and kept his head low.

'What is your bidding, masters?' he asked softly.

'YOUR TIME OF TRIAL HAS COME,' the voice said. 'A DEMON WILL ATTEMPT TO TAKE THIS CITY. YOU ARE TO STOP HER.'

'I will do your bidding. What form will she take?'

'SHE IS A FIRE DEMON. WE KNOW ONLY THIS. DO NOT FAIL US.'

D'Scover dropped again to one knee as the figures began to break up and the cloud swirled around the room and was gone. Outside the sky cleared and Adam could see the people in the streets below.

'Fire.'

Suddenly D'Scover turned and walked briskly from the room with Adam scuttling behind. Halfway down the stairs he stopped and took a key from a strip of leather around his waist and thrust it into a small crack in the brickwork. A hollow sound of metal against stone crunched within the wall and dust fell as D'Scover pushed open a low door. Inside Adam recognised many of the books now still under D'Scover's protection. They stood on thick oak shelves around every bit of wall. Each book was held securely with a strong dark chain that hung from their spines – each chain just long enough to reach the table in the middle of the room. The chains clanked as D'Scover pulled them out one at a time to consult different texts.

This went on for hours. D'Scover was trying in vain to trace a possible weakness in the demon. His hunt went right on until the cry went up. The city was burning.

D'Scover ran back up to the tower windows and looked out over the darkening metropolis to where its heart now glowed red. He ran back towards the stairs and headed down, and Adam followed.

The journey to the fire was clearly difficult for D'Scover – by Adam's reckoning, he had already held his shape for a number of hours and his strength could not possibly last much longer. Moving through the crowds was wasting valuable energy needed to confront the demon. People swarmed out of the city now in all directions and the heat had begun to grow fierce. From the bridge, flames could now be seen rising into the evening sky, carrying sparks high into the swirling smoke. All around him was panic. Most fled the tongues of flame that licked across the rooftops, catching building after building; but some desperately pumped water in the street and carried bucket after bucket to douse their houses.

D'Scover pushed on closer to the thunderous heart of the fire. The heat rose and the smoke soon became impossible to see through, but still he walked on until he stood alone in front of a wall of scarlet flames. Then he stepped through. Adam stood outside the ring of fire, and looked around. A few people scrambled to safety behind him, but as he walked forward, only one other figure remained on the edge. Adam squinted through the haze but, by the time he focussed through the smoke, the figure was gone. He took a deep breath and reminded himself that none of this was real – and he too walked into the blaze.

Inside all was strangely still and quiet. The roar of the fire had died down, and was now replaced with a low murmur that sounded like anguished voices at a great distance. It was as though the voices had long since lost the strength to cry out and only moaned softly at their distress. All around rose the seething walls of fire, rippling like stormy waters.

'I know you are here!' D'Scover shouted. 'Show yourself, demon; your time has come.'

Adam looked at D'Scover's face and saw the determination in

128

it, but a tremble in his voice betrayed fear. He held the sword aloft and turned round, staring into the inferno. For a moment, behind D'Scover's back, the flames darkened as if cooled from outside. A small tear appeared, widening bit by bit until Adam could see a pair of pale hands push through. For a second he could see a face through the tear in the flames. It was the face of the girl in the last Hypnagogia, the witch girl. The wall of fire flared with a blistering white heat and the girl was gone and Adam turned his attention back to D'Scover.

A little in front of D'Scover a thin trickle of ash began to fall from the air. Though it seemed to have no origin, it very quickly grew and angry red sparks danced over the surface. The pile increased and a flicker of fire began to appear from the floor, rising up the ash and cloaking it in a shimmering garment of crimson and yellow. With a final flourish of curling smoke and crackling light, a stunningly beautiful woman appeared in front of them. She was tall with hair and clothes of flame that flowed out and around her in a furious halo. She stretched out long thin arms the colour of wood ash and a white sprinkle like grey rain fell to the floor as she moved. The skin of her face was the same ashen colour as her arms, but her lips and eyes glistened with the rich dark hue of the crimson sparks that had formed her.

'Does my shape please you?' She had a voice that sounded like hot syrup. It made the hair stand up on the back of Adam's neck. An involuntary shudder ran up his spine and he felt captivated by her beauty. He wanted to look away from her and run, but was rooted to the spot and wondered if D'Scover felt the same.

'You cannot influence me, demon!' D'Scover shouted above the murmur of the flames. 'I am here to dispatch you, not to listen to you.'

The woman walked round the circle and small tongues of flame licked out and jumped into her infernal clothing. She lifted an elegant hand as she walked and ran it delicately through the blaze as though trailing it through burning oil.

'Why do you call me demon?' she asked softly, turning back towards him, her dress gleaming as she moved.

'I speak as I find. You are a demon and you cannot trick me with your words.' He held his sword defiantly, with the point towards her.

She smiled and, with a gesture from her, the wall roared and claws of fire leapt out towards D'Scover, stopping within a hair's breadth of him.

'I am no mere demon, I am Elemental. My sisters and I existed long before the time of humans. We shall be here long after you have gone.' Her voice was as smooth as liquid yet bubbled with fury like the flames around her. 'You are a fool if you think that you can stop me. This world is already ours.'

'Then I will die in the attempt!' he shouted and swung out with his sword.

The Elemental moved backwards and partially merged with the flames which reached out and covered her like protective arms. The blade swept wide, missing her completely.

'Forgive me, child, but you are already dead.' She smiled with a look of pure malevolence and D'Scover stumbled backwards.

Stepping out from the flames, her face darkened and her eyes burned blood–red, shining with pure evil.

'I tire of this game,' she said angrily. 'I give you one last chance before I Disperse you for a final time.'

'It is not your choice; my destiny is already marked.' D'Scover once more raised his sword aloft. 'Come, demon, this dance is mine.'

For all of his brave words, Adam could see from the tremble running down the sword just how scared D'Scover really was and, with his hindsight, he knew that the battle was already lost.

The Elemental drew up her arms and the flames turned black around her and licked higher than Adam could see. Her face grew distorted with hatred as she turned and drew a blood-red ball of fire from the air above her head.

D'Scover spun round and the air filled with the song of swung metal as his weapon cast a silver circle around him. The blade this time made contact and swept through the Elemental at the waist, causing her to fold and crumple to the floor. As she fell, she screamed and the flames around her howled an ungodly wail as if they too had felt the cut of the blade. D'Scover took a few steps back, stunned by the sword's effect. But the Elemental lifted her head and the twisted smile on her face chilled Adam to the bone.

'Strong words, boy.' Her words were thick with anger. 'You almost *believe* that you can kill me, but you'll need conviction stronger than the weak mind of a boy to defeat me. My patience with this farce has ended.'

She drew herself to her feet and, as she took a deep breath, grew taller until all that could be seen was a moving column of fire that seared Adam's skin.

'This isn't real, it can't harm me.' He shouted the words out loud, trying to convince himself.

D'Scover had been pushed back by the flames and had his back to the firewall which reached out for him with a thousand tiny scorched hands. His own arms hung limp by his side and the now blackened blade of his sword trailed through the ash on the floor. Staring up, he was obviously transfixed by the movement of the flames. In his eyes Adam could only see the reflection of the roaring column and saw nothing of the man he had come to think of as a friend.

'D'Scover, you can do this, you've got to pull yourself together!' Adam screamed uselessly.

Far above them the Elemental laughed and her breath came down with the hellish smell of sulphur and brimstone. Adam looked up as a drop of hell fell towards them. The Elemental's foot crushed them both and the world was seemingly snuffed out.

'The Senior Council stepped in. I was placed in Dispersal a second before she struck and that saved me from destruction. It was my mistake; I assumed that she was a demon, but she was worse than that. The Council placed a restriction charm on the heart of city and, when the oxygen ran out, the flames subsided. The city burned at its heart for five days; all who saw her died. Today it is still remembered as the Great Fire of London. The Senior Council spent decades sorting out the scars she left on the city and erasing the traces and memory of those who died. I, however, will never forget.'

D'Scover finished his tale and the Hypnagogia slipped from Adam like a thick blanket on an icy night, leaving him cold and shaking. He sat up and pulled his arms around his body.

'I saw her again,' Adam said through chattering teeth. 'The witch girl, in the last Hypnagogia, the same one. How can that be? Is that just my imagination or did you put her there?'

'I did not put her there consciously,' D'Scover assured him, 'but she must have been in my memories; she must be there for a reason.'

'So who is she then?'

'I am not sure, but it is clear that we must find out.'

'Do you think that she's dead too?'

'No, I do not think so.' D'Scover shook his head. 'The time between the two events you have seen was too great for her to have lived through both. I have a theory that she carries a timeless spirit; many witches do.'

'You seem to enjoy confusing me,' Adam grumbled. 'Can't you just speak plain English?'

'When her body dies, her spirit is reborn in another from her family,' he patiently explained. 'It does sometimes happen in powerful witch families.'

'So what now?' Adam asked..

'Now,' D'Scover said, ripping the air apart for the library key once more, 'we find out who this witch really is.'

Chapter Thirteen – Witch Hunt

The library door closed behind them and D'Scover began searching along the shelves.

'Anything I can do?' Adam asked, running his finger along a jumbled collection of book spines.

'You could look too,' D'Scover said over his shoulder.

'I don't know what I'm looking for.'

'Nor do I exactly, but we shall know it when we find it. We are searching for a book that will give us a ritual to discover the whereabouts of someone who can help us,' he said without turning back to look at Adam. 'It is a Ritual of Finding and therefore will want to be found. We simply have to look with the right eyes.'

'You've finally lost it, you know that, don't you?' teased Adam. 'What does all that even mean?'

'If we are meant to find it, then we shall, but only if we look with care,' D'Scover replied flatly.

'Right, I'll take your word for it,' Adam said.

He turned his back on D'Scover and began to slide single books out from the densely occupied shelves. They seemed to enjoy this handling and most offered a dusty flutter as he separated them from their neighbours. Some even curved their spines like waking cats and gave off a creaky stretch as he carried them to the table.

After a while Adam realised that he had drifted into talking to them, offering a little phrase of comfort or praise as he looked through them.

'Wow, you're handsome, aren't you?' he would say to one and, 'Don't worry, all be over in a minute,' to another. After many hours, a jostling pile of freed volumes sat on the desk and yet he still had no idea if they were closer to finding what they were looking for. D'Scover seemed deep in silent concentration in the darkest corner of the room as he pulled book after book from the shelves, quickly flicked through their pages and slotted them back in place.

Adam leaned back in his chair and stretched. 'I wish one of you could help me out,' he sighed, and swung his feet up on to the desk.

At first he thought that it was his own movement that caused one of the books on the top of the pile in front of him to ruffle, but it did it again a moment later. Feeling distinctly foolish, he leaned over and stared at the cover.

'Can you help me?' he asked softly and, once more, the pages fluttered in their bindings.

He picked up the book that he had already examined and laid it in his lap where it puffed itself up like a chicken fluffing its feathers and settled down again. Adam opened the front page and looked at the frontispiece that he had already scrutinised.

'I don't get it,' he muttered. 'I've already looked right through you and found squat. Are you hiding something?'

The pages of the book began to flick past as though caught by a stiff breeze. Adam lifted his hands out of the way to avoid accidentally stopping the rapid search through the volume. After a few seconds the pace slowed then stopped. Adam looked carefully at this page, scanning down the lines, desperate for something that might look as if it would help.

'I wouldn't know a Finding Ritual if it jumped out and knocked me on the head,' he told the book. 'You'll have to be clearer than that.'

Slowly one of the pages of the book began to curl in on itself until the outside edge tucked itself neatly into the bindings at the margin. Adam picked the book up, at first assuming that it was upset in some way and had curled up in a sulk.

'Hey, don't fold your pages in half; it'll leave a crease if you get closed up with a page like that.' He reached out to unfurl the page, but then stopped and took a closer look. An idea hit him so hard he jumped with realisation.

'I think I've found it!' he called out. 'Come and have a look at this!'

D'Scover climbed down from his ladder and, with a head carrying a thick crop of trailing cobwebs, came over to where Adam sat.

'I didn't see it at first; it was just there all of a sudden.' He held the book up to D'Scover. 'I asked it nicely, and it showed me – how about that?'

D'Scover looked at the book where the page had curled in half. The words ran from one half of a page across to the next. Where previously it had been two pages of distinctly different text, now there was one legible page – a Finding Ritual. The library was heavy with static electricity which crackled along the surfaces like tiny vivid blue ants. D'Scover stood with the curled-page book resting in the crook of his left arm, his right arm raised palm upwards in front of him. As soon as he started reciting the words on the pages, the room grew dark. Clouds which once drifted benignly over the building stopped and gathered in churning masses outside the glass. Adam could not hear D'Scover's words, but he had learned that there was no need to shout rituals for them to be effective – just believing the words as you spoke them was enough.

The Ritual continued and a low hum filled the room, making the bowls of D'Scover's collection jiggle and dance on their tables, adding the clink of china to the noise. Adam covered his ears, but the hum was inside his head. He looked at D'Scover to see if it was affecting him too – but he remained still, moving only his lips as he continued with the Ritual. D'Scover held his hand up in the air and a ball of light began to form in the open palm. It throbbed with an intense brightness almost too much to look at and lifted to revolve just above the surface of his hand. The hum began to subside, and the ball gained a round and frosty surface, trailing blue vapour as it turned.

'I think it is ready.' D'Scover's voice made Adam jump.

'What do we do with it?'

'This,' D'Scover said, and took a few steps backwards away from the hovering ball of light.

The blue vapour began to cloud around the light ball giving it a diaphanous halo. Adam could make out shapes within the mist beginning to grow and spread out around the light ball. He moved closer.

'It looks like … a tiny world!'

'It is *our* world, give it time,' D'Scover said.

Inside the ball the Earth began to rush towards the mist, the image magnifying rapidly as it did so. Adam reeled with nausea as he tried to focus on the swiftly changing view. After what felt like an agonisingly long time the ball slowed and Adam could make out England through the veil of clouds. This continued to magnify until the image settled itself on just one part of the country.

'But Cornwall is still a big place,' Adam said, realising where the ball had chosen. 'How's this gonna help us? What are we looking for anyway?'

'I have told you, we need some help. Have patience. Look now,' D'Scover said.

The image stopped and focused in, now moving at such a slow pace that it almost escaped the eye. It closed in on a single village, growing closer and clearer. Adam looked away for a moment to note D'Scover's expression of intense concentration. When he looked back at the ball, it was so tight to the village that they could see people moving about along the tiny streets. The village wrapped itself round the arms of a peaceful-looking harbour where the sea bumped its head against a strong defensive wall. A quiet Cornish town with the usual sprinkling of tourists and locals. All were spending their lives under the watchful beady eyes of the seagulls circling the harbour in an endless search for food.

'I know this place,' Adam gasped.

'How?' D'Scover asked. 'How can you know where this is?'

'I was fostered for a while, to a family who thought they couldn't have kids. Good place until she got pregnant and they sent me back,' Adam explained. 'Anyway, they took me on holiday; they had a holiday cottage just outside this village. The place is called Polcastle. How weird is that? I mean, what're the odds of that happening?'

'The odds are very good if it is meant to be.'

'What do you mean?'

'Destiny,' D'Scover said flatly.

It would take a few hours to find an agent in Cornwall who could gain access to a safe computer for a Hotline. The time had rushed past and most working offices were long closed up for the day. Office computers provided the safest route over which to Hotline: there were so many of them and they were unwatched at night. A Hotline did not leave any trace on the hard drive and many computers were left on overnight so it was often possible to find a way through. However, finding one of the computers left on in a rural area was by no means simple. They had no choice but to sit down for a long wait.

D'Scover managed to convince Adam to pass the time in Dispersal as he had spent far too long maintaining his substance already. The boy had not yet walked among the living unnoticed and, though there was no time to practise, he would have to do so very soon.

When he was alone, D'Scover cleared away all the remaining books from the table in the library and prepared for his own Dispersal. Back in his office he called through to Emma in reception.

'I shall be placing myself in Dispersal shortly; could you carry out an alert if my clearance call comes through?' he asked her via the hands-free phone on the desk.

'Yes … sir,' she replied. She sounded hesitant. 'Sir, before you go into Dispersal, could I have a quick word with you?'

'Of course.'

Emma came into the office and stood nervously by the desk, looking around and avoiding eye contact with D'Scover.

'Well, come on, speak. You are not normally this reticent,' he told her. 'What is on your mind?'

'It's difficult, sir. I don't want to cause any trouble, but agents are pressing me to talk to you.'

'Spit it out.'

'It's the boy, Adam. Some of the other agents are wondering why you're spending so much time on his training. I mean, after all, it doesn't normally take *you* to train a new Shade, it's done by one of the other longstanding agents. It's got them all talking. Gossip has reached me and they're all saying the same thing. They want to know if he's to undertake a Trial and if he's the boy from the Vision,' she blurted out, hardly taking a breath.

'Well, word does get around, does it not?' D'Scover replied. 'Take a seat.'

She sat down opposite him, more at ease but still avoiding eye contact.

'I will be honest with you; the boy does have some of the attributes for him to fulfil the requirements. However, you are aware of much of the history of the Brotherhood, and so you know we have been here a number of times before. I cannot tell you if he is the child of the Vision or not. He is undergoing a more intense training period than most Shades do and I do not normally take on agent training as you know, but he is very young and needs an authority figure he can trust. He seems to trust me and so it has fallen to me to train him. As for a trial, that is up to the Senior Council to arrange and I cannot second-guess them.' He leaned back and looked at her frowning face. 'Does that explain things a little better?'

'Yes, sir, but …' she mumbled.

'Come on, say what you want to. I need to Disperse whilst I still have some time to myself.'

'I've been handling a lot of calls from agents around the country recently.' She looked at her lap. 'All of them have been dealt with, but it … it just seems there has been … been a lot of activity in places that you wouldn't … expect,' she stammered.

'Meaning?'

'Well, spirits who've previously been considered dormant or harmless or even just folk tales are up and causing trouble. Nothing drastic, a few broken vases, thumps in the night, footsteps overhead, that kind of thing – but it seems to be getting worse.'

'Go on.'

'Last week I had a report of a woman who had been pushed out of a window by a ghost, and another from someone who woke up scratched and bleeding, like a cat had attacked her, and this morning …' she hesitated '… blood, from taps, bleeding into the bath.'

'Why was I not told?' he asked.

'It wasn't a problem, sir. As I said, the reports were all easily dealt with by agents in the field.'

'And so why mention it at all?'

'I wondered if it was just us, so I called a few friends at other offices around the world and they have it too. Reports are flooding in about dormant spirits who've become active and are causing problems.' She finally looked up at him. 'Is it the beginning of the end times?'

'What makes you say that?'

'That's what the Vision says, doesn't it? That the end will come and that after the final Trial the Brotherhood will no longer be needed and we'll all have to take the Final Dispersal.'

D'Scover smiled and leaned back, aware that his substance was slipping from him and his hands had already taken on a gauzy appearance.

'The Vision concerns itself with change, not destruction. You know that the Senior Council do not wish anyone to know the exact wording, but you can be assured that the presence of Adam here does not mean the end of the agency. There are always times when old spirits get more active, and it is a normal sign of the flux in the beliefs of the living. When there are times of trouble around the world, they seek something to believe in and that always makes the old ones wake up and shake about a bit. It will fade as it always has. Now …' he sighed, 'I am exhausted and if there is nothing else, I would appreciate it if you could lock us down until my call comes through.'

Emma stood up. 'Yes, sir. I'll call you as soon as your clearance is granted. In the mean time you can be safe in the knowledge that everything is moving smoothly ahead with the arrangements for the manuscript from America.'

'Thank you, Emma,' D'Scover said. 'Efficient as usual.'

When he was alone again, he gestured to the balcony doors, waiting while they slid back, allowing a rush of cold air to fill the room. He stood for a moment on the balcony, watching the flickering sulphur-yellow lights of the city below before he too went through the motions of his Dispersal and cast his substance out into the sky.

The half-moon cast little light upon the man-made, swollen belly of earth that was Silbury Hill. There was just enough to throw a distorted round shadow on to the stone-strewn landscape. Halfway up the circular path that wound its way around the hill a fleck of silver bounced from the ground, and vanished as quickly as it appeared. Another spark appeared and skittered across the grass, then another, and another. More and more sparks spewed from the grass and soon two fountains of brilliant, glittering light rose into the inky sky and joined each other to form a dazzling archway. From the arch stepped a cowled figure that walked on up the spiral path, closely followed by another and another, slowly climbing the hill in silence. Twelve dark figures assembled in a circle around the partially collapsed summit.

'Bring her here.' The voice was more a memory of a voice than an actual sound. 'We must hear what she has to offer us.'

'But it has never proved useful in the long term,' came another voice from another part of the circle. 'Why should this instance be any different?'

'The time is different. This is a time of great change; that fact alone is enough to ensure that we hear every bit of possible information. The Senior Council rest their success on knowing everything they possibly can. It is part of our remit to listen.'

A number of the cowled figures nodded in agreement.

'We should be in majority agreement,' the questioner said. 'It is our way; it is written.'

'This is so. Shall we hear this woman speak?'

Ten members of the circle lowered their heads in a single nod of consent; only two remained still.

'It is agreed by the majority. We shall summon her.'

A low chant spread through the group and a circle of blue-black sparks, barely visible in the darkness, began to form in the middle of the assembly. In unison the Senior Council raised their hands, palms facing towards the churning darkness in front of them, and suddenly, with a loud crack, an indistinct human shape appeared. She turned around and about within the confines of the circle, her incomplete substance hovering above the collapsed crest of the hill. As soon as she realised where she was, she dropped to her knees.

'Masters,' her voice was little more than a whisper, 'I am at your service.'

'WE HAVE SUMMONED YOU,' the Senior Council now spoke in unison, 'TO HEAR THE INFORMATION YOU HAVE OFFERED TO US.'

'Yes, my masters. I am, as ever, happy to serve,' she replied.

'TELL US OF THE BOY AND THE KEEPER OF THE TEXTS.'

'I am aware that you, that all of us Shades, need more

141

information about this child. It is important for us to know as much information as possible and D'Scover is so secretive that we could end up knowing nothing until it is too late to intervene,' she blurted out. 'D'Scover believes completely in the boy and will do anything to ensure that he is the child of the Vision.'

'ALL OF THIS IS KNOWN TO US. WHAT ELSE?'

'I believe I can find you more information, given my unique access to D'Scover … if I could just be allowed access to the Texts …'

'ENOUGH. THE COUNCIL CANNOT, AND WILL NOT, BREAK THE CONDITIONS APPLIED BY THE KEEPER OF THE TEXTS. THAT WILL NOT HAPPEN WHILST THE COUNCIL STILL EXISTS. HOWEVER, WE WILL ENSURE THAT YOUR SUBSTANCE WILL BE ASSISTED SO THAT YOUR MOVEMENTS CAN BE MORE FLUID. YOU SHALL FIND OUT AS MUCH AS YOU CAN ABOUT D'SCOVER AND THIS POTENTIAL. WE SHALL SUPPORT YOU…FOR NOW.'

She lowered her head once more. 'I shall endeavour to do this for you, masters. I will ensure that your trust in me is well founded.'

But her sycophantic words were wasted as the Council had already begun to chant and her partially held substance was already dissipating. Within seconds, she was gone.

'It is done,' a single voice within the Council spoke. 'We have given support for this action. This is a transgression of our rules. A deeply tragic day for the Brotherhood.'

'No,' another spoke, 'this is a necessary evil linked to the changes coming. Time will tell if this act is in itself a symptom…or a cause.'

The Council turned their backs on the now empty crest of the hill, and slowly walked back down the pathway and through the arch, which then blinked into nothingness.

Adam arrived back in the office before D'Scover. His Dispersal had not been as satisfying as the previous one. He had thoughts on his mind and could not give himself fully to the experience.

He could not shake the image of the witch girl from his mind, and desperately hoped that they were going to find her. He had to keep reminding himself she would not know him, would not be the girl in the visions, and probably would not even look like her. But she would be someone to talk to, a friend even.

The office was in darkness when he re-formed by D'Scover's desk, but even in the still silence he instinctively felt that something was wrong, that he was not alone. Staring into the darkness trying to make out who was there, hoping for a movement, he was suddenly forced to shield his eyes as a flash of light cracked through the room and a gust of wind buffeted him. Blinking, he dashed to the intercom and called through to see if Emma was still in reception and was relieved to find she was.

'Call D'Scover back?' he shouted.

'I've had his permission to do so when the clearance for Cornwall is a hundred per cent safe, but it's not yet,' she said. 'Is it urgent?'

'Yes, it is. Call him now, please.'

D'Scover could see it the second he arrived back. 'This room has been searched,' he said flatly when he regained his substance.

'I thought so,' Adam said, 'but how? I thought that this office was secure?'

'I thought it was too,' he replied. 'Did you see anything at all?'

'Blue light, pop, whoosh, gone. That's all, I'm afraid.'

'And you are sure the light was blue?'

'Blueish, yeah.'

D'Scover walked out through the open balcony doors and strode rapidly down the length of it. Adam ran out after him.

'Don't you want the key?' he asked.

'Not if we are still being watched!' D'Scover responded with an angry whisper. He stroked the wall gently, his fingers running down the non-existent cracks, and heaved a sigh of relief.

'They did not find it,' he said, 'but do not mention it out loud ever again. I will sweep the office electronically for standard

143

surveillance devices, but just in case we must be careful about what we say from …'

As they both turned to walk back to the office, a dark shadow burst from the office through the open balcony door and launched out over the city. D'Scover Dispersed in an instant and surged out after the rapidly vanishing smear of colour. All Adam could do was peer out into the thin morning light.

The first lilac fingers of morning stretched up over the city and created a vivid backdrop for the confrontation that was taking place in the sky. The grey shape of D'Scover expanded way beyond his regular size and filled the space in front of the building, surrounding the escapee. He wound round and round in an angry serpentine cloud, twisting and turning about the partially Dispersed interloper. As the sky began to turn blue above them, D'Scover closed in. With a sudden torrent of energy, the cloud blackened and a thin column of purple and white light soared upwards and out of his reach. D'Scover expanded across the sky, scattering his substance as wide as he could, but it was to no avail. The intruder had escaped.

D'Scover gathered his substance once more and came to stand on the balcony next to Adam.

'Do you know who it was?'

'No.' D'Scover shook his head. 'And at this stage I do not wish to speculate.'

'But you have an idea?' Adam pressed him for an answer.

D'Scover ignored the question and pushed past him. 'If you will excuse me for a moment, I must talk to Emma and arrange for the office to be checked fully.'

He strode off at his usual brisk pace with Adam in hot pursuit. Once they were both back inside the office, D'Scover turned and slammed the balcony doors, sealing them with a silver slick of sparks from his fingertips. When he marched back into his office, his expression was even darker than usual.

'Despite the situation here, we must leave for Cornwall right away,' he grumbled as Emma walked into the office behind him.

'The destination may not be secure for very long. I cannot tell what information our interloper has managed to gain from their visit, but I cannot take a chance. They may already know about the girl and that means that she may no longer be safe. We must travel at once.'

'I'm so sorry, sir,' Emma apologised. 'There was no sign that the seal on your office was broken. I really can't explain how this breach of security happened.'

'Emma, I do not have time to talk to you now,' D'Scover said. 'This was a very professional job; we will talk about security when I return. Prepare the Hotline for us so that we may use it right away.'

'Yes, sir,' she said in a subdued tone. 'If anyone calls through for you after you've Hotlined, where can I tell them you are?'

'Tell them nothing.' He looked back at Adam who waited nervously by his desk. 'No,' he called after her, 'tell them I needed a change of scenery, and tell them I have gone to the sea.'

Chapter Fourteen – Freedom Farm

'I can't do it, someone will know.'

'Of course you can do it; you have been practising and you are very good at it. No one will know.'

Adam and D'Scover had Hotlined to a small school on the outskirts of the village of Polcastle. In this cluttered classroom someone had forgotten to shut down the computer overnight. The small building had only three classrooms and no residential caretaker and was perfect for their purpose.

'You can see right through me,' Adam grumbled as he paced round the schoolroom, turning his hands over and over again in the air. 'I'll look like I'm made of tissue paper if I go out there; it's too bright. Look at me!'

D'Scover looked instead out into the sharp morning sunshine across the empty playground. Night had retreated and the brightness of the clear air was stunning.

'All will be fine, trust me,' he replied. 'I have seen what you can do; you just have to have some faith in your abilities. The beauty of moving around in daylight is that nobody expects a ghost in daytime. Any problems like blurring or an interruption to your substance they will write off as a problem with their own eyes brought on by the low and bright winter sun. Anyway, you have no choice; I need you to help me find the girl.'

'What use will I be?' Adam asked. 'I don't know how to use that ball thing and if we're caught, it could ruin everything.'

'You have been here before,' D'Scover said flatly, 'and so it is your fate to be here again.'

'*Riiightt* …' Adam sighed. 'You and your fate thing again. OK, but you have to get me out of there quick if you think anyone has sussed me.'

'Agreed,' D'Scover said. He walked towards the door and, in an effortless, vaporous waft, melted through to the outside world. Adam could see him standing in the playground through the mottled sea-blown glass of the school windows. He walked to the same spot himself and, taking a deep yet essentially useless breath, he concentrated hard until he became a shadow of his own form and was able, with a bit of a wriggle, to pass clumsily through the door.

Polcastle was busy, despite summer being a long way off. The day shone bright and clear with unseasonal sunshine, but a sharp and icy wind still blew in from the sea, causing people to pull their jackets tightly round them as they walked. The gusts blew across the village, tossing litter high into the air where it fell under the ruthless examination of the seagulls wheeling in the air. D'Scover strode ahead down the hill towards the centre of the village. Adam trotted behind, keen to keep the focus on D'Scover in the hope no one would notice he was not as solid a presence as he would like.

The village was full of life and even out of season people bustled around the many touristy shops as the two of them tried to make their way through the main street. It took all of Adam's concentration to make sure that he did not allow anyone to bump into him for fear of them realising his great secret. D'Scover seemed to glide through the crowds, each person missing him in an effortless waltz in which he took the lead.

'How do you do that?' Adam called out, always a few steps behind.

147

'There is no mystery, just a few hundred years of practice,' he replied, 'and never forgetting our Prime Rule – concentrate.'

Adam followed him through the village and out the other side up on to a hilly park overlooking the silver-green band of the wide river running out to the ocean. D'Scover made his way up the hill to a bandstand that seemed to overlook this whole corner of the county. Here he stopped and looked around, trying to get his bearings.

'Well?' Adam asked. 'What do we do now? Should we go to a graveyard or something? Do we start with dead people?'

D'Scover squinted into the sun and said nothing.

'Do we just wait here? Will she come to us or what? I mean, is she even a she? Is she even a person?' Adam babbled on. 'Could she be a dog?'

The dog Adam had been looking at ran up to D'Scover and sat by his foot and stared up at him with a trusting and earnest expression. D'Scover looked down at it and ruffled the hair between its ears.

'Hey!' Adam asked. 'How come the dog doesn't bark? I thought dogs would be able to tell that we're, well, you know, dead.'

'He does know,' D'Scover said without looking back, 'he simply doesn't care. We pose no threat to him, but he would probably growl at malevolent spirits. Have you never seen an animal stare at a blank space or growl at apparently nothing?'

'Not that I remember,' Adam replied.

'That is because you saw the spirit it was reacting to, you just never realised it,' D'Scover said. 'Further proof, if you needed it, that we are all in the place we are meant to be.'

He stood back up and watched as the dog ran off across the field to its owner. Then he cupped his hands together to form a bowl shape. Despite the bright sunlight, Adam could see a glow forming within D'Scover's curved fingers. When he opened his hands again, there, in one palm, lay the blue sphere that Adam had last seen back in London.

'This will show us what we need to know.' D'Scover held the

148

ball out. Almost at once it began to throb light in a slow but steady rhythm. D'Scover turned around in the park and the throb slowed even more until it was barely detectable.

'It is the depository for a powerful incantation. These are almost impossible to maintain over a long distance hence the containment sphere wrapped round it,' he explained.

'You mean the ball?' Adam asked. 'So the finding, reveal, thinga-majig is inside?'

'Inelegantly put, but accurate nonetheless.' He turned back the way he had come and the throb increased. 'The pulse will speed up as we get closer to our destination, but you must stay close as I may need to move quickly to follow its lead. We are looking for a living person and they could be walking around as well – that always makes matters more difficult.'

D'Scover strode off down the hill, apparently oblivious to the crowds of people with dogs and kites littering the muddy slopes. Adam concentrated hard on his shape once more and tried to remember that running was the most natural thing in the world for a boy to do – a living boy, that is. He stumbled and rolled forward through a small spiky bush. Two dog owners turned and began to come over to where Adam lay half sunk into the slope of the hill.

'He is fine,' D'Scover called out to them as he pulled Adam upright before anyone could notice his apparent lack of legs. 'Children are so clumsy, are they not?'

The men smiled, waved and turned back to their pets.

'Do not try so hard,' D'Scover told him as he once more resumed his long stride. 'I find that people do not look at youngsters very much and so most of those we pass shall only notice me. If you relax, it will be easier for you to keep your substance. Do not worry about what your feet are doing. When was the last time you looked at someone's feet?'

D'Scover was right about people focusing on him, though. A tall and very pale man wandering around a seaside village on a crisp February day with only a light jacket to keep him warm and holding in front of him a glowing blue ball that seemed to pulse is an uncommon sight even in the more artistic parts of Cornwall. All eyes seemed to be on D'Scover and Adam could concentrate on making sure his own legs did not slip into the ground, or that he didn't accidentally pass *through* something instead of *around* it. Once or twice he failed to notice a bollard or a particularly high kerb and his foot (and in one instance a whole leg) passed straight through it.

Finally they reached the outskirts of the village. They had walked along the coast road and the sea stretched out like a blue slate towards the horizon on their right. The land banked steeply upwards, but Adam found this no easier than downhill walking; it was all much more difficult than he had imagined it would be and he was finding holding his substance enormously difficult. He had to concentrate hard as he walked down the road and was relieved when the buildings around became fewer and fewer until they were eventually on little more than a country track.

'Have we got much further to go?' Adam called out.

D'Scover turned towards him and Adam could see that the ball was now throbbing to a rapid beat and the mist inside was furiously swirling about like a tiny but very angry sea.

'Wow,' he grinned, 'guess not!'

D'Scover stopped outside a large wooden gate that had been painted in many different colours a long time ago. The paint now scabbed over the surface and fell to the floor as he reached out to touch it. The sign hanging loosely from the top bar said FREEDOM FARM.

'I know this place,' Adam told him. 'They ran a kind of summer play scheme for kids on holiday – arts and crafts, that kind of thing; one of my crappy foster parents brought me here when I was about six. It's run by a couple of old hippies, some kind of commune, everything equal and all that. The locals think they're a bit of a joke; d'you reckon the girl is here?'

'I know that someone here can assist us,' D'Scover said, swinging the gate wide.

The path to the farm was little more than a dirt track and Adam noticed D'Scover no longer bothered to walk over the ruts and instead wafted through them. They had both been holding intense substance for over four hours and Adam was finding it increasingly difficult to appear solid. D'Scover took small short cuts – like wafting through the ruts – and this enabled him to last much longer.

Adam felt as though he was growing more diaphanous and ghostly with each passing minute, and he knew it would not be much longer before he had to admit defeat and Disperse. In the safe confines of D'Scover's office he had been able to hold his form for much longer, but no one living could see him there and so he did not have to pay such attention to detail. Out here in public a transparent hand or missing foot would give the game away. The thought of having to hang on while D'Scover explained it all to the person who was going to help them was terrifying.

'How will we explain to them?' Adam asked.

'We should not have to,' D'Scover replied enigmatically.

'What?'

But there was no time for a reply; ahead of them a young girl of about Adam's age was running up the track towards them. She stumbled in her haste and her long, brown hair fell over her face as she regained her balance. As she ran, she glanced over her shoulder occasionally to where a tall, willowy woman slowly followed. She called out something to the woman, but the sound was lost to the breeze.

'It's her!' Adam gasped as his stomach seemed to flip. 'She's the witch from those memories, the Hypnagogia. How's that possible? How can she look exactly the same?'

'As I suspected,' D'Scover answered somewhat smugly, 'her spirit is indeed carried forward.'

He strode on to meet her, but Adam, fearful of losing substance

151

in front of the girl from his dreams, held back for a moment. She reached D'Scover and, gasping for breath, stopped in front of him.

'Follow my lead,' she panted. 'I know more or less why you're here, but we have to do this carefully. Just go along with whatever I say.'

'Of course,' D'Scover replied, unfazed by the whole scene.

'What are your names?' she gabbled quickly.

'I am D'Scover and this is Adam,' he said.

'OK, I'm Edie. Right – no time for anything else, here goes.'

The woman had arrived at their little gathering and smiled a broad grin, slipping her arm round Edie's shoulders.

'Moon,' Edie said to the woman, 'this is Mister D'Scover and this is my friend from school, Adam. Mister D'Scover is the teacher who's going to escort us to London, for the Environmental Writing Festival. The one I told you about, remember?'

'Oh yeah,' Moon replied. 'Eden told us that her teacher would call, but she never said you were so …' She gave him a cautious smile as she broke off mid-sentence. 'Anyway, will you come up to the house? You must be terribly thirsty after your long journey.'

'I am afraid I have very little time, Mrs …?'

'Call me Moon, everyone does. We all take the name Freedom when we give up the restrictions of the ratrace, but everyone simply calls me Moon. Surnames bind us to others when we should be free to express our individuality, don't you agree?'

'If you insist,' D'Scover replied with reserve. 'I am afraid we have run right out of time as we are quite late anyway and so we will have to ask Edie to hurry with her bag.'

'She's been ready for two days. I've never known anyone as keen to go to school as my daughter. I'm sure I never wanted to, but as I was raised here on this farm, I've had very little formal schooling. It's never done me any harm. Ah well,' she waved her long fingers in a dismissive gesture, 'each to their own.' She turned back to the girl. 'Edie, will you sort your own stuff out? I have to go to the village. I'll see you in a week?'

'Yes, shouldn't be more than a week, should it, Mister D'Scover?' Edie asked.

'A week should be sufficient,' he replied.

'OK, no hassle, see you,' Moon replied, flinging her arms round Edie. 'Take it easy in that big city, babe. Don't go coming back with any mad ideas!' she laughed.

With a brief hug and kiss on top of her head, she separated from Edie and walked on up the track, humming an unrecognisable tune.

'Nice woman,' Adam said, desperate to say something.

'Yeah, bit messed up in the head, and not much of a mother, but she's all I've got,' Edie replied, watching Moon walk out of the gate. 'So, how do we get to London?'

'Well, you being so young has rather killed my plans,' D'Scover said.

'I'm not that young,' the girl replied indignantly. 'I'm older than I look – I'm fourteen.'

'Nevertheless,' D'Scover replied, 'I had hoped you would have a vehicle of some sorts, but we have to use public transport now. You cannot travel alone, I do not feel that it is safe. Travelling with you will require a lot of energy and I will need to Disperse first, we both will. Do you have somewhere my young friend can rest? This has all been a bit of a strain for him.'

'Sure, there are loads of outbuildings. We can go to the barns by the river; no one uses those at this time of the year.' She flicked her long knotty hair over her shoulder and gestured for them to follow her.

'How does she know about us?' Adam whispered to D'Scover as they followed her across a muddy field towards three rickety wooden buildings.

'Because nothing's been a surprise for me since I was three,' Edie called out to him without looking back. 'We can talk in the barn.'

She heaved open the heavy door and the sound of tiny scuttling animals filled the air for a moment before silence rested on the huge space within. The remains of the sunlight forced its way through the pencil-thin gaps in the wooden panels, casting golden stripes across the hay-strewn floor. Edie walked over to a jumble of hay bales and, climbing up behind them, she kicked two down to form a makeshift seat. Jumping into her resting place, she leaned back and looked at the two misfit characters standing in front of her.

'So, Mister D'Scover, and Adam, what's your story?' she grinned. 'Tell me and I'll see if it all fits together with what I already know.'

'Would you mind telling us your story first?' D'Scover asked. 'We have a lot at stake and must first be sure that you are the person we are looking for.'

'Short version?' Edie queried. D'Scover nodded.

'I'll do my best.' She took a deep breath. 'But it's not exactly a short story. My full name is Eden Joy Freedom, but everyone calls me Edie. My mum says we're from a long line of healers, but despite her best efforts, she's never managed to do anything better than stick a plaster on a cut knee. I've known I was different since I taught myself to read when I was three and I always knew what people were going to say before they said it. When I was seven, I had my first full vision. It was dark and violent and it changed my life forever. I saw my history, my *real* history. I saw my ancestral past through the eyes of all those who'd carried my life force before me. What was worse was that I could hear what people were thinking. I knew the world for what it really was: a dark and dangerous place full of mistrust, deception and brutality. When I came round, everything had changed. My whole life changed in one day.

'I became interested in finding out why I was different and so I did my own research. What I discovered was that instead of *healer*, the books said *witch*. I'm happier with it now, but it took time to get used to. I've kind of come to accept it and understand that I'll never be normal. I'm telepathic and my gift is pretty powerful. I have strong visions – flashes of the future – and that's how I knew you were coming here. That's about it really.'

'Can you do spells?' Adam asked.

'Not really,' Edie explained. 'Witches are actually linked to nature more than the spirit world. We have a strong bond with the Earth and plants, so our powers are all linked to an understanding of the natural world. I have some control over the flow of water and I'm able to influence localised weather, move clouds, and make gusts of wind and the like. That's about it.'

'Sounds like a lot!' Adam was impressed.

'Now,' she said, 'what about you two? Short version?'

'The short version, miss, is that we are part of a Brotherhood that has existed for almost five hundred years, and we need your help to find out about something that has not happened yet,' D'Scover replied.

'Hmm, that *is* the short version, isn't it!?' She leaned forward and stared at Adam. 'I think that your friend's having trouble staying with us,' she told D'Scover.

They both looked at Adam who had almost given up trying to hold his substance and the sunlight was throwing light straight through him.

'We need to work out a way of getting all the way to London and he looks about as substantial as a bride's veil,' she said, nodding towards Adam. 'Is there anything you can do about him?'

'Hey!' Adam snapped. 'I'm right here!'

'Well, you could've fooled me,' Edie giggled. 'We can't go anywhere with him looking like that, can we? People will see right through him – and I mean that literally!'

'He will require some time to get his strength back, an hour at the least, two would be better,' D'Scover said.

'No problem, you can stay in the barn if you want,' she offered. 'Do you need to rest too? Moon has gone to visit friends so she'll be gone for the rest of the day.'

'It is not essential for me to rest fully yet, but a little time would help in case of any delays later,' he said. 'We must talk first about how to get you to London.'

155

'I … don't think I can hold on much longer,' Adam interrupted.

'Then you must Disperse and we will call you back when we are ready to leave,' D'Scover said.

'Thanks.' Adam stood back, looking for somewhere to perform the Ritual.

'Don't worry about me,' Edie said. 'You wouldn't believe the things I've seen!'

'OK,' Adam said.

He stood to one side, acutely aware of Edie's watchful gaze upon him, but he was only just able to maintain himself. He took a deep breath and, as he exhaled, he became fainter and fainter until he was merely a shadow. Muttering his Dispersal Ritual under his breath, he closed his eyes and the Dispersal took hold. His body became droplets of grey before darkening to red and spinning in a whirling mist, scattering itself to the corners of the barn.

'Wow!' Edie said. 'Cool! Can he still hear us?'

'If he wants to,' D'Scover told her, 'but he is exhausted so probably not.'

'Does he have to do that often?'

'Every few hours,' D'Scover replied. 'We all do.'

'We? You mean you ghosts?' Edie asked.

'We prefer not to be called ghosts; that word has a bad reputation. Ghosts are unskilled and unaware, trapped in the wrong place; we are agents for an organisation called the Brotherhood of Shades, or just Shades, if you prefer.'

'Touchy ghosts, sorry, *Shades*, just what I need.' She patted the hay next to her. 'Sit down and tell me how we're going to get to London.'

D'Scover walked over to her and, despite his obvious distaste at this informality, sat next to her on the dusty bale.

'I honestly do not know. Is there public transport available?' he asked.

'There's the train, and I have money, so the ticket's not a problem, but you say I'm not safe? I have to admit that a day ago

I was hit by a very powerful feeling of being pursued. You'll just have to travel with me.'

'Sadly I cannot do that. Travel in the conventional way is not possible. We have to use a computer to travel or …' He hesitated. 'No, we will have to think of something else.'

'What were you going to say?' Edie frowned.

'I was going to say it might be possible to use a living person to carry me back to London.'

'You want someone to hitchhike inside?'

'Put a little more simply than I would have liked, but that is the basis of it, yes.'

'Why don't you want to do that?' she asked. 'That sounds like a laugh!'

'It relies on too many random factors. It would mean finding someone who is travelling alone to London and who will not mind having no recollection of their journey. It is very risky.'

'How important is it that we get to London?' she asked.

'Good point. It is vital that we get you to my office.'

'Do we have any choice?'

D'Scover thought for a moment. 'No,' he answered with reluctance.

'Train it is then. I'll find you someone who's going our way when we get to the station. Shouldn't be too hard. I just have to take a peek inside someone's head and get someone who's planning on sleeping the whole way.'

'Can you do that?'

'Sure. Can't you?'

'We are dead, not telepathic – that is an entirely different thing and clearly why we need you. Without you, our best chance would be to remain in partial Dispersal – the vaporous state you saw Adam in – and hope to hear what we need to hear.'

'Well, I can, so it's decided. I take it you can walk as far as the station?' she asked.

'We can travel a couple of miles in each direction from where we were first placed.'

'What do you mean?'

'We normally travel these days by computer; it is very convenient, but we can still only move a few miles in each direction once we have arrived. I have learned to travel further, but Adam is …'

'Newer to the game?' Edie grinned. 'Where did you pop in to?'

'The school building.'

'That's fine, the train station's only a stone's throw from there,' she said. 'Do you want to do your ghostly thing before we go?'

'Dispersal, and yes, I would like a couple of hours if that is possible? I will need all of my strength if I am going to occupy someone all the way home,' he explained.

'Sure,' she nodded. 'What about Adam?'

'I will have to send him back to the office first.'

'OK, I'll get my bag sorted and come back in two hours,' Edie said as she stood up to leave. 'Oh, one more thing. Who's watching you?'

'You have sensed that?' D'Scover frowned. 'My office was searched just before we Hotlined here, but I do not know who it was. I was hoping you would be able to help us with that.'

'No, sorry.' She shook her head. 'Whoever's watching you is very gifted. I sense a presence, but I can't pin down exactly who it is. I kind of had a feeling that it's a woman, and display cabinets, glass and wood...but it's so hazy, it's weird actually. Normally I can tell right away what I need to know, but this has got kind of fuzzy, unclear.'

'What do you think that means?' D'Scover asked.

'It means I can't help,' she shrugged. 'I think they're blocking me as I've tried a number of times to pin them down, but can't. That means that they're either a natural who doesn't know they have the ability to block, or they're extremely skilled and are doing it deliberately.'

'Either way, secrets are being kept and we do not know by whom.'

'Looks that way,' she agreed. 'Anyway, you'd better have your rest, dispersing thing. I've got packing to do.'

D'Scover waited for Edie to leave and looked around the empty barn. Wisps of straw drifted in the air and, in the silence, small creatures began to relax and scuttle from their hiding places once more. He stood still as a mouse ran through his foot and across the floor. Raising his palms upwards, he began to give himself up to his Dispersal. Within a matter of seconds, he started to break up into deep grey globules that swirled in the dying fragments of sunshine before shattering into the air, causing the dust to whirl about in the space where he once stood.

From her viewpoint just outside a loose panel in the side wall of the barn, Edie watched him vanish before turning and running back towards the farmhouse with a huge grin on her face.

Chapter Fifteen – Edie

In her room it took Edie only minutes to be ready. Her bag had indeed been packed for days as she had known this visit was coming, and all she needed to do was stuff her mobile into it. For the last month she had felt a sense of impending menace that had been growing stronger daily. That morning, in the early hours, it had been almost overwhelming and had inspired in her a barely controllable feeling of panic. She had to use all of her powers of concentration to quell the desire to run from this unknown threat.

These detailed flashes of the future had been a routine part of her life for so many years and she no longer questioned whether or not they actually made sense. In the beginning they had been simple glimpses of what someone was going to say or where something had been hidden. She could tell whether someone was lying straight away, and if someone had a secret that gnawed inside them, she could feel the pain it created as it ate away at them.

Edie had spent her life up to the age of nine travelling around the world with Moon. For most of these years she featured more like luggage in her mother's life than a child. When her hippie grandparents passed away, Moon inherited the farm and took Edie back to live there permanently.

Living at the farm made her unusual character easier to mask as the other people there routinely attempted to gain a more spiritual aspect to their lives. Crystal readers and psychic healers seemed to gravitate to the farm and many lived there for long periods of time, or at least until the hard work of running a self-sufficient community ground them down. Most of these people had been fakes; Edie had known this and had tried for a while to tell her mother. Her mother had wanted to know how Edie could possibly know such details about these colourful hangers-on at the farm, but Edie had seen what happened to people with a 'gift'. There were regular psychic events at the farm with fat middle-aged women apparently reaching out to the spirit world. Edie knew that she had no desire to be roped into these events and end up being trawled around the world all over again as some kind of wonder, and so she learned to keep silent and hide her skills.

But despite her best efforts to pretend she was 'normal', her powers grew and distanced her from regular people. In secret she had begun practising her skills and by the time she was eight she had refined them so much that she could turn them on and off as she needed to. She could sense emotions in others all the time, just as clearly as if they were wearing a T-shirt with the details of their life printed on for all to see. With practice, she learned to switch off her ability to see what was going to happen to them. Too often she had seen terrible things in a person's future – illness, tragedy and loss – and she knew that she could not help them or prevent this from happening, so she just shut it out.

It was the powerful flashes that she could not turn off, and these forced their way into her life no matter what she did. Her only warning that it was about to happen was a slight taste of metal, like dried blood, in the back of her throat. She managed to keep these flashes to herself, but had sacrificed friendships to maintain the secret.

What she struggled with most were the dreams. Edie could not recall a time in her life without the dreams, the nightmares. At first, when she was very small, they were cluttered and indistinct. Images of faces and people and places that she did not know, but felt as if she should. As she grew older, she realised that they were memories, but not of this life. These were fragmented recollections of all the persecution and suffering her life spirit had been through to get to this place in her life, this point in time.

Then, when she was seven, everything that her ancestors had suffered rolled over her in brutal and vivid nightmares over which she had no control. She walked in their footsteps and saw into the faces of those who persecuted them. She knew every bit of their pain and lived it over and over again, and it felt as fresh and as real as if it had just happened. As a result of this, she now slept very little; it just seemed safer that way.

Edie's biggest fear was that someone would find out about her and she would be ridiculed in the village. The people who lived on the farm were already thought of as weird by the villagers – a true witch would just be the icing on the cake for most of them. And so she kept to herself and remained friendless.

The flash about the impending arrival of D'Scover and Adam had been very vivid and she was thankful that it had not happened at school as it had swept her away for over an hour. She had seen London and a dark cloud that was looming larger and larger with each passing moment; she had seen Adam and his cold and lonely life and death. She had seen his isolated life as he bounced from school to school, from foster family to foster family, as no one cared enough to deal with this damaged and angry boy.

Edie saw the monastery and its destruction and watched as D'Scover fell into his fiery coma and died. She had seen the rituals and the formation of the Brotherhood and had seen the chaos that currently threatened to engulf it. Though, as hard as she had tried, she had not been able to grasp what it was that actually threatened them, but she knew she could help them to deal with it. She knew she was important to them somehow, and she felt pursued.

When the visions began to subside, Edie found herself slumped over her homework, and began to prepare for the arrival of Adam and D'Scover and made up a suitable cover story for why she would need to leave. Her mother had not argued as she felt Edie was a 'free spirit' and should do whatever she felt was 'emotionally right' for her own well-being. Edie had heard this many times and knew she could safely make her excuses and they would not be checked up on. This casual approach to parenting had annoyed Edie when she was younger, but recently she had begun to feel it was all part of the grand plan that was coming and that ultimately her upbringing had a bigger purpose.

With her bag ready, she managed to get out of the house without having to say goodbye to anyone and ran across the fields to the barn where she had left D'Scover and Adam. D'Scover had already emerged from his Dispersal and was patiently waiting for her in the dusty shadows of the barn.

'I will just need to summon Adam and we can be on our way,' he said.

Edie waited as he muttered some words to bring Adam back from his Dispersal. She felt a low hum that made her ears pop and D'Scover gestured for her to stand back. A deep crimson spiral of glistening globules whorled around the barn, with the vortex growing ever smaller until it gradually formed the shape of the boy once more.

'Why is he red and you're grey?' Edie asked D'Scover.

'It just works that way. Have you not found that in the living world some people seem to be more blue or white than others?' he asked. 'I do not mean skin colour, that is irrelevant, rather that some people seem to represent colour more than others do? Some spirits do have vivid colours, often if they have had a less than pure past or if they have had a violent death. For most of us, our Dispersal colour is grey, white or various tones of blue, but for Adam it is red,' D'Scover said. 'Ah, he is back.'

Adam stood once more in front of them, beaming his confident grin.

'Impressive, huh?' he said to Edie.

'If you like that sort of thing,' Edie said casually, unwilling to admit it was easily one of the most impressive things she had ever seen. 'We'd better get going. We've got a couple of hours before the train leaves and we'll need time to find someone to, er, travel with.'

'We have to stop at your school first,' D'Scover said.

'Why?' she asked. 'We really don't have long if we're going to find someone to hitch a lift with so best not to waste time.'

'I said earlier,' he reminded her, 'that Adam must return to the office and start consulting the Texts. A long train journey is essentially a waste of valuable time; we have little choice in how we travel, but Adam does.'

'Do I have to?' Adam moaned. 'I think I'm getting the hang of this; it's kind of nice to be out in the sun and all.'

'Yes, you do have to.' D'Scover put his foot down. 'In any case, you have no experience of using a living person to carry your spirit. You may as well go back the quick way.'

'The quick way?' Edie asked.

'It is a long story; you will see soon enough,' D'Scover said. 'Now we must go.'

The day had drifted past. The short February afternoon had lost almost all of its sunlight, and the sky now took on a cold, deep blue tone. No clouds cluttered the view to the ocean and a spiteful chill wind ran up the road towards them. Edie shivered and pulled her thick fleece tighter round her thin frame.

'You two'd better look a bit colder,' she said through chattering teeth, 'if you don't want people to think you're weirder than you are – although that'd be difficult, I reckon.'

'Hmm,' D'Scover said and stopped in the middle of the track. 'Is there any way we could be seen here and not realise it?'

Edie shook her head. 'Nah, the only thing nearby is Freedom Farm and even from there you can't see the road because the barn is in the way.'

'Good.' D'Scover raised his palms to his face.

He began to grow blurry as if she was looking at him through smoke. Then, with one swift movement, he swept his hands down and over his body as though he was brushing something off his clothes. Edie looked from his feet to his face and saw that he was now wearing a well-tailored black overcoat that almost touched the ground and black leather gloves over his pale hands.

'Very classy,' she said. 'Looks expensive.'

'Your turn,' D'Scover told Adam.

Adam nervously looked up, unwilling to admit in front of Edie that he had not actually done this before. He had created a bench in the Memoria, and had moved a few things around, but he was still wearing the tatty outfit of jeans and T-shirt that he had died in. In fact he had not changed any of it and had avoided trying in case he lost a grip on what he had. His outfit had not been right for the weather when he died, and it was not right now. He tried to picture what a boy of his age should be wearing, but drew a blank and instead decided on a copy of the fleece that Edie had on, only in black, as he reasoned it would not only be easier to do, but would look better too.

He stood back, mimicked exactly what D'Scover had done, and felt the shapes around him change and flux as he settled into this new image. Opening his eyes again, he could see he was indeed wearing a black fleece similar to Edie's but far too big for him. The sleeves hung over his hands and it came down far too long over his body, reaching almost to his knees.

'Guess I pictured myself a bit bigger,' he grinned, bunching the sleeves up.

'It will suffice,' D'Scover said, and strode on once more. Adam and Edie exchanged a small laugh and trotted to catch up.

'Not bad for your first time, Red,' Edie said.

'How did you know I'd not done that before? Is that your powers again?' Adam asked. 'And why Red?'

'I didn't need any powers for that,' Edie laughed. 'You should have seen your face; you looked scared stiff that you were going to make a total doofus of yourself! I called you Red because it just seems to suit you better and you go red when you do that Dispersal thing. Adam's not your real name anyway, is it?'

'Do I go red? He goes all grey shiny bits; I didn't know I went red. Should've gone red with embarrassment after ending up with a fleece this size!' he said, waving his long, flappy sleeves at her. 'I don't mind what you call me as long as it's not rude. Don't suppose you know what my real name was?'

'No, sorry, I did try to see what it was, but it's just … I dunno … it's like it's lost, out of reach.' She frowned. 'It's like that sometimes. It might come to me; one day it might just pop into my head. Don't worry about the fleece – you look fine. Shame you don't look like him though,' she teased, gesturing towards D'Scover, who was still ahead of them on the road.

'Why?' Adam frowned. 'What do you mean?'

'Because he's so fit of course,' Edie said. 'Did you see the way Moon looked at him? I mean, look at him!'

Adam looked at D'Scover properly and saw for the first time that Edie was right. There was something about him. He moved with a fluid grace and his hair always seemed to be unruly but never actually looked messy. His clothes always fitted perfectly and the dark colours he draped himself in complemented his pale skin.

'I mean, he must've caused a bit of a stir in the village – we don't get guys like him around here often,' Edie gushed. 'He looks like a model or an actor or something.'

'He doesn't really look like that, you know,' Adam snapped. 'I mean, that's just a look he took for himself.'

'Nah, sorry, Red, I've seen him in one of my visions when he was young and he would've grown up to look like that anyway,' she said. 'Some people are just born that way.'

'And some aren't,' Adam grumbled.

'Hey!' Edie laughed. 'Don't go throwing your toys out your pram about it – you're not so bad yourself, you know. You just need his fashion sense!'

166

'Thanks!' He laughed and playfully shoved her.

D'Scover stopped abruptly and turned back to where they stood, his coat curling dramatically out around him.

'I would like to remind you that it is imperative that we return to my office as quickly as possible,' he said sternly. 'The more time we spend on the journey, the greater our risk of detection. We are still unsure of Miss Freedom's role in this, but I feel that it is of great importance. Everything could depend on her safety and we are far too exposed this far from the Texts and the relative security of my offices.'

Suitably chastised, the two hurried to catch up. The walk to the village was far less tedious than the walk out to Freedom Farm. Edie tried to contain herself, but was so full of questions that it was impossible to remain silent.

'You don't feel the cold?' she asked as they still trailed behind D'Scover.

'No, I think that I did at first, but he says that was just because I remembered what cold was like and so if I knew that I should be cold, then I was. Does that make sense?' he said.

'I think so. What about food – d'you eat?'

'No, but I don't feel hungry either and that's brilliant,' he replied. 'I don't miss anything anymore. It's dead weird.'

Edie pictured his death just as she had seen it in her vision, and could understand exactly why he wanted to forget what it was like to feel cold and hungry.

'How long have you been, you know, like this?' she asked.

Adam stopped walking and a thick frown contorted his face. 'You mean dead?' he replied. 'I don't know; what's the date?'

'It's the twenty-third.'

'Still February?'

'Yeah.'

'It's been about two weeks.' He shook his head in amazement. 'I can't believe it's only been two weeks; it feels like forever.'

'You're aware of time passing?'

167

'Sort of. I mean, I don't really have days as you'd know them, but if I spend enough time holding my substance, I do notice the nights passing, so it's possible to hang on to time,' he tried to explain. 'I don't know about in the long term, but for now I'm roughly aware of the days.'

'What d'you miss most?'

'Shouldn't your psychic powers answer all of these questions for you? I mean, shouldn't you just be able to look inside my head and find out for yourself?'

'It doesn't work.' Edie frowned. 'I mean, it works with everyone else but not you two. With you two, I don't have the same level of control of what I see, I just get random images. I suppose that means that it doesn't work properly with dead people. I can see things that you've seen, but I don't get any solid visions about you as people. I can see some things connected to you, but they seem to be in your past. I can feel your emotions in the past, right up to where you ...' She broke off.

Adam stopped in the middle of the path. 'You were going to say that you could see up to where I died, weren't you?'

Edie nodded.

'You know what happened to me? How far back do you know?'

'I only saw your death,' she lied. 'I haven't tried to see your past.'

'Well, leave it that way.' Adam began to walk off. 'That's my business, OK?'

'Sure, no problem, Red,' she called after him and trotted to catch up. 'Anything you wanted to ask me?'

'Yeah,' he turned to face her, 'did you know that your ancestors have been linked to the Brotherhood for centuries?'

'Kind of,' she nodded. 'I mean, I've found enough references to show my family were around monks and stuff, and one ancestor was killed during the Dissolution. It seemed weird that witches were linked to monks, but my ancestors were written about by loads of religions, mostly when they were trying to execute us. I had the vision about you two and everything kind of slotted into place.'

'Did you see his death?' Adam gestured towards D'Scover.

'Yeah, that was when I saw what he looked like younger,' she said. 'When was it? Sixteenth century would be my guess.'

Adam nodded. 'I'm not sure of the exact date, fifteen thirty something.'

'Why's he a man? Didn't he want to be young anymore?' Edie stared ahead at D'Scover, and the dark swathe he cut through the streets, as they descended into the village. 'I mean, don't get me wrong,' she continued. 'There's nothing wrong with being old, but why not stay young?'

'He has his reasons,' Adam told her. 'It's complicated.'

'Aren't you tempted to do that?' she asked. 'You could be anyone you wanted to be.'

'Nah.' He shook his head. 'I need to deal with all the other stuff first. Holding a shape that I know this well is difficult enough, let alone choosing a new one.'

D'Scover had stopped outside the school hedge, waiting for them both to catch up. 'When you two have quite finished, we have work to do,' he frowned.

The school playground rested under a clear, starry sky by the time they arrived, and thankfully no one was around to see D'Scover and Adam as they melted through the door and into the school building, leaving Edie outside to wait alone. She slipped into the shadows and leaned against a wall.

Inside the classroom the green glow of the computer's standby light gave the room an eerie quality. Adam had found that his eyes worked just as well in the dark as in the light now, but darkness gave everything a slightly creepy feeling until he remembered that *they* were the ghosts. D'Scover slipped his CC from his pocket and rested it next to the keyboard while he tapped into the Brotherhood's network to establish the Hotline.

Adam walked around the classroom, looking at the artwork displayed on the walls: a bright and cheerful collection of paint-ings on the theme of springtime that the art teacher had surely chosen so that they could all chase off the last of winter. Jolly little houses with smiling flowers waving over bright green lawns. A nice friendly school with normal children to paint pictures for a caring teacher's wall. Adam sighed.

'Adam,' D'Scover called out, breaking into his musing. 'When you get back to the office, I want you to use my computer to find out if there have been any unusual ghost reports from around the world. Not the general reports of wandering women in black or Romans in the cellar kind, it has to be out of place or aggressive, poltergeists and violent hauntings, that kind of thing.'

'What? How d'you expect me to do that?' Adam asked. 'I can't just call up agents like you can.'

'You know how to use the Internet, do you not?' D'Scover asked him. Adam nodded.

'There are a number of sites that deal with this sort of thing; most of them are bookmarked. A most valuable resource is a site run by a magazine called the *Fortean Times*. They have this type of news from all around the world and you will not have to wade through pointless news of the living. It will cut through the rubbish for you and give you the reports you require. You will need to use your CC to unlock my computer as most of the functions are shut out in case the office is ever infiltrated. I have already set it to accept your CC's identity code; simply drop it into the slot on the right-hand side of the keyboard. Is that clear?'

'Yeah, suppose so, but I'm not going to pretend I'm happy about it,' Adam grumbled. 'I don't see why I can't travel back with you two.'

'You do not have to like it, just do it. This is a serious business and we need more information within a limited timeframe. Miss Freedom and I shall be back in the office by nightfall as soon as I have managed to cast off whoever gives me a ride back.'

He stared back at the school computer screen, which was rippling with a familiar black surface decorated with the occasional crackling blue spark.

'Your Hotline is ready.' D'Scover waited for Adam to come and stand by him.

As soon as Adam placed his hand on the screen, the Hotline began to take hold. Blue sparks rushed up to meet his fingers before spreading up his arm and breaking him down into a mix of blue and red glittering embers whirling in mid-air before disappearing into the screen with a final *pop* as the last of him vanished.

Outside Edie stood upright as D'Scover reappeared through the school wall.

'Did he get off OK?' she asked.

'We must hurry; we have wasted enough time already,' he snapped at her and walked off in the direction of the village. She remained in the same spot, leaning casually on the wall.

'I think we'll waste less time if we head in the right direction, don't you?' she said sarcastically.

D'Scover stopped walking and turned back to Edie once more. 'You may think this is all a grand game, young lady, but there is more at stake here than you realise,' he growled. 'If you have quite finished, could you get us to the station before we waste any more time?'

'Fine,' she muttered. 'It's this way.'

The station was busy. Parcels were being unloaded from a goods train standing in the station and people milled around the small, antiquated building.

'Why are there so many people?' D'Scover asked.

'It's the last Sunday in half-term, so the family types are trying to get back home before school starts again; also there are only three London trains a day so they're pretty busy all year round,' she explained. 'Lots of business types stay in London during the week, so they head down on Sunday night. One of them is probably our best bet.'

There was only one platform and the tiny waiting room was filled with people virtually shoulder to shoulder, huddling into the tiny space for warmth.

'Do we have to go in there?' Edie asked. 'It always stinks of sweaty bodies and I hate tuning in to people when they're so crowded together, makes my head thump.'

'We have no choice. It is imperative that we find someone who is going our way,' D'Scover said.

'Well then, could you look a little less, well, noticeable?'

'I do not understand what you mean,' D'Scover said, looking down at his long black coat, perfectly fitted suit and expensive-looking shoes. 'Is not my clothing smart enough?'

'Oh, it's smart enough. It's just …' She sighed. 'Never mind. I'd better go and buy my ticket; the train's due any time.'

Edie walked over to the ticket office while D'Scover stood and looked uncomfortable in the background. He even attempted a smile at the ticket seller.

Rather than wait for Edie to open the waiting-room door for him he hoped that no one was looking and held his hand round the handle and concentrated for a second. A light fuzz of blue sparks rolled round the handle between his hand and the metal and he turned it, opening the door and going in. A wave of heat from sweaty human flesh rolled over D'Scover and he stepped backwards as he took a moment to shut it out. He hoped no one had noticed him reeling back, but looking around, he could see no one had looked anyway as everyone was doing their best to avoid eye contact. D'Scover tried to guess who would be going all the way to London, but without Edie, he had no chance and was grateful when she joined him a few minutes later.

'Time to play your part,' he whispered. 'Find us someone.'

'OK.'

She peered through the masses and tried to focus only on each individual. Wishing she had something to lean on, she started to trawl through the minds of the people in the crowded room. Dipping into these collected minds made her dizzy and nauseous at first, as she was overwhelmed with the emotions of this mixed crowd of strangers and knew if she did it for too long, it would cause her pain. She felt their distress at being late home and their annoyance at the cramped room and this washed a wave of discontent through her.

Their feelings and senses blurred together until Edie had to take a deep, calming breath to try to smooth them out into separate streams of consciousness. Closing her eyes, she isolated first one, then another until she could sense them all as individuals. She tried to shut out some painful memories that came to the surface in some of their minds, unwilling to sink too deep into the tragic mire of their lives. She only wanted to know where they were going, not where they had been. At last she could feel two men travelling alone who were thinking about London, and how they would travel on from the station at Waterloo. Edie named these two Mr Lanky and Mr Chubby.

First she fixed her thoughts on Mr Lanky, who wore an obviously expensive and well-fitted suit, as she thought this man would fit D'Scover quite well – although she was not yet exactly sure how that would work. Her main motive was that he looked like the kind of person she could spend a long journey with; he looked intelligent and had soft crow's feet around his eyes of the kind that her mother called 'laugh lines'. In fact he looked just the kind of person she would have chosen for a dad. She concentrated on him, but all the while looking at her own feet so as not to raise his suspicions.

It had been a long time since Edie had gone out of her way to plunge into someone's thoughts like this, and as such, it took her a little while to even out the thoughts of the rest of the people around them and isolate only this man's mind. When she finally had his thoughts to herself, she saw his world and it churned her up inside. Here was everything she wanted in life: a smart house in a London suburb with a scruffy dog running in the back garden and a couple of big brothers to watch out for her.

Edie shook off his life and tried to only pick out how exactly he was going to get home, but quickly realised he would be of no use to them. She saw him arrive at the station and walk briskly across the forecourt, looking around for someone who was obviously meeting him from the train. This would be no good for D'Scover as the man would not have the time to be steered to the office.

Mr Chubby was leaning back against the wall from his seat in the corner – he was obsessively thinking about finding somewhere to have a cigarette and to distract himself he popped chunks of chocolate into his mouth and washed them down with large gulps of Coke. Edie was not looking forward to this man's thoughts as she had already picked up brief snatches of his tedious job and mundane life and his endless ill health. He was thinking about how late home he would be and she could see a large house a long way out from London. He would be catching a connecting train from the city. This was very good for D'Scover as Mr Chubby could be taken to the office and put back on his way hopefully without meeting anyone who knew him.

Edie delved further to make sure that Mr Chubby was not on a tight schedule and that he only had one train to catch; it would not be fair to abandon him in London just because of a missed connection. He must have travelled this way a lot as he seemed to know the times of all the trains and his thoughts roamed speculatively about whether or not to stop off in London for dinner before catching a later train home.

'That guy,' Edie whispered to D'Scover. 'Mr Chubby in the corner. He'll be perfect; no one meeting him and he's looking forward to sleeping the whole journey.'

'You will have to see if you can get him outside alone,' D'Scover said. 'That is going to be really difficult.'

'Not really, I have an idea.'

'Be quick. I will meet you outside,' D'Scover said as he gestured to Edie to open the door for him so that he could leave.

Edie leaned against a patch of window and pretended to stare out at the track, but watched Mr Chubby in the reflection. She closed her eyes and pictured the grey mass of the ocean she knew so well. She took the gentle swell in her mind and began to churn it up and rush it towards the shore. Picturing the sound, she splashed it around her target man's thoughts until the image of him in her mind hung wet with spray and water dripped from him. Conjuring up a beach so real that she could taste the salt of the water and hear the hiss of the tide as it sucked back along the sand, she placed him right on the shoreline. She forced him to think only of the water and the sound it made as the ocean rolled in its relentless ebb and flow. Then she brought on rain and the whisper of it skimming off the cliffs and breaking up the sea around him.

Mr Chubby sat up, stretched, reached down for his overstuffed bag, got up and left the waiting room.

Outside D'Scover watched him leave and stroll across the platform.

'How did you do it?' D'Scover asked as they followed at a suitable distance.

'Easy – long train wait, bottle of Coke and a vivid memory of the sea – enough to make anyone need the toilet!' she said.

D'Scover nodded and followed the man along the platform. The toilets were squalid and D'Scover was grateful that he could not smell them. He waited by the sink, pretending to wash his hands and hoping that no one else would come in and see the water run through his hands rather than over them. Mr Chubby dragged his bag out of the cubicle and dropped it at his feet at the sink next to D'Scover. D'Scover turned to walk away and pretended to stumble over the bag; Mr Chubby reached out instinctively to catch him as he pitched forward; it was the opportunity that D'Scover needed.

As the man lifted his palms, so did D'Scover and for one second they stood like that – palms to each other's chests, frozen in a foul-smelling public toilet. Then, almost imperceptibly, D'Scover breathed in and the familiar blue sparks began to crackle under his hands. By the time Mr Chubby looked down to the hands flat on his chest it was too late to resist. D'Scover's hands had begun to melt into the body of the other man and were already absorbed to the wrist.

'What the …?' Mr Chubby gasped and stepped backwards.

D'Scover stepped with him and plunged his arms into the hapless man and, as he broke up into a whirl of cobalt crackles, he became totally absorbed by him. For a few moments the sparks skittered over Mr Chubby's body, making it appear as if he had grasped a live wire – then they were gone and the man stood alone in the lavatory. He turned to the mirror and leaned in close to get a good look at himself, taking special interest in his eyes which now glistened with D'Scover's dark and piercing gaze, before picking up the bag and turning to leave.

Outside Edie had found a space on the end of a bench and was sitting with her head tipped back against the wall, taking in the last of the clean Cornish air before boarding the train. Right on cue the train rolled slowly to a stop in the station and the doors hissed open as people began to stream from it.

'I suggest we find a seat.' D'Scover leaned over Edie, casting a shadow as he blocked the platform lights. She opened her eyes and looked up at him in his new guise.

'Fantastic!' she laughed. 'No one would ever guess. Have you got his train ticket?'

D'Scover rummaged in his new pockets and came up with a wallet stuffed with receipts and little else. Further examination of his bag turned up a small amount of cash, several bars of chocolate, two cans of Coke, a variety of still damp clothes and an envelope containing the ticket for the return journey. D'Scover read it carefully.

'How long before the train leaves?' he asked.

'Ten minutes, why?'

'Because you need an upgrade. It seems that our friend likes to travel first class.'

Chapter Sixteen – Friend of the Texts

It had started in the storeroom of the British Museum Reading Room. Museum staff arrived in the morning to find that books had moved from where they had left them and items were jumbled up on the shelves. Then the shelves in the Reading Room itself had books in the wrong places each morning.

The librarian blamed the staff and the staff secretly talked about how the librarian was losing her mind. For months everyone skirted around the issue and tried to pretend it was not happening. Each morning the librarian would arrive and pick up the books discarded on the floor and re-shelve them. She would tidy the disorganised shelves and get on with the day. The final straw came the day some of the most precious archive books were meddled with. Two priceless books, each over two hundred years old, were found lying on the floor several metres from their home shelves and a number of archive boxes lay on the floor with the contents spilling out.

'I will not work under these conditions any longer!' she shouted at the museum director as she tossed her resignation on the desk. 'Museum staff are constantly taking advantage of library privileges and leaving the place in a mess. I have tolerated it for long enough, but the ruination of archive material is more than I can bear. We have priceless material arriving for display at the end of the week and I am not prepared to take responsibility for it if this continues. I am not prepared to stake both my reputation and career on the slim chance that someone will stop taking advantage.'

'Please, Mrs Foster, try to calm down. Please take a seat.' The director gestured to the chair opposite her desk. 'Who is taking advantage? Please explain and I will do everything in my power to stop it.'

Mrs Foster lowered her tall body into the chair, greatly resembling a folding ruler as she did so, and then frowned harder at the director.

'I arrive each morning to a terrible mess,' she snipped on. 'Well, I suppose I can't expect some of these young idiots to understand the value of a well-ordered system. I can put up with that, after all it's part of my job to tidy these books away, but the archive material is a different matter. I simply cannot tolerate such wanton destruction.'

'Mrs Foster, I am aware that this must be most distressing for you, but surely you must be mistaken.' The director tried to placate her.

'How can I be mistaken? The manuscripts and older texts are *always* shelved or boxed at the end of each day before I lock up. For three days now I've arrived to discover the library in disarray. I've found manuscripts left out on the table, boxes pulled from the shelves, and now some with the contents tipped out on to the floor.' She sighed and leaned back. 'I can't face such destruction. I know it's none of my staff, and so the only conclusion I can draw is that it's one of the general museum staff.'

'I understand how you feel,' the director said. 'We'll put a stop to this right away.' She leaned forward and picked up the telephone, hastily punching four numbers into the keypad. 'I'll talk to … hold on … is that you, Geoffrey?' she spoke into the telephone. 'I'd like you to email up the library security camera recordings, please.' Replacing the handset, she returned her gaze to Mrs Foster. 'We'll sort this out and you have my assurance that once we discover the member of staff who's doing this, they'll be most seriously reprimanded.'

'I appreciate your co-operation, and I suppose I could consider putting the past behind me – as long as the guilty party is punished,' Mrs Foster said with obvious reluctance. 'But I still don't know how they got into a locked storeroom. I really think that this is more serious than we're both presuming; we may have to face the fact that a thief is in our midst.'

'That is indeed a serious matter, but before accusations are made …' She was interrupted by the bing of an incoming email. 'Now we shall see. Here's last night's recording. Let's have a look.'

She opened the file and a grainy fisheye view of the library came up.

'Nothing out of the ordinary here,' the director said. 'Let me fast-forward a bit.'

The image flickered as it skimmed through the night, but everything in the library seemed quiet and totally normal.

'It looks fine. Maybe it's someone who comes in early, or maybe it happens … wait, what was that?' Mrs Foster pointed at the screen.

The director slowed the video to normal speed and they both craned in for a better look.

'There, what's that?' The director asked. 'Good grief! It can't be.'

Both of their jaws fell open as they watched the screen. One by one books floated from the shelves and lay in mid-air with their pages ruffled as if caught in a gentle breeze, then they were tossed to one side or jammed back into the shelves next to where they had been hovering. Book after book laid itself open for scrutiny by something that could not be seen.

'I don't believe what I'm seeing,' the director gasped. 'It must be a trick of the light. The room's so dark and I can't quite see, but …'

'I'm sure it can be easily explained, the security system has obviously been hacked, but I think we'd better keep it to ourselves for now,' Mrs Foster said in a strangely calm voice. 'If we tell anyone about this, they'll think we're insane.'

'But what can we do?' The director could not take her eyes from the screen, captivated by the books and boxes apparently moving unaided through the room. 'We have to do *something.*'

'It's clever camera trickery, I'm sure of it. Don't worry, just leave this to me.' Mrs Foster reached into her pocket and slipped her hand round the small black cube nestling within it. 'I know just who can help us.'

'Good to see you again, Adam.' Emma greeted him with a warm smile as he reassembled in the office. 'D'Scover has instructed me to lock down the place until he's back, and you've some work to do, I think?'

'Yeah, thanks.'

'No problem. He also asked me to patch through the day's reports so you can add them to your research.'

'Cheers,' Adam said.

He slumped down in D'Scover's chair and, as the secretary left, listened to the slight suck of the door as the room was locked down.

The Internet had been Adam's companion for so long when he was homeless that he had become a bit of an expert. During his stretch of living rough he had spent as much time as possible in the public library, because it was warm and free. The librarians had seemed to know he had nowhere else to go and let him use the Internet for as long as he wanted. This gave him plenty of opportunity to learn his way around.

D'Scover's computer was easy to access as he had indeed already set it to respond to Adam's CC and it blinked into life as he clipped the box on to the keyboard. The screen loaded up with the search engine's home page and Adam drummed his fingers on the desk, thinking about how to approach the research. He linked the site for the *Fortean Times* and called up the most current news. Page after page loaded up with tales of ghosts and hauntings from all over the world. Ghosts no one had reported for decades were seen wandering corridors, and even city streets, all reported by terrified witnesses. There were so many reports that Adam hardly knew where to begin.

'Right,' he said, 'I need to start more locally.'

He searched for entries for London and the site found over a hundred for the last month. He clicked on the first page and began to scan the information and make notes of dates and details, but the sheer quantity soon began to overwhelm him. After a long couple of hours he sighed and pressed the intercom to speak to Emma.

'Where can I find today's stuff?' he asked her.

'I'm just sorting them out for you, Adam,' she replied. 'Sorry about the delay. I'm afraid there're rather a lot. I'll patch them through; you'll find them in the folder named "Daily" on the computer.'

'Thanks.'

Adam cleared the screen, and brought up the daily reports and was once more surprised by the sheer volume. There must have been a good few hundred there from all over the country. Something big was happening, he didn't need Edie's psychic powers to work that out, and sitting here staring at a screen was not going to get him closer to the answer. He felt he almost knew what it was, like a word on the tip of his tongue; he knew he had seen something that would explain what was going on – or would at least help them. Closing his eyes, he took a deep breath and tried to recall what it was he had seen and where.

'Damn it, just can't quite think,' he said to himself.

He slammed his hand down on the table and his CC jumped from its place in the keyboard, causing the screen to snap into darkness once more. 'None of these reports seem to have anything in common, apart from the fact most of them haven't caused any trouble for at least a century. It's all like muddy water, all mixed up. I can't get a clear view.'

He stood up and paced around the room, trying to think, looking out over the city as if it might reach out and hand him the answer.

'This is like trying to find something in a book without an index. How am I supposed to know what's important and what …' He trailed off and a thin smile flickered across his face. 'A book, that's it.'

He walked to the Madonna painting and, mimicking the complicated pattern of movements he had seen D'Scover perform, he pulled the library key from around her neck. Stunned at how easy it had been, he watched as it settled like a living thing into his palm as he walked back to the desk and the intercom.

'Can I get out on to the balcony?' he asked Emma.

'Yes, but I have to open the doors from here. D'Scover left instructions that the balcony doors should remain sealed when he wasn't here,' she replied. 'But I'm sure he wouldn't mind the doors open while you're here. Need some fresh air?'

'Yeah, it can get a bit stuffy in here,' Adam lied.

'That's exactly what I told him!' she chuckled. 'They're open for you.'

'Ta.'

Opening the balcony doors made the wet air of the city rush through the room, stirring the paper on the desk. Adam stepped out on to the broad paved strip and walked towards the library door. Hesitating briefly, in fear of what might happen should the door not recognise his hand, he pressed his palm against the wall in what he hoped was the same spot D'Scover had used. He was enormously relieved when the thin vein of silver ran around the brickwork and revealed the library door.

The room beyond was too dark to see for a moment. Adam waited for his eyes to adjust before remembering that it was all in his mind and if he believed he could see in the dark, he could. Walking to the table in the middle of the room, he stood and looked up at the ancient Texts lining the walls and wondered where to begin. Then he had an idea.

'Now,' he said, feeling distinctly foolish, 'you books know me, and you know D'Scover. He's cared for you for centuries and now it's time to pay him back. Something's happening in our world, and the world of the living, and we need your help to find out what it is. I'm trying my hardest to find out, but I can't do it alone.'

The books stood silently on their shelves, and Adam felt his face grow red.

'What was I thinking?' He sighed loudly. 'I mean, how could a load of glued paper and ink possibly help me? For a mad moment I thought you'd understand me. Seems I got it wrong.'

Adam turned to leave the room, but was stopped in his tracks by a large dark-brown volume hovering in front of him with its cover looking at him. A single red eye stared out, a cold glower at first, but as Adam watched, it wrinkled at the corner as though smiling at him. He stepped aside as it drifted past to land on the table, fluttering its pages open. Adam took a step forward and read aloud from the open, highly decorated page.

'And at once the creatures of the field and birds of the air were compelled to work together so that the world might resolve itself into one great place where all life depended on one another for survival,' Adam read aloud. 'I get the message.'

He turned round and spoke to the now jostling and fluttering books on the shelves. 'We *can* do this together. Thank you.' He took a deep breath. 'I'm sure the reason behind this is an old one. We've been thinking far too recently. If someone is controlling old ghosts, it must be someone who's been around long enough to know of them, or someone who has access to the files. D'Scover told me that right through history the living have been trying to get hold of you for the power you contain. Do any of you have an idea about what's going on? D'you know anything that can help?' Adam pleaded.

A movement on a high shelf caught his eye and a thick volume bound in deep blue leather and heavily decorated with silver embossing slid from the shelf and descended towards him. He laid his palms out flat and the book landed gently in them. Adam waited as the book opened to the frontispiece and showed its title.

'*Alchemy in Tudor England*,' he read. 'So this'll give me a clue? Looks like it'll take a bit of reading, can't you narrow it down?'

The book skimmed through its pages, curling them back one by one, the movement growing faster and faster until Adam could no longer focus on the pages and they became a creamy blur. Eventually the pages began to slow down and came to rest at the start of a chapter headed with a scrolled font that made it look as though the book had been handwritten.

'John Dee,' Adam read. 'I think I remember seeing something about him, or I read something about Queen Elizabeth the First and him – is that the same one?'

The book flicked over another page and there was a small, watery portrait of Queen Elizabeth I.

'Hey, I was right. So something about this guy will help us out? OK, I'll take your word for it. Maybe D'Scover can shed some light on that one. D'you mind waiting for a bit until he gets back?' he asked the book.

It closed again and, lifting from his hands, laid itself on the table next to the red-eyed book.

'I have a big favour to ask,' Adam announced to the whole room. 'I need to look at the Vision again to see if anything in it can help us, but I don't know the words to make it appear so I just have to ask to see it. Would that be OK? Could I please see it again?'

The book on the table closed and slowly blinked its eye before rising from the table and slotting itself neatly back on to the shelves. A thick rumble of thunder ran through the building and Adam looked up at the sky through the glass pyramid that was the roof. He remembered the first time he had seen the Vision and, knowing what would come next, he took a step backwards. A vortex of clouds studded with letters and words filled the centre of the room above the table. He watched as the words bumped and sparked off each other with flickers of crimson fire before rising and becoming darker and more condensed until the cloud dispersed, leaving a single black book slowly revolving in the air.

It drifted down, leaving a thin, ash-like trail, and came to rest gently above the table in front of Adam.

'What an entrance – that was beautiful!' Adam gasped and the book ruffled its pages in what could only be described as pride. 'Can I see the Vision, if that's OK with you?'

The book opened its creamy pages and the clouds outside parted to reveal a single shaft of moonlight that once more bounced around on the gold details of the pages as they flickered through, coming to rest on the Vision page.

'Nice touch, very dramatic,' Adam said, and the book gave another pleased shiver. 'Now what's the exact wording of this thing? I can't read Father Dominic's code. Can you help me out?'

He stepped closer to the book and leaned into the light for a better look. The words started to blur as if water had been spilled on to the paper and the ink was running. Adam continued to watch as the words pooled together in an inky puddle in the middle of the page. A thin black thread of a line reached out from the puddle and started to take the shape of words. Adam smiled and began to read aloud.

'In times of chaos, a great division will split the Brotherhood. Faith shall weaken and many shall be lost forever to the void. In this confusion of spirits, darkness shall rise silently and take upon a form known to many. This force shall command the elemental spirits and countless spirits of ill-passage. This evil will take hold whilst others look away, but a trinity shall see all and one shall be triumphant. The one who overthrows shall have known nothing of the wickedness of the living world and shall have died unsullied by the mire of the living. This innocent shall raise a blade, forged in purity and crystal fed, and shall strike down the demons that rise to overthrow the living world. This shall be the Sentinel and their form shall be true and shall be that of a child.'

He sat down by the table and the book rotated towards him and lowered itself to his eyeline.

'Well, what do you lot think?' he asked the full shelves. 'It sounds different from the last time. You showed me the full version, didn't you? There weren't any gaps. I don't know about you, but I think D'Scover's got it all wrong. I can't be the one that this Vision talks about. I didn't die knowing nothing of the wickedness of the world. I died cold and alone on the streets of a crowded city. I've seen some terrible things. I've lived a short life full of stuff that would pass as evil in any faith. No, it can't be me, so that means that it can't be time for the Vision. That does it. No point in training or anything. D'Scover can let the Senior Council know there's no need to put me up for a Trial. It's not time for the Vision, is it?'

The book jammed itself towards Adam once more, pushing into his chest.

'Ow, calm down,' Adam said, pushing it back towards the table.

As he looked down at the words on the page, he could see that they now glowed angrily back at him with ink that had become the colour of dried blood.

'How *exactly* did you get in here?'

The voice made Adam instinctively grab the book from the air and draw it close to his body.

'D'Scover!' he gasped. 'You scared the life out of me.'

'Interesting choice of words there,' D'Scover said sarcastically. 'And you still have not answered my question.'

'Oh,' Adam sputtered, 'I just copied what you did and it let me in.'

'You should not have been able to ...' D'Scover stared at the book that Adam still held close against his body. 'How ... how did you get the Master Text? No one but I can access that text.'

Adam looked down at the book and loosened his arms, allowing it to rise from them and settle back once more, hovering above the table.

'I don't know really,' he said quietly. 'I asked nicely and it came to me.'

'Indeed,' D'Scover said. 'You certainly have a way with these works, I commend you on that, but you are never to access this room without my express permission. If these books were to …'

'Yes, I know, if they fell into the wrong hands, it could be disastrous,' Adam interrupted. 'But I'm the wrong hands, am I? I thought it might help us find out what's going on. Did you have a good journey? Where's Edie?'

'She is sleeping in the office. The journey was long and very dull. Public transport is barbaric. Thankfully my human transportation preferred to travel first class so that at least minimised the horror of being so closely crammed in with others.'

'It can't have been that bad,' Adam scoffed. 'It's a train not a prison.'

'Suffice to say I am truly glad that I no longer require a lavatory.'

'Oh, nuff said,' Adam grimaced. 'So what's Edie like?'

'Inquisitive. She has asked what must be close to a hundred questions about the Brotherhood and life after death, if you will pardon the obvious cliché.'

'Did she ask about anything else?' Adam said, trying to look as if he didn't care.

'You mean did she ask anything about you?'

'No,' Adam blurted in hasty protest. 'I meant, did she ask anything about what's going on?'

'No, but I asked her,' D'Scover replied. 'She feels she is meant to be here and can help, but she does not know exactly why her life has led her here. She does, however, feel that it is something only she can do. She is a great believer in destiny.'

'You two have a lot in common!'

'I would not have put it like that.' D'Scover looked around the room and his eyes fell on the leather-bound book that still hovered patiently above the table. 'I think that it is time this room was sealed once more, do you not?'

'Sure,' Adam said and held out the hand into which the silver outline of the key still lay.

D'Scover looked down at the shimmering pattern on Adam's palm.

'I think you can handle the sealing of the room, as you have such a bond with the books,' he said, turning to leave. 'Put the Master Text away. I will see you in my office.'

Alone once more Adam felt a nudge in his back and turned to see the Master Text fluttering its pages behind him.

'I get the hint; you can go back to … well, wherever it is you go,' he said.

The book rose into the air high above the table and the thick dark mist of tiny black and red fragments grew around it. As the mist expanded, Adam watched the words rise and mingle together, twisting out of shape as the cloud began to spin.

'Oh, and thanks for all your help, I really appreciate it,' he called out to the text that was now retreating into the mist.

A warm red pulse spread through the cloud for a second and, with a small popping sound, the book was gone.

Adam walked to the door, turning back just before he left. 'Oops, nearly forgot you.' He saw the blue book waiting patiently on the table. He held out his palms and the book gently drifted towards him. When he tucked it under his arm, it gave a small wiggle and settled down.

'Thanks, you lot,' he said, and reached out to the red-eyed book that had been the first one to help him. When he ran his finger down its spine, it arched in recognition. 'And especially thanks to you for convincing the others to help me.'

He left the room and stepped into the crisp air that whipped around the balcony. Raising his hand to the wall, he pressed it against the brickwork and waited while the mercurial track reversed its course and sealed the room, leaving only an insignificant brick wall at the end of a weather-beaten London balcony.

Chapter Seventeen – The Queen's Magician

'At this stage I am not prepared to get the police involved any more than I absolutely have to. There is, after all, nothing stolen, is there?'

The director of the Beinecke Rare Books and Manuscripts Library leaned back and looked up at the frowning face of the librarian. She scared him a little. Her arrogant and imperious nature combined with her striking beauty had always made him nervous around her, but this time he was determined not to be undermined by her.

'This library is purpose-built and one of the most secure in the world. Imagine how it would look if we went around making a fuss about supposed burglaries where nothing's taken,' he said in his soft transatlantic accent. 'We shall have to assume that this is a clever student prank and nothing more.'

'But the mess?' The librarian was angry and her narrow face grew redder and redder as she spoke – her New York-accented voice rising to a sharper pitch with each sentence. 'My computer was wiped of everything. Thankfully I back everything up, but we have no way of knowing just what they might do with the information they could have gotten hold of.'

'I really don't feel that one crashed computer can be regarded with this level of suspicion. I'm assuming that you didn't keep information about the security system on there?' the director asked.

'Of course I don't!' she replied indignantly. 'And that PC is not even networked so they couldn't have linked into any other systems from it, but that's not the point. There was a huge amount of information about the manuscripts, their shelving codes and details of what's in the archive and what's out on loan. They could pick a library that's more susceptible and aim to steal something that's on loan.'

'For crying out loud, you're making this sound like an international incident when all we're actually talking about is a bit of a mess in your office. Are you sure you haven't upset someone recently?'

The frown on the librarian's face grew deeper.

'As you may or may not know, I am not very well liked and I have not been attempting to win a popularity contest,' she said. 'Here it's my primary function to maintain order and to make sure the manuscripts are well cared for and kept safe. It's not always easy and sometimes toes must be trodden on.'

'So it could be anyone on the faculty?' the director muttered to himself.

'I beg your pardon!' she barked.

'I think that we should talk to the faculty and see if they can offer any insight into this. They may be aware of anyone who was planning a prank.'

'I do not see how this can be a prank.' She spat the word with disgust. 'Have you seen the display cases yet?'

'No, maybe you'd better show me those now.' He stood up, grateful for the opportunity to usher the angry librarian from his office.

He followed her up the main stairs and out on to the central floor, which housed the display cabinets. The golden glow of the last rays of afternoon sunlight falling through the thin marble panels cladding the building gave the library an eerie atmosphere. He always thought this effect, combined with the air so still and warm, gave the library a feeling that was a little like being inside a jar of honey He hated this stifling sensation.

The librarian marched on impossibly high heels with quick, angry steps to the first display box – a glass-sided cube with a book resting open inside it.

'There,' she said indignantly, pointing to the book. The director leaned over the case and examined the creamy pages of text.

'I'm sorry, I just can't see anything wrong with this book, am I missing something?' he said as he peered into the case.

'Yes,' she snorted, 'it's obvious. This book is turned to a different page!'

'A different page? Are you sure?'

'Of course I'm sure; I have a strict routine for turning these pages so the binding is not stressed by being open at the same page for too long. This volume had only just had its pages turned. That one,' she pointed to the next case along, 'was due to be changed on Friday. But they've *all* been changed.'

'And there's no one else who might've changed them?'

'There's no one else who *could* have changed them. I have the only key and it was at home with me. These cases are bombproof and tamper-proof and each one carries a link to the alarm system. As far as security is aware, no one came in here at all.'

'I see.'

'I want these cases fingerprinted to track down who's bypassed the security system, and then possibly we can find out why.'

The director stood up straight once more and tore his gaze from the case. 'As I've said before, I do not wish to have the police crawling all over the place unless it's absolutely necessary and I don't feel that the situation warrants it.'

'But the books, my office …' she stammered.

'However,' the director interrupted, 'I do know someone who may be able to help, an Englishman I used to know. I'll email him and see what he has to say.'

'Thank you,' she said, clearly not pleased with his decision. 'I suppose that'll have to do for now. Who is this person anyway?'

'He's an … um … international archivist, an expert in ancient texts, and has seen pretty much everything in his long career. We worked together a few years back in another building I was responsible for. His name is Toby D'Scover.'

'Are you angry with me?' Adam whispered.

Edie was asleep on the couch and Adam was trying his best not to wake her. Despite the quiet, she was sleeping fitfully, her eyes jerking in an uneasy dance behind her closed lids.

'No,' D'Scover replied curtly.

'But I did kind of break into your library, and went through your books without asking.'

D'Scover slid the balcony doors closed, but did not turn back to look at Adam who stood, still clutching the dark book from the library.

'They are no more my books than they are yours,' he said, staring out over the city. 'I am merely the Keeper; if they had something they wished to show you, that is at their discretion. You would not have been able to enter the room at all if it was not meant to be.'

'There you go with that fate and destiny stuff again. I just don't get it,' Adam snorted.

'It does not matter; you do not have to understand it for it to happen.' D'Scover spun round to face Adam. 'No, your access to the Texts does not worry me. I am more concerned about the increase in ghost activity. I have had a number of reports from living agents who have the care of certain important buildings and they are witnessing an increase in activity, even the reactivation of once dormant spirits.'

'But you said yourself that this happened before,' Adam reminded him.

'Yes,' D'Scover agreed, 'but never on this scale. Have you noticed a pattern in any of the reports you inspected?'

'No, apart from the fact that there are a number of libraries that've had archives disrupted.'

'Libraries?' D'Scover was interested. 'I would like to see the full details of those reports.'

'But it was just a dozen or so reports out of hundreds,' Adam exclaimed.

'Even so, I would like to see them,' D'Scover insisted. 'What did the Texts show you? You seem to be clutching that volume very tightly.'

Adam looked down at the book in his arms and it wiggled slightly as if to remind him it was there.

'Oh yeah, it's all about alchemists in Tudor times.' He loosened his arms and the book lifted from them and slid through the air, coming to rest on the desk. 'Show Mister D'Scover the pages, please.'

The pages once more flickered open and speeded up, wafting the other paperwork on the desk before slowing down at the pages Adam had already seen. D'Scover walked over and laid a careful hand on the pages to steady their movement before reading his way through the text.

'John Dee, a good man, misunderstood,' he muttered.

'You knew John Dee?' Edie's voice startled them both and they turned to see her sitting up on the couch.

'Hey, sleepyhead!' Adam laughed. 'Long journey?'

'Yeah,' Edie grinned. 'I don't last as long as dead people, I need my sleep – and anyway, I seem to remember that you need your rest too.'

'Wow, you do wake up in a bad mood, don't you?' Adam joked and returned the grin.

'What do you know of John Dee?' D'Scover interrupted their banter.

'I did a school project on the Tudors last summer. We had to pick a Tudor person and write about them. I chose John Dee.' She yawned and stretched. 'Pretty amazing coincidence, isn't it?'

'Oh no!' Adam clutched his head in an overdramatic mocking gesture. 'Please don't get him started on coincidence! He thinks that there's no such thing – it's all fate and destiny.'

'Well, Red, it makes sense, you have to admit it,' Edie said. 'Although I already believe that I'm here with you for a good reason.'

'Oh God, I forgot you were another one who believes in all that crap!' Adam slapped his forehead in mock disgust.

'We have work to do.' D'Scover, the voice of reason, brought them back to the book.

Edie stood up and walked over to the two of them and the book that D'Scover still held.

'John Dee was alchemist and advisor to Elizabeth I, and so that makes it the sixteenth century – were you still alive then?' she asked D'Scover.

'A typically candid question, Miss Freedom, and the answer is no,' he replied. 'The Brotherhood had been founded, but I was just another small part of it. The Senior Council were not yet fully established with ten members organising just over a hundred Shades. I was a working Shade and was sent to meet Dee to see if I could convince him to join the Brotherhood.'

'Stop!' Adam blurted. 'This sounds like a cool story. Don't tell her – show her! You can do it for the living, can't you?'

'Yes, but in the circumstances it would be quicker to just explain the basic details,' D'Scover said.

'But you might miss something that the Hypnagogia will show her,' Adam insisted. 'It could be important, you know, fate and all that.'

'Hypnagogia!' Edie said. 'The bit between waking and sleeping; old witches used to use that to influence people. What d'you do? Please show me.'

'Very well,' D'Scover sighed, 'take a seat back on the couch, and you might as well join her, Adam, but I warn you – to show you all the details it will be a long Hypnagogia.'

'I bags the warm end of the sofa!' Edie ran back to where she had been sitting.

Adam walked over and sat next to her while D'Scover pulled over his desk chair once more.

'Do not worry; it all looks real but it is not,' D'Scover explained. 'None shall be able to see you, including the image of myself, and you will be unable to touch anything. You can pass through solid objects and people, but it takes a while to accustom your mind to it; you have to keep reminding yourself that it is like a dream. As Adam said, the experience is very vivid and you may feel it is real. Because you are still within the living world, and because of your gifts, you may feel even more connected to the illusion. You will not be able to stop it. Only I can do that and I will do so if I feel that you are under too much stress.'

'I wasn't nervous before, but I am now,' Edie said, but she tipped back her head and closed her eyes all the same.

'Now I must ask you if you are sure you wish to go through with this?' D'Scover asked her.

'How could I not after that build-up?' Edie grinned without lifting her head. 'Bring it on!'

D'Scover took a deep breath.

'*In the early summer of fifteen eighty-three the Brotherhood became aware of a new element in the London scene that made them sit up and take notice,*' he began. '*An alchemist and mathematician by the name of John Dee had been causing a stir by relating his conversations with spirits, or angels as he believed they were. He had been working in London for some time, but, due to his dramatic revelations, he found himself in fashion with the elite of the London set and this drew him to the attention of Queen Elizabeth the First …*'

Edie felt the words wash over her and the sounds seemed to throb in and out of her hearing range. It was almost as if she was on a swing, drifting backwards and forwards towards D'Scover as he spoke. Soon the words became even less audible and faded with each swing until she was aware that she could not hear them at all. She had hardly noticed that she was no longer sitting on the couch, but on a low wooden bench inside a crowded coffee house filled with smoke and noise. Turning, Edie could see that Adam was still sitting next to her and that he too was marvelling at their surroundings.

'How does he do this?' Edie gasped, still twisting and turning on the bench to get a better view of everything. 'Am I dreaming or awake?'

'We're on the edge of dreaming,' Adam replied. 'I think he does it by drifting from speaking proper sentences into disjointed words that explain what we need to see, and our minds fill in the gaps from what we've read about this stuff, you know, in books and that.'

'It explains why it sounded like his voice came and went. He wasn't speaking in sentences at all,' Edie said. 'I thought it was my imagination, but it makes sense; you can get a lot across if someone can see where they are and just have lists of objects to fill the image. Suppose it's like hypnotic suggestion.'

'I try not to think too hard about it,' Adam said. 'Does my head in.'

'What do we do now?' Edie asked.

'Just go with the flow,' he shrugged. 'It worked for me the last two times.'

They sat still and looked around the room at the organised chaos going on all about them.

The room was large and scattered with low tables that were barely lit by several massive iron candelabras that hung on great hooks from the ceiling. These monstrosities of twisted metal were liberally stuck with grey fatty candles, which spat and crackled as they burned, giving off a pallid yellow light. Around the tables sat men, all dressed in rich and elaborate costume, and all swigging repeatedly from large pewter flagons. They wore long velvet jackets of the deepest shades of red, blue and light-absorbing black with ice-white lace that spilled from deep cuffs. They were obviously impatient for something and many highly polished black boots stamped the floor as the men made raucous demands for entertainment.

'Look at the bling on him!' Adam pointed to a man who wore an elaborate black wig studded with the fire-gleam of rubies. 'It must be difficult for him to lift his head.'

'Yeah, but the smell's awful,' Edie said, holding her nose. 'Don't these people ever wash?'

'Not much, washing this stuff must've been murder,' he said. 'Guess they just got used to it. Anyway, it's just our imagination – the smell.'

'Tell that to my nose!' She wafted her hand in front of her face.

A very large woman, wearing a white wig piled high on her head like a snowy peak, wove her way through the crowd until she was standing right in the middle of the room. She shook open a large fan of deep blue feathers and wafted it around to gain the attention of everyone in the room.

'I have a pleasure for you, gentlemen of the Court of Bacchus!' she called out and received a riotous wave of laughter in return.

'This is like some kind of fancy gentlemen's club,' Edie explained. 'What can D'Scover want here?'

'Every time I've been in one of these Hypnagogias he's been here too. He must be around somewhere,' Adam said. 'We should have a look for him; after all they can't see us.'

The laughter died down and the mountainous woman spoke once more.

'For your distraction this evening I have managed to secure the attentions of someone who has the ear of our Queen.' She swung her bulk to one side to reveal a man who had been standing behind her. 'Master John Dee!' she exalted.

A tall thin man, with a long white beard and flowing robes of shimmering green, stepped forward into the circle of space around the woman.

'Master Dee will astound you all with his prophetic visions and feats of magic,' the woman continued, wafting her immense fan around. 'He will produce marvels the like of—'

'STOP!' A shrill voice interrupted her mid-sentence. 'This man is not John Dee.'

'Look!' Adam whispered to Edie. 'It's D'Scover. So that's not the real Dee? Why would she say it was him if it wasn't?'

'He was very well known in society circles. I suppose it'd give her some kind of status if she had the real one at her party,' Edie reasoned.

'Of course he is Dee. Mark his appearance, who else could it be?' The woman spoke in a mocking tone. 'My concern is more with who you are than he. Why are you at this gathering, Master, er—?' She waited for his reply.

'My name is of no concern to you,' D'Scover spat, 'but I do know *that* is not Master Dee and the trickery here is yours if you tell your patrons otherwise.'

'I think my fellows will believe me far more readily than they will believe a stranger who does not even know his own name,' the hostess said mockingly.

The crowd laughed again, a hearty and spiteful guffaw that rolled around the room.

'Now,' she continued, 'I think the time has come for you to leave us.'

She raised a fat hand and gestured to two huge men standing in the shadows behind D'Scover. They stepped forward until they were standing right behind him. D'Scover turned and looked up at the two men and took a few steps back.

'There is no call for aggression. I will leave of my own volition,' he said, and walked to the door.

'Come on,' Adam said to Edie. 'We have to go with him; this is his memory of those events so we have to stay close.'

They followed D'Scover to the door and out into the street. The party rose in volume again and the sound of laughter followed them out on to the street. Once outside, the door was slammed behind them and with it the light that had spilled out from inside was abruptly removed.

'It's so dark, how will we find him?' Edie tried to peer through the blackness of a London night. 'What I wouldn't give for a few streetlights!'

'We just have to see if we can … there, there he is!' Adam said and pointed to where the figure of D'Scover could just be made out briskly walking down the muddy street with his cloak snapping behind him.

They followed him through the darkness, desperate to gain ground and get closer to him, but he moved so fast that it was almost impossible. After a short distance the clouds parted overhead and a sharp white blanket of moonlight fell through the streets. The party had been in a wide avenue with tall trees and elegant houses that rose up around a large square; the streets they now entered were quite different. Here the stench of the river was all-pervading and it hung over them like a hot, foul blanket. The houses crowded in on each other and the gaps between them became dirtier and smaller as they walked on. D'Scover had slowed down now and walked at a steady pace through the silent streets as though the anger he had felt earlier had worn off. Adam and Edie felt more relaxed about following him and no longer worried about losing him.

'I wish I'd been able to do this when I was doing that project at school. I would've aced it,' Edie said, staring around, trying to take in every detail of the streets around her. 'You know what I don't get though?'

'No,' Adam replied, 'what?'

'How can we both see the same thing here?' she said in a puzzled voice.

'I don't know if we do.'

'What?' Edie stopped for a moment. 'You've lost me.'

'Well, who's to say that we're seeing the same stuff now?' Adam said. 'I might see different colours or different objects, but because they're on the edges of the illusion we don't know that we're seeing different things. I reckon that's how it works anyway. You've done a whole project on this period so you probably have a better idea of what London looked like than me. I might see a totally different street scene, but the main details will be the same because D'Scover has given us those images.'

'Pretty complex stuff.'

'As I said, it does my head in if I think too hard about it,' Adam laughed. 'I think I'll give up thinking for now in case D'Scover drives me totally off my head.'

'You're not wrong! Speaking of D'Scover, where is he?' Edie said.

The street in front of them was empty; D'Scover was nowhere to be seen. Adam and Edie ran ahead and stopped just in time before they fell over the wharf into the Thames. The black slick of the river ran slow in front of them, but no boats were floating across it and so he could not have taken that route. They turned round and listened hard for any evidence of footsteps, but the only sound was the soft lapping of the river against the legs of the wooden piers that stretched out over the water.

'So what now?' Edie asked.

Adam shrugged and looked all around at the buildings fronting the water with a heavy frown on his face.

'Hey!' he said, with a sudden flash of inspiration. 'I've been here before, last time when D'Scover showed me all this. I know where he is!'

'Where?' Edie asked.

'There.' Adam looked up and Edie followed his gaze.

Above them rose the tower of the building Adam had followed D'Scover into in the last Hypnagogia. The city around it was different, he had last seen it nearly a hundred years in its future, but it was unmistakably the same tower. It reached up above the river, casting a long moon-shadow across the foul water. Around its base wooden scaffolding still stood and the remains of the day's building work littered the floor. The convent buildings were not attached to the tower as they would be in the future, but the door to the tower was in the same place in its base. Adam showed Edie the way into the building and, after steadily climbing the narrow, winding stairs to the top of the tower, they emerged into D'Scover's lofty room.

'This is earlier than when I was last here, but it looks pretty much the same,' Adam said. 'I suppose he doesn't need much in the way of personal stuff.'

'I dunno, he has all those bowls and paintings,' Edie replied, 'so he must've started collecting those later.'

'Or he's not mentioning them now, so we can't see them in this illusion,' Adam said.

D'Scover was standing by the glassless window, looking out over the sleeping city. A wind blew up around the tower, whipping dead leaves through the windows. The wind grew until a now familiar dark cloud swirled through the tower, forming twelve distinct shapes in the room.

'What are they?' Edie asked.

'The Senior Council,' Adam explained. 'They're the ones at the top who control the Brotherhood.'

'I thought that D'Scover—' Edie started to say.

'Don't ask him, he gets real tetchy about it,' Adam cut in. 'This must be important if they're here; last time I saw them they were warning him about a demon.'

The shapes became more solid and once more the room was ringed with tall, cloaked figures. This time Adam felt a surge of confidence and ran forward into the circle where D'Scover had already dropped to one knee in reverence.

'What're you doing?' Edie called out.

'I want to see what this lot look like; I was too freaked out by it all last time to do it.'

He walked round the ring and peered under the heavy cowls to see what was underneath.

'And?'

'Nothing,' Adam replied. 'It's like there's nothing in there but darkness.'

'I suppose that they're representations of the people they were,' Edie mused. 'I mean, there's no real reason for them to be here at all. They could just send an image to represent themselves. It could even be because D'Scover's never seen them either.'

'Surely he must have an idea who the Council members are?' Adam said, still peering under the cowls.

'Probably not and, as this is D'Scover's illusion, that means that he doesn't know what they look like.'

The wind died down and the dancing leaves fell to the floor.

'RISE.' Cold voices boomed through the room. D'Scover stood and adjusted the sword on his belt.

'WHAT DO YOU HAVE TO TELL US OF YOUR SEARCH FOR THE MAN DEE?' the voices asked.

'I have not been able to ascertain his whereabouts, masters,' D'Scover answered, still keeping his head bowed. 'He does not seem to be in the city and my restrictions mean that I am unable to search further afield. I have heard he has taken a house somewhere further up the river, but that is not confirmed.'

'IT IS NOW,' the voice replied. 'YOU ARE TO GO TO MORTLAKE AND SEEK EMPLOYMENT AT HIS HOUSE THERE. THE DETAILS ARE ON YOUR TABLE.'

Adam and Edie automatically glanced over to the desk and watched as a layer of blue and silver sparks crackled up the side of a quill which stood erect and began to scratch words upon a half-curled piece of parchment.

'Thank you, masters. How am I to get there?'

'THE SENIOR COUNCIL VIEW THIS MATTER AS ONE OF GRAVE IMPORTANCE. WE HAVE BECOME INCREASINGLY CONCERNED ABOUT THE NATURE OF THE INFORMATION THIS MAN IS GATHERING,' the massed voices of the Council members explained. 'WE MUST KNOW IF HIS CLAIM OF CONTACT WITH SPIRITS IS INDEED TRUE. WE HAVE DECIDED THIS MAN'S LIBRARY AND PERSONAL NOTES MUST BE EXAMINED AT ANY COST. THE COUNCIL SHALL SUPPORT YOUR CORPOREAL ESSENCE FOR THE DURATION OF THIS TASK. YOU SHALL BE ABLE TO MOVE AT WILL THROUGH THE CITY AND BEYOND.'

'Yes, masters, I shall make preparations to leave at once.' D'Scover bowed low. 'But I fear I may not be able to gain employment in his house. I am experienced in the Texts as you well know, but this man is most private and will take none into his confidence, not even the Queen.'

'WE AGREE THAT YOU MAY NOT FIND EMPLOYMENT IN HIS HOUSE AS YOU ARE,' the voices continued, 'BUT THE SENIOR COUNCIL FEEL THAT THERE IS ANOTHER WAY.'

D'Scover looked up into the dark, empty cowls and, as Adam and Edie's mouths fell open, a thick black cloud rolled around him, obscuring him from their view.

'What's going on?' Edie asked. 'Is he in danger?'

'Your guess is as good as mine,' Adam replied.

The human-shaped cloud in the middle of the circle began to shrink in size so that it almost looked as though it was dropping through the floor. A series of small pops and crackles emanated from the cloud, sending silver sparks cascading out to dance across the floor before vanishing. The Senior Council remained in a wide, silent circle around the sparkling black cloud, with no sign of movement. Eventually the cloud began to break up and Adam and Edie could just make out the figure of D'Scover still standing inside – but now he looked somehow further away. The cloud dissipated and there he stood, still wearing the grubby green tunic and hose that he wore before, but without the bloodstained legs; the heavy sword hung from his waist – only now it scraped on the floor. Turning to each other, they both spoke at the same time.

'He's a boy again!'

Chapter Eighteen – A Vision in White

'Why's it dark now?' Edie twisted round, straining her eyes in the blackness.

The space around Adam and Edie had gradually dimmed until all they could now see was each other. They were both aware only of slight flashes of images around them – one moment a river slicked past them and was gone again, then open fields and now a town, just a blur of walls and tumbledown cottages.

'I think he's skipping bits, taking us somewhere else – Morelake – was that the name of that place he's being sent to?' she asked.

'Mortlake,' he corrected her. 'It's a place much further along the Thames, but I guess it would've still been a village during Dee's life.'

Almost as if prompted, the images around them began to settle and solidify once more and when the illusion was fully re-formed, they stood in a small village square surrounded by the bustle of a market. Adam immediately began to scan the crowd for D'Scover and quickly found him heading towards a track leading away from the crowds.

'There he is!' He grabbed Edie. 'Quick, let's get after him.'

They both ran through the crowd, closing their eyes to run through the people that blocked their way, until they were just a few steps behind D'Scover on the path. They followed him to another settlement, but this was quite unlike the houses they had seen before. The house itself was normal enough, a farmhouse of decent proportions with a tidy vegetable garden and the brilliant white flash of boiled linen drying on the walls around the perimeter – it was the rest of the building that stunned them.

Attached to the main house were low buildings that seemed to have been added in haste by someone who had only seen houses in pictures. They resembled houses in that they had four walls and a roof, but they were so crudely made they looked more like a child's playhouse than the home of one of the greatest minds of the age. These extensions to the house seemed to lean against each other for support and looked as though a decent wind would carry them off across the fields.

'They say that intellectuals are the most eccentric and they're not wrong, are they?' Edie laughed. 'Is this really Dee's house?'

'Must be,' Adam said. 'Let's try and get a bit closer.'

They ran through the wall and across the lawn until they were up against the house. They systematically began to peer in each of the windows around the ground floor. But despite their best efforts, the gloom of the interior revealed nothing of use and they could not decide which wall to walk through.

'We have to find him,' Edie moaned. 'Where would you keep books safe in a rickety old house like this?'

'Maybe you'd keep them in a room without windows?' Adam pointed towards the jumble of other buildings that sprouted from the main building. 'They could be—'

He was interrupted by a loud banging noise from the front of the house. Gesturing for Edie to follow, he ran back round to the gardens.

A young boy was knocking on the door of the main house, running an impatient hand through his messy black hair as he waited for someone to open it.

'Adam!' Edie shouted. 'It's him!'

They ran closer to be sure they would miss nothing of the impending conversation. By the time they reached the door, a tall, wiry woman had answered it and was already talking to D'Scover.

'I do not think that my husband is seeking help, boy,' she said, 'but as you have come all this way, I will ask him. Wait in the gardens to the back, but mind my vegetables or I will have your hide.'

She disappeared into the house and D'Scover wandered round to the back, closely followed by Adam and Edie. They did not have to wait long. A few minutes later a shout came from one of the flimsy-looking buildings on the far side of the property.

'YOU – BOY!'

They all turned to look and there in the doorway of the furthest building stood a tall thin man with a long, pointed beard. He fitted the physical description of the man they had seen at the party, but his face carried a wearier look. In this tired face the only signs of vitality were his eyes and these shone with a hard stare on D'Scover. Dee was dressed in a shabby, long black robe liberally peppered with ash and covered in small burn holes, some of which still smouldered. The woman stood alongside him wearing a gentle smile and, glancing down at his robe, patiently bent down and patted out the smoking patches.

'Master Dee,' D'Scover said, and bowed low before walking to where the great man stood. 'I come to offer my services.'

'You, offer your services to me?' Dee began to laugh, a loud, rattling laugh that seemed to fill the garden. 'What can *you* do for *me*, boy?'

D'Scover looked up and his face carried a look of absolute confidence.

'I can read, sir, English, Latin, French and Greek and some of the Germanic tongues, and I can write the same,' he said.

'Can you now?' Dee looked surprised. 'Well, we shall see about that. Follow me.' He walked back into the building and his wife, smiling indulgently, beckoned for D'Scover to follow.

'He likes you,' she whispered to D'Scover as he came to the door. 'He trusts his first impressions always and he would not invite you in if he did not like you.'

'Thank you, mistress,' D'Scover replied. 'I hoped that it would be so.'

Inside the room it was dark and hot with an acrid stench that should have made D'Scover's eyes water. Adam and Edie followed Dee and D'Scover through into another room even darker than the one they had left. No external door or window cast light into this room and momentarily they were blinded by the gloom. They listened to the rustling of Dee's robe as it dragged across the floor and a vivid yellow flare of flame suddenly lit the room. The shadows danced across the floor, falling away from a jumble of equipment the like of which Adam and Edie had seen only in movies.

'It looks like the lab of a mad scientist!' Adam laughed, walking round the large central table.

This table dominated the room and it was overloaded with all manner of glass containers and pipes. There rose from the table a confection of glass tubing that looked so fragile it almost defied gravity by remaining upright. These tubes twisted and turned on themselves, curving once in a while low to the table so that the flames of a candle could brush a swollen bulge in the pipe. Glossy copper piping shone under the table in great coils, looking like metallic snakes frozen in mid-strike. Throughout the glass, and dripping from the copper, were great globs of a silver liquid that clung to itself in perfect gleaming beads.

'Mercury,' Adam said. 'Isn't that, like, really poisonous?'

'Yes, the air in here must be totally toxic,' Edie replied. 'No wonder he thought he saw angels.'

'Angels?'

'Yeah, one of the things Dee is known for is that he believed that he had conversations with angels, archangels in fact.' Edie watched Dee move around the room and light more candles. 'Actually, not surprising if he was breathing in all this mercury vapour; he would've hallucinated all sorts of things. It would've killed him in the end.'

'But what if he really did see angels?' Adam asked.

'You're dead,' Edie reminded him. 'Seen any angels?'

'No.' He shook his head. 'Good point. Hey, I remember that D'Scover said Father Dominic spoke to angels too; maybe that's the connection here.'

'Or maybe Father Dominic licked his lead-covered paintbrush too many times and he was hallucinating too,' Edie said.

'Boy,' Dee said. His voice was thick with phlegm and the sound made them want to cough. 'So you claim you can read?'

'Yes, master. I was raised in a holy order and I was taught texts.'

'Holy order?' Dee suddenly flew at him and grabbed him by the shoulders. 'Amongst the Sisters? Are you sent from them?'

'No, master,' D'Scover protested. 'I was raised amongst the Benedictine Brotherhood at St Albans.'

Dee let him go. 'I have no tolerance for the holy sisters; they are too keen to pry into my collection. I am tired of their attempts to steal my library and discredit me, sneaking around with Elizabeth's questions, talking to the Court …' He trailed off, seemingly forgetting D'Scover was there.

He gave a little cough to remind the man of his presence.

'Well, boy,' Dee snapped himself out of it, 'we shall see if your arrogance lives up to your claims, shall we? I warn you, I do not have time for liars; if you can read as you claim, I may have some use for you.'

The tall man turned and placed both hands on a section of wall panelling behind a large iron candlestick and pushed hard. The wood gave an almost imperceptible click and revealed itself to be on hinges. Dee pulled the section forward and the panel folded back on itself to expose the rows of bookshelves hidden there and the books crammed into them. He reached into the crowded shelves, pulled out a large brown volume and blew dust from it. Cradling it in his right arm, he flicked through the pages until he came to one that made him smile; he raised the book and offered it to D'Scover.

'How come he can hold the book?' Edie asked. 'He's still a ghost after all and I can't see that crackly light that normally comes just before he holds something.'

'Dunno,' Adam shrugged. 'Must be the Senior Council's doing; they're giving him their strength, remember.'

D'Scover looked down into the book and frowned.

'What is the matter, boy? Can you not read this text? It is simple Latin and should be well within your grasp if your claims are true.' Dee smiled under his white beard.

'Reading it is not a challenge, master, but I am ashamed to read it aloud,' D'Scover mumbled.

'Tell me, boy, what do you read there?' Dee demanded.

''Tis a potion, sir, or recipe for one.' D'Scover's voice was barely audible.

'Go on, tell me in full,' Dee persisted.

''Tis for ...' D'Scover faltered. 'It deals with matters of love, sir, and with how to make a girl's head turn to you ... even if she is already betrothed to another.'

'HA!' Dee laughed a short burst and banged his hand upon the table so hard it set the glass tinkling. 'You can indeed read, boy; you may be of use to me.'

He took the book from D'Scover and replaced it on the shelves before pulling the panel back across and hiding the books from view once more.

'I do not pay a regular wage, but you may earn a penny or two for good work, you will not go hungry and you will always be warm,' Dee said. 'I expect loyalty and discretion. If you do not give it me, then I have many friends and I am sure you are aware of the fact that even the Queen's spies owe many favours to me.'

D'Scover nodded and watched as Dee shuffled around, snuffing out candles one by one.

'Go back to my wife,' he said, 'and the kitchen girl will feed you and find you somewhere to sleep.'

With that, the last candle was extinguished and the room was in darkness. He shuffled past D'Scover, turning back so that his unkempt hair created a halo when silhouetted in the thin light from the other doors beyond.

'Understand this though, boy,' Dee said, his voice now much lower and more malevolent than before, 'I do not make idle threats and I will tolerate nothing more than absolute loyalty. If you betray any of what you see here, you will fall harder than you ever would have imagined possible. Do I make myself understood?'

D'Scover nodded furiously in the thin light.

'Excellent!' Dee said, his voice full of cheer once more. 'Away to my wife now. I have work to continue and shall see you later when you are fed.'

He shuffled off into the dark maze of other rooms leaving D'Scover standing in the doorway alone. He waited for a moment, throwing a brief glance behind him into the room, before running off to find the kitchen with Adam and Edie in hot pursuit.

Before they reached the kitchen the image started to blur once more. They could just see a girl step from the gardens towards the kitchen, her apron held up at the hem full of apples.

'Look!' Adam called out. 'It's you!'

The image was fading fast, but it was clear this was yet another incarnation of the life spirit Edie now carried, another of her ancestors.

'Amazing!' Edie gasped. 'It's like watching an old film of myself! I suppose working in the house of an alchemist would be the perfect way for a young witch to secretly learn her craft.'

'Why doesn't D'Scover remember you from this time?'

'Dunno, but I'm guessing he's never been exactly brilliant around girls.'

'I can believe that!'

The image of the girl continued to fade until all around them was a faint blur that grew ever darker.

'He's skipping bits again, look,' Adam said.

He pointed through the darkness to what was forming before them. There in front of them was a silent scene, played out as though on a stage, of Dee and D'Scover in Dee's workroom. D'Scover swept the floor as Dee talked in an animated fashion, moving around the glass equipment, tapping and touching sections as he did so. The scene smudged and the colours ran into another scene of Dee and D'Scover sitting in front of a table loaded to breaking point with books; both seemed to be scouring the pages for something.

The scenes changed again and again, speeding up as they did so. They watched as D'Scover became closer to Dee and gained his confidence even more. The passage of time speeded up and they saw many visit Dee in his crowded house. Edie leaned on Adam's freshly strengthened shoulder to steady herself as the images began to slow down and form a room around them.

'Looks like we're here again,' Adam said.

'D'you think this is nearly over?' Edie asked. 'I'm starting to forget what reality is like.'

'Yeah, well, I—' Adam stopped short as Dee burst into the room closely followed by D'Scover.

'Quickly, boy, the carriage will be here soon and we must be ready to leave,' Dee urged. 'My trunk is almost ready; put these remaining books in and bolt it securely.'

'Your library, master,' D'Scover asked. 'What will become of it?'

'I have left instructions with someone I trust in the village to guard my house well,' he sighed. 'We shall have to hope that his word is good and he will take care of it.'

Dee walked to the panels that concealed the bookcases and rolled them back to reveal the books within.

'It has been my life's work to gather these volumes,' he said, caressing the spines of a few books. 'And now I am forced to take my leave of them and to place them in the hands of a man with less education than a coachman.'

Dee spun round to look at D'Scover and his face burned with a look of anger and hate that made Adam and Edie shudder involuntarily.

'The royal house shall regret this move to force me and my counterpart from the country,' he raged, angrily slamming the panel closed behind him. 'One day they shall realise that Kelly and I are privy to great truths from the hearts of angels, and they shall all be doomed for their failure to allow us freedom of movement.'

'Who's Kelly?' Adam asked.

'Kelly was a con artist, basically,' Edie said. 'Somehow he managed to convince Dee he could hold a seance and get in touch with angels when he wanted to. He got Dee to observe and write about it all and he was totally sucked in.'

'Well, it can't have all been a con,' Adam protested. 'Otherwise why would we be seeing this now? Something here must be important.'

Dee reached out an arm and swept it across the table, forcing the complicated tangle of glass to fall to the floor and shatter on the hard stone. Adam looked down as the rain of shards cascaded through his legs, but the scene in the room seemed to transfix Edie.

'They shall not have my work,' Dee said through gritted teeth. He dumped a large fabric bag unceremoniously on the table and began to stuff it with parchment and books from his desk.

'Master, where will you go?' D'Scover asked.

'I have a friend in Prague who has gained me an audience with King Rudolf. I shall find work in his court,' Dee said. 'At least he is not a fearful ignoramus! These fools here in England who jump at the beck of the girl we call Queen shall mourn my leaving. Well, to hell and to damnation with the lot of them.'

Dee returned to his desk and began rummaging around in the huge mound of loose papers for something. It cascaded like an avalanche over the side of the desk and skidded along into the mess of broken glass and spilled mercury.

'Blast, where is the monk's book? I cannot leave without it,' Dee muttered angrily to himself. 'That fat nun may have slandered my name, but she will not seize my book.'

'Which book, master?' D'Scover asked, bending to look under the desk.

'The one I showed you before, the coded one from the monastic house.'

'Here, master.' D'Scover bent over and pushed aside a pile of paper. 'Here it is.' He held up a book for Dee to take. It was smaller than most of the books in the library and bound only in a crumpled cover of creamy vellum around diaphanous sheets of white paper. Dee looked visibly relieved to find it and snatched it from D'Scover, holding it tight to his body.

'Why d'you think he's going away?' Adam asked, turning back to Edie.

Edie stood next to him, but as Adam looked at her, he felt he was only looking at an empty shell – Edie seemed to have gone. She stood stock-still and her wide-stretched eyes had a glazed look as she stared into the distance.

'Edie?' he said. 'Edie – EDIE!'

He began to shout, took her shoulders in his hands and shook her. She rocked stiffly backwards and forwards as if she was a rigid doll and her eyes seemed fixed on something way beyond Adam's vision. He let her go and she softened and crumpled to the floor with her eyes still wide and staring. Behind them, the illusory Dee continued to pack to leave and D'Scover fussed around with the spilled paper, but Adam only had eyes for Edie. Kneeling down beside her, he concentrated on solidifying his own hand, gripped hers tightly and closed his eyes.

'Don't leave me, Edie,' he begged, 'we've only just found you, come on, hang on.'

He wrapped both of his hands round hers, hoping to force them into the real world with his tight grip, and willed his thoughts to D'Scover.

'C'mon, D'Scover!' he shouted. 'Get us out of here.'

Adam took a deep breath and focused on her cold hands in his and pictured the office, imagined the walls rising up around him and the couch beneath them. He gave his whole being to making this image in his mind real and, when he opened his eyes a moment or two later, he was back in the real world.

'*Carriage, books, trunk, glass, rain, fear, haste, boat, sickness, destruction, books …*'

D'Scover still mumbled in his soft voice, his eyes closed, deep in the illusion himself.

'D'Scover!' Adam yelled. 'Something's wrong with Edie!'

'What?' D'Scover shook himself back to an alert state. 'How did you remove the influence of the vision?'

'I dunno,' Adam snapped. 'Does it matter? Edie needs help.'

D'Scover stood up and leaned over Edie where she sat with her head slumped backwards over the cushions of the couch. Her eyes still stared at nothing and she was quite still. D'Scover took her limp wrist, felt for a pulse, then he reached out a hand, and a small mirror appeared in it. This he held over her mouth and with her breath the surface immediately steamed over. Adam sighed with relief.

'She is fine,' D'Scover said. 'She told me about this during our train journey. She is having a psychic episode. She said once in a while they can be very strong and quite overwhelming like this. She may have seen something in the Hypnagogia that provoked this.'

'So what do we do?' Adam asked, horrified by Edie's stillness.

'Nothing,' D'Scover replied. He clicked his fingers and made the mirror vanish again. 'Just make sure she is comfortable and wait for it to pass. She will be tired when she comes out of it, but it should not cause her any damage. I hope she learns something useful.'

'*Should* not cause her damage?' Adam spluttered. 'How can you be sure?'

'We cannot, but she seemed very sure of these episodes when she told me about them.'

'It's horrible,' Adam said, leaning over her. 'She actually looks deader than I do.'

'Hmm,' D'Scover mumbled from his seat at the computer where he had once more called up the reports that Adam had seen before. 'I have some work to do now. I suggest you Disperse until Edie revives. You should take every opportunity for rest as there is no telling when the Trial will come.'

'Oh, the Trial,' Adam said. 'Actually, I was meaning to talk to you about that. I don't think that—'

'Enough,' D'Scover cut in. 'That is enough for now, you must Disperse. There will be time to talk later.'

Adam fell silent, raising his hands before him and, with a confidence that suggested he had been doing it for centuries, muttered his Ritual and scattered himself in his trademark scarlet beads before vanishing altogether into his Dispersal.

D'Scover did not turn to watch him go, engrossed instead in the screen before him. Report after report rolled across it and all seemed to have one thing in common: defunct spirits were being resurrected. Some of these ghosts had not been reported in over a century and yet here they were again, wandering corridors and clanking chains with all the style and grace of a cheap horror movie.

These were not the ghosts of the new and yet also did not seem to be the antiquated ghosts that had become accustomed to modern ways and adapted. These were the ghosts of the old worlds resurrected. They were striking fear into the living that saw them as they walked in the darkness, dripping spectral blood and wailing. One of the biggest areas of increase was in the sighting of headless ghosts, screamers and poltergeists. These ghastly phantoms were terrorising some of the older houses and castles around the world and people were fleeing their homes in terror.

The Brotherhood was being swamped with pleas for help from living agents and other Shades who were sending message after message back, asking for information. As D'Scover paged through these reports, another CC message flashed up on the screen – he cancelled it and carried on reading, but the message came back again. Again he cancelled it, but it flashed up one more time. Curiosity won and he clicked on it and raised Marcus's ident screen.

'What do you want, Marcus? I am very busy.'

'I have to see you; I have to tell you something, it's really urgent,' Marcus whispered. 'Call me in now – you have to do it. Please get me out of here and I'll explain everything.'

'Very well,' D'Scover sighed, 'but it had better be good or I will Disperse you myself. Do you have a secure line for me to bring you in?'

'I've managed to get into the webcam in the ant colony – will that do?'

'It might be a bit choppy on transmission as a video stream is not as smooth as a clean data feed, but it will do,' D'Scover said. 'Can you be sure you will not be seen?'

'Oh yes, I'm sure of that; the museum's been closed today – that's one of the things I need to tell you.'

'Very well, stand ready.'

'I can't stand. It's a glass case and not all of me fits in,' Marcus said, taking furtive glances around. 'I can *lay* ready, does that count?'

D'Scover rolled his eyes in frustration and tapped the keyboard. The image of Marcus blurred and a crackling and vivid blue cloud began to take shape in front of the desk. First the legs formed and then the shape sputtered and sparks flew around the room. D'Scover tapped the keyboard a few times and the image seemed to strengthen and start re-forming once more. D'Scover waited until a fully formed Marcus stood in the room in front of him.

'Still makes me feel a bit sick,' he said.

'What is all this about, Marcus?'

'Something's going on at the museum,' Marcus said proudly with a smug expression on his face.

'You will have to be more specific. I do not have psychic powers.'

'Well, I keep hearing voices, at night in the shadows, and no one's there.'

D'Scover sighed. 'Marcus, I really do not have time for you if you are just angling for another transfer.'

'No, absolutely not,' Marcus insisted. 'I do hear voices, and I'm not cracking up. I think they're keeping their substance low so they can Disperse in a second – clever trick.'

'I am listening,' D'Scover said and turned away from his computer. 'Tell me more.'

'They talk about searching for something, but I'm not sure what. They've been all over the place by all accounts. They know where one of the things they're looking for is, but they need something that goes with it. Last week they went to a place by Newquay – or at least that was what it sounded like.'

'I do not think they were saying that,' D'Scover said. 'What are they looking for? Better still, who are *they*?'

'Now that I might be able to help you with – I think that one of them's the bloke I've been lumbered with. Fifth earl of thingy, totally barking and a flash uniform, but he has a greedy streak a mile wide and I think he's up to something. I've seen him sneaking around a lot.'

'I am familiar with William Lawton, a gambler but betrayal does not seem his style,' D'Scover mused. 'You said *they* – who is he acting with?'

'Can't tell, never seen the other one and they always whisper.' Marcus shrugged. 'I think it's the Ice Maiden – she's the woman who controls the museum, the one who dealt with me when I arrived there. They were keeping their substance very low, almost at the point of Dispersal, but I'm sure it was a woman. I've never seen Lawton with anyone else but her, and she's really strict about movement around the building. I don't think anyone could get in here from the outside without her knowing about it and kicking up a stink. I just know something's going on. He was nowhere to be found one night last week and then I heard the voices planning that trip somewhere, Newquay or something. Can they do that travelling around thing without you knowing?'

'Strictly speaking, yes,' D'Scover said. 'Although it is difficult and more than noticeable and I am surprised that the Senior Council have not picked it up.'

'Maybe it's because so many other spirits have gone crazy; maybe they can't tell who's doing what.'

'How do you know about the rise in activity?' D'Scover asked.

'Have you heard from the museum lately?' Marcus laughed. 'The place is a nuthouse. Cases smashed, the library's been messed about with and stuff has even gone missing. The living had the security cameras pointed at everything and all they could see was stuff moving around on its own. They even closed the museum for a couple of days to see if there was a fault with the cameras and the security systems.' Marcus frowned and realised what D'Scover had said. 'Hey, you mean this's been happening in other places too? I thought it was just the museum.'

'No, it is not just the Natural History Museum; it has been happening in other places,' D'Scover said. 'We are experiencing some problems with an increase in hauntings.'

'Maybe the voices are involved somehow?'

'That is a distinct possibility,' D'Scover said. 'Now, if that is all, I had better send you back.'

'No way.' Marcus jumped to his feet.

'What do you mean?'

'I'm not going back there,' he protested. 'It's bloody awful there, and now they're sure to know that I've been to see you.'

'You have no choice in this issue,' D'Scover said dismissively.

'If you send me back,' Marcus said in an oily fashion, 'I won't tell you what *they* are looking for.'

'I may well consider reallocation when there is time, but right now I am considering Final Dispersal and then attempting memory retrieval from your scattered substance,' D'Scover said menacingly.

Edie stirred on the couch, sitting up and blinking away the psychic episode. She licked her dry lips and looked around in a bemused fashion.

'Hey!' Marcus pointed at Edie. 'I thought she was dead! I didn't like to say anything, but I did think it was a bit odd to have a corpse just laying around on the sofa, but who am I to question you?'

D'Scover stood up and walked over to Edie, picking up a glass of water from the desk as he strode over.

'How do you feel?' he asked as she sipped the water.

'Mrrr,' she mumbled.

'What did you say?'

She took a large gulp of water and swallowed hard. 'Mirror,' she blurted. 'One of the things they're looking for is a mirror.'

'Hey, how did you know that?' Marcus asked.

'She *is* psychic,' D'Scover said. 'So maybe we will not need your help after all.'

He turned back to Edie. 'Did you see anything else?' he asked. 'Anything that might help us find these people.'

'A building, white, very white, and two staircases wrapped round a shiny white building.' She sipped more water and her eyes slowly drifted open and shut as she struggled to stay awake. 'It was like a building inside a building, but all white and shining, pure white and above it …' Her head lolled back and her eyes closed.

'Edie, you must help us.' D'Scover gripped her shoulders. 'Please try and keep going; you can sleep all you want afterwards, but you must help us now.'

'Hmmm.' Edie shook her sleepy head awake. 'A library, lots of books, but a roof that is blue, blue like a duck's egg. They need a book too. But the white, outside but inside too, it's all white. Above that … above that …' She drifted again and her head slumped on to her shoulder.

'Edie,' D'Scover said firmly, and shook her again.

'Mmm, yes, I'm awake,' Edie slurred.

'What is above it?' he asked with insistence. 'You said something about above.'

'Above,' she repeated. 'All white, walls and floor and two staircases curving up.'

'You said that, but what else?'

'Spider web,' she mumbled, 'like a spider's web, high up above it all, all over the white, shining white, white and inside the room books and the blue ...'

Her head dramatically dropped right back and she fell into a deep sleep, snoring lightly.

'Damn the frailties of the living!' D'Scover said angrily. 'I shall just have to wait until she has had her rest then try and make sense of all of this.'

He stood up once more and turned back to find Marcus grinning widely behind him.

'What on earth is that inane expression for?' D'Scover asked.

'Oh, I've got plenty to smile about,' Marcus chuckled. 'You see, *I* know exactly *where* she's describing!'

Chapter Nineteen – Ancient Sisters

In a small dark office, lit only by a reedy yellow light emanating from the lamp posts outside the window, a computer monitor gave off a surge of static electricity as it sprang to life. A dark cloud fell like a shadow from the screen and began to expand. It crackled with violet light that deepened to the edge of black as it swirled around the room. The room filled and the cloud began to break apart, gradually taking on the shape of a single cloaked figure that walked off into the empty corridors.

'What's this book about?' Adam asked as soon as he was fully re-formed.

'We do not know exactly what it contains,' D'Scover said.

'Why do these spirits, whoever they are, want it?'

'It was written by Father Dominic, the first person to identify the secrets at the heart of the Brotherhood,' D'Scover explained in hushed tones. 'Later Dee deciphered Father Dominic's code and added considerably to the book, writing between and around the pictures drawn by the father. I was sent to keep an eye on the books by the Senior Council, as you know, but that one was lost when he fled persecution to Prague. It resurfaced in nineteen twelve in Italy after it was found in a chest in a monastery library by a book dealer called Wilfrid Voynich. It is commonly called the Voynich Manuscript.'

'Why is it so important now?'

'I am uncertain,' D'Scover said. 'The book was entirely written in Father Dominic's code and, apart from Dee, no one has ever managed to unlock it. Voynich worked on it for twenty years before he sold it, by then a broken and bankrupt man. Others have worked on it throughout the decades, and there have been hundreds of theories about it – even ridiculous ones that suggested it predicted the arrival of aliens on Earth – but to this day the Brotherhood has managed to prevent it from being sold into private hands. It has never been fully decoded. Eventually the notebook was donated to a library in America and, with a bit of influence from the Senior Council, it was placed in secure storage in the Beinecke Library at Yale University. I have been protecting this book for most of my time in the Brotherhood.'

'That's what they said, the voices in the dark,' Marcus said. 'Beinecke, not by Newquay.'

'Yes,' D'Scover agreed, 'it would seem they are looking for this book, but for the first time in many decades it has been moved.'

'Moved?' Adam asked. 'Where to?'

'Here, to London. Sadly it seems that somehow they have discovered it is now here. I suspect someone has betrayed me. I fear they are heading straight to where the Voynich is. Edie's vision has confirmed it,' D'Scover said. 'With a little help from a friend inside, we will be there in a moment or two. One of my contacts, a living agent, has arranged for one of the computer lines to be left open.'

'How's Edie going to get there? She can't travel like us,' Adam said, looking around the room. 'Hey, where's she gone?'

'Do not worry about her,' D'Scover said without turning away from the screen. 'She is already on her way; we will meet her there.' He tapped the keyboard a few more times and stood back from the desk.

'Are you ready, Adam?' he asked.

'I'm coming too!' Marcus said.

'No, you are not.'

'You have to take me, after all the help I've given you.'

'Your help is not reason enough for me to have you tagging along like a lost pet.'

'OK.' Marcus thought for a moment. 'That means you'll have to leave me here in your *lovely* office with all your lovely stuff... Is that OK for you?'

D'Scover sighed and rolled his eyes in despair. Adam had to turn away and stifle a laugh.

'Very well, you may come with us. But,' he growled into Marcus's face, 'if you cause me any trouble, I will permanently Disperse you on the spot.'

'You can rely on me, sir,' Marcus grinned. 'You'll hardly even know I'm there.'

'Hmmm,' D'Scover mused, 'that remains to be seen.'

He turned back to the computer and, taking a deep breath, tapped the ENTER key. A deep blue wave of sparks rushed out from the screen, enveloping Adam first, who crackled and broke up into red beads of intense light. The wave rolled over Marcus, Dispersing him into bright neon-blue fragments, and finally D'Scover, who broke down into his glistening grey globules before the wave disappeared back into the computer screen.

A small information screen in an empty cloakroom of the British Museum gave off a single blue spark that bounced across the dusty floor, sending a scavenging mouse hurrying to its hole. Other bouncing embers came and soon the small cloakroom was filled with a cascade of them and a hot smell of singed cloth rose from the uncollected coats dangling along the wire racks. The sparks spiralled and whirled around the room and, gradually, separate colours became clear within the maelstrom. Grey first, then red and finally a sharp and vivid blue and D'Scover, Adam and Marcus re-formed inside the room.

'Why do cloakrooms always smell of feet?' Marcus asked. 'I mean, it's not as if they leave shoes here, is it? Or maybe they don't smell of feet – maybe it's because I remember that they smell of feet. Maybe this one smells of roses – what does it smell like to you?'

'I have a poor memory for smells.' D'Scover checked if the way was clear.

'Is that so?' Marcus pondered. 'Do I actually smell feet or what?'

'We don't have time for this garbage,' Adam said, rolling his eyes. 'Where's Edie?'

'We are only a few stops on the Tube from my office,' D'Scover replied, striding across the marble floor of the lobby and stopping in front of a pair of huge oak doors, 'and that means that she should be on the other side of this set of double doors.'

Adam joined him and looked all around the doors while Marcus wandered over and stared into the glass cabinets that flanked the walls of the lobby. He touched the lock and the first set of doors opened easily, revealing the second pair which were stronger and far more secure.

'What do we do about the alarms?' Adam asked. 'We can't just open the door. Look.' He pointed to a wire that skirted the top of the door, trailing off and disappearing into the frame. 'It'll go off as soon as the door's opened.'

'Hmm, good point,' D'Scover said. 'Travelling with the living is always difficult, but it is imperative we have Edie with us as we need her to tell us if everything fits with her vision.'

'Why don't you just make sure the door *thinks* it's still closed?' Marcus said over his shoulder.

Adam and D'Scover looked to where Marcus now stood, peering into a display case, matching the dead gaze of an elaborate Aztec mask.

'What're you on about?' Adam asked.

'Simple trick really,' Marcus said, joining them by the door. 'Used to do it when I was still alive. Oh, only if I was locked out of my own house or something, you understand.'

He took a deep breath and slowly rose into the air until he was level with the exposed section of wiring. He drifted gradually around the door, carefully examining the slim gap between door and frame.

'The security system needs to believe that the door's still closed, yes?' Marcus asked. The other two nodded.

'The trigger for this is a small section where the wiring has a gap in the frame that's matched by a patch of wiring on the door,' he continued. 'This means that when the door's closed, there's a perfect circuit. All we have to do is to create a circuit of our own and it shouldn't set the alarm off. When I was alive, I could do it by finding the gap and slipping in a piece of tinfoil or wire to bridge it. It was time-consuming but effective, and wouldn't work these days, but we've got a much better solution right at our fingertips.'

'Marcus, you do have your uses after all,' D'Scover said. 'I shall take this side, you take the other and Adam, you tackle the lock when I tell you.'

Adam and Marcus nodded in agreement and got into position. Marcus and D'Scover both breathed deeply and each placed his hands as if in prayer. Drawing their hands apart and then cupping them together, Adam could see a ball of sparks resting in the hands of the two Shades. These they tipped towards the door and the sparks danced around the frame until the whole door was ringed with a grey and blue halo.

'That should do it,' D'Scover said. 'Your turn, Adam.'

Adam reached out for the dark, tarnished metal of the door handle and concentrated on generating his own electrical field around the handle and lock. The mechanism gave a few cracks and scrapes in protest, but grudgingly the handle began to turn. A moment later and they all flinched in anticipation as the door opened a small crack – but no alarm sounded.

'About time too!' Edie said as she slipped into the lobby, pushing the door closed behind her. 'What now?'

'Now we have to get to the Great Court,' Marcus said. 'I'm pretty sure it was the place you saw in your vision.'

'What about other security?' Adam frowned. 'I can't believe that there aren't guards and stuff.'

'Well, we should be fine as we can Disperse quickly if we only hold half-substance whilst we move around,' D'Scover explained. 'I can generate a thin electrostatic field around you so that any cameras are fooled. It causes them to freeze for a moment until you have passed, but it only works for technology, not the human eye. You are going to have to use your gift to tell if someone is coming near you and then hide.'

'Give me a minute, and I'll unlock my mind,' Edie said, taking a seat on a low wooden bench.

She closed her eyes and leaned forward, her head in her hands as she concentrated.

'D'you think it's difficult for her?' Adam whispered to D'Scover.

'She told me she has spent the last couple of years perfecting a lock on her gift so she does *not* see into every mind around her,' D'Scover said. 'She says it is terrible to see what everyone is thinking all of the time, and to have their futures laid bare for her.'

Edie lowered her hands and, still frowning, shook her head. 'Nothing, I'll try again.'

She repeated the motions and, after a few seconds, lowered her hands and again shook her head.

'Something wrong?' Adam asked.

'I must be confused, or out of practice. This can't be right,' she said.

'What is it?' D'Scover asked.

'I can feel nine, possibly ten, different minds in this building, but I must be messed up by something.'

'In what sense?'

'Well,' Edie said, 'they all seem to be thinking the same thing. That can't be right.'

226

D'Scover sighed and looked around the lobby, walking towards the stairs that led to the galleries and the Great Court.

'I have a theory,' he said, 'and now is the time to test it. Come.'

'What about the field around me?' Edie asked. 'The one you were going to generate?'

'I have a very strong suspicion that we will not need it,' D'Scover said. 'If I am correct, we need not have worried about the alarms on the doors either.'

'And I thought you didn't have psychic powers,' Marcus grinned.

Ignoring this sarcastic remark, D'Scover made his way to the stairs, closely followed by the rest of the group.

They were in almost total darkness. Feeble blue moonlight tumbled in through a high window and barely illuminated the vast bells on display in the stairwell. They made their way upstairs and reached the first long gallery leading to the Great Court. D'Scover went first, peering round the corner and into the gallery. A security guard sat in a chair on the other side of the door, facing away from them towards the main doors to the Great Court.

D'Scover gestured to the others to pull back into the shadows and he walked forward, straight out in front of the guard. At the last minute Edie, realising what he was going to do, reached out to pull him back, but her hand slipped through him. Silence welled up around them and Marcus opened his mouth to speak, but Adam flicked a single red spark instinctively towards him and he thought better of it and kept his mouth shut.

'You can come out,' D'Scover said from around the corner. The group walked out and joined him where he stood in front of the security guard.

'What's up with him?' Adam asked. 'Is he dead?'

'No.' D'Scover leaned over the guard's tipped-back head. 'What do you see, Edie?'

Edie reached out, placed her fingertips on his forehead and snatched them back quickly.

'Whoa, he's freezing! How can he be that cold and not be dead?'

'Did you see anything in his thoughts?' D'Scover asked.

'Yes, he's seeing the same thing as all of the other guards.' She blew on her cold fingertips. 'He dreams he's patrolling the corridors and knows that everything's fine. He feels quite content and occasionally drifts off to thoughts about his summer holiday.'

'As I feared,' D'Scover said.

'What's going on?' Adam asked.

'He is caught in a Hypnagogic state; he has also been cooled down to slow his heart rate. That should keep a simple repetitive Hypnagogia like this going for much longer without extra prompting. This is a very powerful influence upon him.'

'But didn't you tell me that these Hypnagogic states could only be induced by you or a member of the Senior Council?' Adam asked.

'That is the current assumption. I think we had better continue.'

The group gathered together and walked through the long, empty gallery to the doors leading out on to the floor of the Great Court. When they reached them, they could see that the doors stood slightly ajar and the handle still gave off faint purple and black sparks.

'It cannot be,' D'Scover muttered.

'What now?'

'I fear that our hidden nemesis has beaten us here,' D'Scover said. 'We must remain alert.'

They walked out into the British Museum's Great Court and, as if on cue, the clouds above the building parted and a clear full moon lit the sky, shining in through the great span of glass and steel of the roof. Edie staggered backwards and leaned against the cool of the limestone wall for support as the powerful recollection of her psychic vision filled her head.

'This is it! The white building and the spider web roof, look!'

She pointed up, and Adam nearly fell over as he took in the enormous arc of the roof and the ice-white moon shining through it. The roof had been built to cover the old museum courtyard, and to help protect the Round Reading Room, and was a vast mesh of glass and steel that arched high above them. The walls and floor were as white as clouds and the magnificent space was littered with statues and monuments from antiquity.

In front of them stood the limestone-encased Round Reading Room. It was all that was left of the old British Library, a circular library space filled with dark oak desks underneath a domed and gilded ceiling. The shelves were filled with some of the rarest and most significant books in the world. Countless great minds had studied and read in this room. Here Bram Stoker had researched his Dracula story and Sir Arthur Conan Doyle had fleshed out Sherlock Holmes. To protect the building from the relentless destruction of time it had been wrapped in the same limestone as the rest of the court and now stood gleaming white in the moonlight.

They walked on into the court, reaching the doors of the Reading Room heading past the shutters of the gift shops that nestled under the two vast staircases. These elegant steps curved upwards wrapping themselves round the old library like two protective arms.

'The door's open,' Marcus whispered. 'I think we're too late; maybe we should just leave …'

But Edie was already walking ahead and into the Reading Room.

'Oh well …' He trotted after her. 'Not up for discussion then?'

Inside the library the shelves curved away around them and climbed to the ceiling with high walkways edged with dull brass railings. The shelves were filled to bursting with some of the rarest books in the world, all offering their decorated spines to view. At floor level dark wooden desks fanned out across the floor behind a desk carrying three computer screens. Above them rose the great dome of the building, a beautiful confection of gilded plasterwork framing perfect curves of duck-egg blue.

'It's so beautiful,' Edie breathed. 'I've never seen anything like it.'

'Yes, it is exquisite, is it not? I always find it impressive that the tedious living can have created something that seems so close to heaven.' A cold female voice cut in behind them.

The group spun round as one and there in the doorway stood a hooded figure, framed in the moonlight as a silhouette.

'Who the hell are you?' Adam demanded.

'Oh, Toby knows, do you not, Toby?' the voice mocked.

Everyone looked at D'Scover who showed no emotion on his face.

'I rather feared it was so,' he said. 'There is no further need to disguise yourself; the end game has been reached.'

'How very dramatic,' the figure said, the voice taking on a softer tone. 'You really do know how to play to the gallery.'

Taking a step backwards, the cloaked figure threw back its hood.

'Sister Goodman!' Adam was shocked. 'But how could you …?'

'Toby, it is such a tragedy you had to interfere with my plan. I hoped that this brat would prove to be enough of a distraction to you to keep you out of my way,' she sighed. 'It really is a shame to have to Disperse you all, but I simply cannot have you getting in my way, not now everything is ready.'

'I take it you have broken the Voynich code?' D'Scover asked.

'Not quite,' replied the sister, 'but I do have the key and so the next step will be much easier.'

'Key? I was not aware Father Dominic left a key,' D'Scover said, playing for time.

Sister Goodman laughed and the sound echoed around the Great Court behind her.

'Father Dominic?' she guffawed. 'That fat old fool? He did not know what he had! He spoke to the demon Uriel and, mistaking him for an archangel, wrote down all he had to say. Uriel and his servants dictated to him the methods for keeping the spirits of the dead on Earth, and for controlling the living. He wrote it all down, here in this manuscript.' She waved the small book at them, laughing as she did so. 'Dee thought him the Archangel too – the folly of the living to reach out for their self-created gods for explanations to their confusion. Why do the living need such pathetic delusions? How typical it is of humankind to invent gods in an attempt to try and explain all that they do not understand. And then to believe all of the answers that come from them.' She laughed again. 'Dee and Kelly sought out this book and added to it. Two more ignorant men caught in a trap and feeling as if it was a blessing. Both of them even more stupid than the pious fool who first wrote it.'

'Do not talk about the good father,' D'Scover growled. 'He was a great man, an honest man, and the Brotherhood would not exist without him.'

'Yes, I will give him that.' She smiled a cold and emotionless smile. 'He did create the Brotherhood, but it did not take quite the path that the demons chose for it. Sadly you were the first chosen initiate into the Brotherhood and your vile innocence corrupted it and forced it down quite another path. That was when Uriel came for me.'

'You?'

'Yes, me; who better to keep an eye on the Brotherhood and follow the notebook until the right time? I took my own life a year after you passed into the Brotherhood and my true master showed me the path of my destiny. As I watched my own blood ebb away on the cold stones of the convent floor, I felt the cold grip of death and I knew that I had made the right decision. I passed into the World Between and they whispered to me. The demons who first spoke to Father Dominic knew it might take centuries before they could rise, but the time would come. And it was not long before I knew their desires, they needed me,' she sneered, 'but I needed Father Dominic's notebook, and that was always the plan. Right from the first moment I learned of its existence I knew that it would give me the power I craved, the power to reach out and control the dead and give my master the darkness he required to step into this world. Without it, he is condemned to wait in the World Between. I alone deserve the honour of bringing him and his servants from the shadows. I have suffered and searched for centuries for it and, even before I opened my veins for my masters,

I knew that this simple and battered notebook held the key to controlling the Spirit World. The Senior Council hid the book well after they had retrieved it from Dee in Prague. The Jesuits in Italy kept it concealed until Voynich found it and tried to sell it on the open market. I tried to buy it but could not engineer the monetary funds for the living – a profound annoyance.'

'Is that why you were removed from the Senior Council,' D'Scover asked, 'because of your searches for the manuscript?'

'She was on the Council?' Adam gasped.

'Those idiots,' Sister Goodman spat. 'They said I was spending too much of my time in "private pursuits". Yes, I was removed, but they never actually discovered what I was doing. My removal from the Council made my searches more difficult, but not impossible. I had to rely on other sympathetic agents within the Brotherhood to help with the hunt for it. I have been able to use secured lines from the Natural History Museum thanks to the help of two sympathetic Shades there, and recently your secretary has proved most helpful when I needed to gain access to your office. She has been a mine of useful information.'

'Not Emma?' D'Scover asked. 'Please tell me you have not corrupted Emma?'

'Not her,' Sister Goodman scoffed. 'Her pathetic loyalty to you ran true. No, your new girl, Julie. She is keen to get ahead and gain power for herself. She told me that an important text was due to be moved from the Beinecke. I had followed the Voynich for so long that I had almost given up hope of ever gaining access to it. It had been a long struggle to keep track of it and when it finally ended up being donated to the Beinecke, and held there sealed and well-guarded, I thought our plans were permanently delayed. But, with some distractions for the Senior Council, kindly created by yourself and your idiotic companions, and a few hundred old spirits stirred up for good measure, we managed to gain access to the Beinecke computer and find out the Voynich was coming here. Coming to the very place that held the key to finally breaking the code.'

'The key!' Edie gasped, clutching her head in pain as an image burned across her memory in a searing flash. 'The key is the black mirror that I saw in my vision, an obsidian mirror. It belonged to Dee and it is here – in the British Museum. She needs it to decode the manuscript!'

'Ah.' Sister Goodman smiled her cold rictus grin once more. 'This must be your little witch – how charming of you to bring her along. What more proof do you need that the witch trials should have continued? Tell me, my dear, what do you see of our future?'

'I know that good beats evil every time,' Edie snapped.

'Oh, how very quaint,' the sister replied. 'And tell me, witch child, who defines good and evil in your neat little world?'

'We all do,' Edie said angrily. 'In our hearts we all know the difference. You don't understand because you're missing a heart.'

The sister laughed again and Edie gave an involuntary shudder at the chilling sound.

'As you are well aware,' she laughed, 'my heart has not beat out a rhythm for over four hundred and fifty years, a situation that suits me nicely. I have no desire to walk amongst the pathetic flesh of the living.'

'What about the Vision?' Adam defiantly shouted. 'You know you'll be beaten.'

'Vision?' She spat the word with venom. 'You really do not understand, do you, child? There is no such thing; I have always believed it to be a lie to keep us all under control. I merely used Toby's belief in the Vision to distract you all. You know in *your* heart there's nothing special about you. You are, and always will be, a fouled little boy who nobody wanted, not even his own mother. Now, if you will excuse me.' She took a step away from the door. 'I have work to do and you, my dear Toby, have an appointment to keep with an old friend.'

She folded her cloak back and tucked the manuscript into a cloth bag under her arm. They caught a glimpse of the round black slab Edie had described from her vision. Sister Goodman laughed her chilling cackle and the sound dissipated as she vanished into Dispersal, leaving violet sparks flying around the doorway.

'What did she mean, "old friend"?' Adam asked, looking around the library. 'And where's Marcus?'

'He must have taken the opportunity to flee,' D'Scover said through gritted teeth. 'I should have known the coward would not last. Come, she must not escape with that book.'

The three of them ran for the door and entered the vast silence of the Great Court, but this time something was different. The moon was now partially obscured by torn fragments of black clouds and only brief shards of light broke through to penetrate the glass roof. The air inside the court felt heavy and hot and Edie felt the hairs stand up on her body with the static electricity buzzing around them.

'What's that smell?' she asked. 'I can hardly breathe.'

'What does it smell like?' D'Scover asked.

'Rotten eggs,' Adam and Edie said together.

'Brimstone, sulphur – keep your eyes open, and be prepared for anything.'

The three of them took a few more steps out into the court, stopping opposite the library doors, between the bottom treads of the two huge staircases. A thick cloud overhead plunged the court into sudden darkness. Edie reached out for Adam's arm and was relieved when he boosted his substance so she could hold on to him. The air pressure in the court began to build and Edie felt as though a great weight had been placed upon her.

'Something's coming,' she gasped and clutched her head. 'I can't stand it for much longer. I can hardly breathe. The pain in my head is almost unbearable.'

'I can feel it too, like pressure building before a storm,' Adam said. 'Who's coming?'

'Not *who*,' D'Scover said softly, '*what*.'

A sudden hot wind rushed around the court and the floor beneath them heaved and pitched so that Edie could not keep her balance and she tumbled forward and fell over.

'The floor!' she shouted, holding up a dripping hand. 'It's all wet – look at the stairs!'

They all turned to see rivulets of water cascading down the stone steps. The water gathered at their feet and spilled out past them, quickly covering the floor in a creeping lake.

'What the hell is this?' Adam asked. 'Some kind of earthquake? It must've cracked a pipe.'

'An earthquake in Russell Square?' Edie said doubtfully, trying to avoid the puddles forming round her feet. 'Get real.'

But Adam was not listening to her as his attention was caught by a dark mark spreading across the white floor in front of them. It started as a small charred spot and gradually grew to form a full circle on the floor.

Edie sniffed the air. 'Something's burning. D'you think something caught fire when the ground heaved? A gas pipe?'

'No,' replied D'Scover, staring straight ahead, 'far worse. Get in the library and shut the door. And do not come out under any circumstances.'

His voice remained calm, but the way he spoke made Adam and Edie act unquestioningly and they began to back away towards the open door of the library. Edie slipped in the water on the floor and her wet trainers squeaked under her as she tried to regain her footing. Adam reached out to steady her.

The circle on the floor in front of D'Scover now darkened and a thin yellow flame ran round it as if a fuse had been lit. The flame licked a little higher and a little darker and Adam and Edie waited in the doorway, captivated by the dancing light. A rush of wind through the court fed the flames and they suddenly surged upwards and whirled in on themselves like a fiery tornado. They twisted and contorted and gradually the figure of a woman formed within the fire and the Elemental that in 1666 had confronted D'Scover in the crowded streets of London stepped out from the inferno. The hypnotic figure of Fire once more stood before him.

Adam and Edie were frozen to the spot, too afraid to move. Adam had been terrified by this creature when he had seen her in the Hypnagogia but here, in front of him, the spectacle was truly awesome. Her beauty was overwhelming, but her crimson eyes bore such cold hatred that they belied the fierce heat she generated. He looked to Edie and could see the heat turning her pale cheeks a vivid red. But Edie did not look away and her eyes carried a look he had not seen before – one of pure determination.

'It is the little boy again,' the Elemental said, and in her voice echoed the sharp cracking of bones in fire. 'I drove you back once, child, and I shall do so again. The days of the living are numbered – why do you persist?'

'Because I know that I shall win,' D'Scover said. 'This time the victory will be mine.'

He took a deep breath and smoothed his hands over his body and the man in front of Adam and Edie changed. His modern tailored suit disappeared to be replaced with the outfit he had worn the last time he had taken on this battle. A man still, but with his simple clothing punctuated only by the sleek silver flash of the sword at his side.

'Why has he changed?' Edie whispered to Adam.

'I dunno, but he always has a sword when he's dressed like this so maybe that's why,' Adam whispered back. 'Maybe it's the only way he can have a weapon.'

'You cannot win, boy,' Fire said, and as she smiled, the heat rose so suddenly that the glass in the gift shop windows hissed and cracked and fell like a hard rain to the floor. 'I, like you, have not come alone. I have my sisters with me this time.'

She gestured with her two long and flaming hands to the paired staircases and D'Scover instinctively turned to look up, first one way, then the other. At the top of the stairs appeared women, on either side, each as physically stunning as Fire, but quite different in appearance. One shimmered with a deep blue light that glowed from within, changing as the seconds passed from blue to green to grey and to blue again in a moving liquid wave of colour. The other female was harder to focus on as her shape shifted and moved, whirling around in a tempest of clouds that danced across her gown.

'My sisters, Water and Air,' Fire said as they took an exaggerated bow.

'I thought there were four Elementals?' Edie whispered to Adam.

The ground beneath their feet shifted again with a fearsome rumble and a deep crack split the floor wide open between Fire and D'Scover. The limestone heaved wide and the cement splintered with a deafening roar. The white floor of the Great Court fractured, sending dusty fragments high into the air, which slowly rained back down.

'You had to mention it, didn't you?' Adam shouted above the chaos.

Within the chasm in the floor, a dark shape began to emerge: long and thin, it flickered over the edge of the rift and took hold. One hand of slender, dark-brown fingers clawed the edge of the crack, and another soon joined the bony set. The hands tightened and pulled the rest of the body from the pit, lifting it to the floor to stand alongside its sister.

This figure was shapely and slim like her siblings, but there the beauty ended as her body was made of all things underground. It was formed of earth the colour of chocolate shot through with thick red seams of clay and lumps of rock and moss. She was clothed in rotted leaf matter and this ragged covering was all that shielded her nakedness. Rising to her full height, she tossed her head from side to side, shaking free what at first glance seemed to be matted reddish brown hair.

'Her hair!' Adam gasped. 'It's moving.'

They both stared as the hair waved and writhed on its own as the fat worms that made it up tried to bury themselves again. Earth tossed the squirming mass once more and smoothed her body down with both hands, causing clods of dirt to fall from her on to the floor. She cocked her head to one side and looked past D'Scover to where Adam and Edie stood behind him.

'Who is the little living one, sister?' she asked, and in her voice they heard the cold and hollow sound of wet stones sliding against one another. 'I am so very fond of the recently deceased, and my worms are hungry. May I have her?'

D'Scover turned and shouted angrily at Adam and Edie who stood as if frozen by the door of the library.

'GET INSIDE AND SHUT THE DOOR!' he bellowed. 'AND STAY INSIDE NO MATTER WHAT.'

Without further prompting, the two of them ran inside the library and slammed the heavy door shut behind them, leaving D'Scover to his fate.

Chapter Twenty – The Reading Room

'What do we do?' Edie panted, short of breath and long on fear. 'We can't just sit in here and wait for him to be killed.'

'He's already dead,' Adam replied, pacing around behind her.

'Oh, this is no time for your stupid comments,' she snapped. 'Why d'you find it so hard to grasp reality? Sometimes I wonder if you ever lived at all.'

'Cheers for that!' Adam grumbled. 'How would you feel if you'd been used to cause this mess? I was just a distraction to hide the fact that Sister Goodman was sneaking around looking for the Voynich. That means all this is wrong, the Vision, the Sentinel, all rubbish. I knew it, I knew it all along.'

'No.' Edie gripped his arm. 'No, you're wrong, Red. I've seen it, remember? We're here for a reason. Sister Goodman may not have realised it, but she was another part of the path to the Vision. Don't you see? It doesn't matter if she doesn't understand it or believe it, the Vision will still happen.'

'And if it doesn't?'

'Then it isn't the right time,' Edie reassured him.

'Damn it, you're putting so much faith in this fate and destiny thing. I can't do that. I wish I believed it as much as you do, but I don't.' Adam slumped down to sit on the floor.

The Reading Room was a perfect island in the chaos that was going on outside. Inside the books remained silent and calm on their shelves and the only sign that something was not right were occasional thumps and flashes from outside, and the fact that heat was gradually building up in the room. Edie stood close to the door and put her ear to it to listen to the sound from the Great Court, but recoiled as the door was too hot to touch.

'There must be something more we can do,' she said. 'Think! You were the one who saw the full Vision – is there anything in it to help us?'

'I dunno,' Adam said, pacing up and down in frustration. 'I can't remember. There's something about a trinity and the saviour being a child and …' He frowned hard, screwing up his eyes in frustration. 'I dunno, I really don't remember.'

'You know something that can help us. Somewhere in your head, something in your memories can get us out of this,' Edie told him. 'Otherwise why are we even here?'

'Please, not the fate thing again,' Adam said in an exasperated voice. 'You heard Sister Goodman – I'm not even meant to be here. She told D'Scover about me just to distract him from the real issue, the search for that book. This is all a mistake so how can fate or destiny or whatever be involved at all?'

'I don't want to argue with you, not now anyway,' Edie sighed, 'but I do believe that we're *meant* to be here. As I said, I saw this place.'

'I suppose so,' he mumbled, 'but I can't think of anything … I can't remember anything that might be useful. I've gone totally blank. Maybe it's all locked away in my head, but I just can't seem to—'

'Wait!' Edie ran to him. 'That's it – locked away in your head! I can try and see inside your thoughts and find out if you know something that can help.'

'How can you do that?' he asked. 'You said you can't read the thoughts of ghosts.'

'I can't generally, but it's not as if I've had many to practise on. Maybe if I really concentrate on you, I might get something.' She looked around for a table with a good view of the door in case anything came through. 'Come and sit here.'

'What good will this do? I don't have a brain, do I? I'm dead, remember. How can you read a mind that's not there? We should just go out and take our chances.'

'Easy for you to say, you've already died once, but I know I've got plenty to do in the land of the living before I join you,' she told him. 'If you have thoughts, then I can read them, and you do clearly still have them. Stop wasting time. Sit down, I need to concentrate.'

Adam moved grudgingly away from the door and joined her at the table.

'You need to concentrate too,' Edie said. 'You must focus all of your strength on your mind. Make your thoughts clear.'

'You say that like you've done it a thousand times.' He slammed his hands down on the table. 'But how the hell can that work?'

'I don't know.' Her voice was soft and calm. 'But unless you've got a better idea, what choice do we have?'

Adam shook his head and leaned forward and closed his eyes attempting to clear his thoughts. Edie tilted her head forward as well and pressed her forehead against his, pushing all of her will into seeing what lay in the deepest recesses of his memory.

'Sister, is this the boy you dealt with before?' Earth's fearsome voice rattled deeply round the court. 'I imagined him smaller and … fleshier somehow.'

She walked over to where D'Scover stood and leaned down from her great height to look him in the face. She cocked her head and examined him closely. D'Scover looked defiantly up into her muddy face; he could see every grain of dirt that had combined to form her and smell the cold aroma of decay and corruption on her breath.

241

'I think he is enchanting.' She smiled a smile that looked like a knife slash in muddy ground. 'I think he looks like a dear little corpse. More animated than the ones I am used to. I think that my faithful friends would like to get hold of you,' she said, stroking her wormy hair. 'Or maybe they would prefer the girl child, the little witch?'

She licked her lips and D'Scover watched a glossy red beetle scuttle out of her mouth and run across her cheek before disappearing inside her ear.

'NO!' D'Scover yelled. 'YOU WILL NOT TAKE ANYONE.' He drew his sword and, clutching it in both hands, stood his ground in front of the library doors.

'What does he think he can do?' Earth asked her sister. 'Can he possibly think that he can fight us alone?'

'Because he believes he has fate on his side,' Fire laughed, and wafted over towards her sister, charring a burnt trail on the floor behind her. 'He actually believes it is his destiny to win.'

'Let me take him. I will show him how false his thoughts have been,' Earth pleaded with her sister.

'No,' Fire answered in softer tones, 'I have waited a long time to taste this revenge. The last time we met I was cheated of the chance to finish him off. This boy is mine.'

She threw out her arms and an impenetrable circle of flames arose all around, cutting Earth off from the two of them. Turning back to D'Scover, she smiled and he felt the heat cover him like a thick blanket. Suddenly he wanted to lie down, to give up on all of this and just Disperse once and for all. His eyes closed slowly and his head began to loll around sleepily.

'Ah,' Fire whispered, so close to him now that he could see the small fires that danced together to make her body shape, 'see how you want to sleep? You do not want to fight me anymore, do you? You are so tired. Why do you not come to me and let me keep you safe and warm in my embrace?'

She stretched out her arms to him and beckoned for him to

242

come closer. His arms drooped and suddenly the sword seemed unbearably heavy. His shoulders strained to keep the weapon in the air and pointing in her direction.

'Come to me, I can make everything better.' She breathed the words and the warm air rolled around him. 'I can make you feel like you belong to someone, like you are safe and loved. Is that not what you want?'

He looked at her as she drew closer; his sword now crashed down with the point on the ground. She was so beautiful and, for a moment, he could not believe her capable of anything other than good – of anything other than creating this wonderful warm sensation that rushed through his body as though he was alive again.

'Come to me, come to me,' she repeated in soft tones, luring him in.

As she reached out her hand for him, he looked up into the flames that licked around her, making the shape of her body, and saw something else. Within the flames were the hideous, distorted faces of those spirits she had taken before. Poor lost souls Dispersed by her and drained of what little energy they had left so all that remained were twisted images in their last agonising moments of death. D'Scover looked up into the faces in the inferno and the horror of it tore through him and snapped him from his dreamlike state.

He staggered backwards, dragging his sword across the floor. Fire snatched an arm out through the air and one of her long fingers scoured across D'Scover's cheek, burning a deep mark where it ran. He recoiled and stumbled further away from her until the fire licked up his back, but the pain of the wound she had inflicted had returned him fully to his senses. Clutching his sword, he raised it with renewed ferocity and ran towards her, screaming and hacking the air from left to right. She now stood her ground and smiled a patronising grimace at him.

'I CANNOT, AND WILL NOT, LET YOU WIN!' he screamed.

As he bellowed, he put all of his concentration into bolstering his substance and a cluster of blue sparks began to build round his hands, enveloping them as they held the sword. Slashing the air in front of him, he ran forwards the vast circle of fire. As he reached her, a wave of blue sparks flew down the blade and sheathed it in a halo of sapphire light. D'Scover hefted the sword over his shoulder and, with a mighty swing, he lashed out at Fire.

At first he thought he must have missed her as nothing seemed to have changed, but she looked down and the expression on her face turned to one of shock. Across her stomach there now ran a deep black gouge, charred and smoking as if she had been partially extinguished by his sword. D'Scover looked to the blade and saw that it was glowing white-hot at the tip and was sheathed in blue light.

'What have you done?' she gasped and it was her turn to stagger away. 'How can this be?'

Her circle of flames retreated with her and D'Scover had to run after her to stay out of the fire wall as it closed in behind him. Lifting his sword, he hacked out at Fire before she had time to recover and another appeared – this time across her chest, cutting deep from shoulder to hip. She clutched at her wounds and an unholy scream echoed round the court. She clapped her hands together and a ball of fire rolled from her fingertips; this she hurled towards D'Scover, but he dodged it easily and swung out his sword for her again. This time he made contact across her legs and she collapsed in front of him. He lifted his sword for the final cut, but in her desperation she had one last trick and threw out her hands, causing the veil of flames to drop.

'SISTER!' she screamed. 'HELP ME – IT IS THE SWORD.'

D'Scover turned to see Earth bearing down on him, her face now the colour of dried blood, baked by the heat of her sister's flames.

'WHAT HAVE YOU DONE TO HER?' Earth bellowed.

She swung out her arm and caught D'Scover off guard and the impact sent him and his sword skidding hard across the floor. His limp body slid across the floor through the dirt and water, with his blade following. Free of D'Scover, Earth bent over her fallen sister and was joined by Air and Water.

'LEAVE HER ALONE, YOU WEAK IDIOTS. HOLD YOUR-SELVES IN READINESS UNTIL I SAY OTHERWISE,' Earth shouted to her sisters. 'I CAN HEAL HER.'

She laid her infernal sister out on the floor and, stepping through the flames trickling from her limp body, began to press Fire's wounds closed. The two remaining sisters slunk back after their chastisement and returned obediently to their places on the stairs.

All had turned their attention away from D'Scover as he had been cast across the floor. His bolstered substance had taken the full force of Earth's strike and the blow had thrown him far from where Fire lay to where a large limestone plinth had finally stopped his progress. He collided heavily with its base and became partially embedded before he lost consciousness.

The images were far away at first, like long-forgotten dreams that return when triggered by a taste or smell. Drifting images of places he had seen or people who had helped or hindered him during his life. Edie tried to force these images away so she could move into newer territory. She had no desire to see again how he had died and these old images were wasting time, but she knew she could not rush it for fear of losing the link altogether.

More images came through, of cold and a hospital, of nurses talking and a long corridor – and blackness. In her mind she walked in this vast empty space that seemed to have a spotlight just on her. This was the most realistic image she had ever seen in someone else's thoughts. She could feel the softness of the floor beneath her and the gentle breeze against her skin, but there seemed to be no end to this blackness. She could no more see what was under her feet than she could see what was at the edge of the void.

'Adam?' she said experimentally.

Her voice echoed around the space and bounced back to her, obviously unhindered by any obstacle. She waited a few moments and stopped walking.

'Adam, can you hear me?' She tried again, and once more, her voice rebounded on her.

Suddenly she could see something, a sharp spot of light that cut through the blackness in front of her and lay out like a path. She followed it and, as she did so, she could hear snatches of speech and the soft tinkling sound of a woman's laughter. The pinpoint of light grew bigger as she got closer until eventually it looked like a small, round yellow hole that seemed to hang in the void. She walked to it and peered in. Inside there was a garden, with a child playing in a sandpit while a woman laughed.

Edie was overwhelmed with the complex jumble of feelings in this memory. Deep emptiness and angry resentment accompanied this image. Locked here, deep in Adam's mind, a child played in complete innocence and it was tearing Adam apart. Edie knew this was not the memory they needed and too much time dwelling on it might make Adam lose heart altogether.

'ADAM!' Edie screamed at the top of her voice. 'THIS IS THE PAST, WE'RE WASTING TIME, AND WE NEED TO KNOW WHAT YOU SAW IN THE LIBRARY – HURRY.'

The darkness suddenly flooded with light and the images rushed past her at breakneck speed. Images of D'Scover and his instruction of Adam, the office, Freedom Farm and the euphoric power Adam felt in his Dispersals and then the library. The images slowed and stopped and the walls of D'Scover's library locked in place around them until Edie found herself standing in the unfamiliar room. She turned round and saw Adam talking to himself.

'Red? Can you hear me?' she asked, but he did not reply.

She stood back and watched as he gestured to the shelves and the books responded to him and descended into his hands. He moved slowly around the room and then reached out for one that had appeared from a dark cloud of sparks and smoke. He looked down as it hovered in front of him and he frowned at the pages. His speech was indistinct, as though he could not remember the specifics of what he had said, and Edie could not grasp what he was saying.

'Adam, we *must* know the Vision,' she said out loud, 'the exact wording, try.'

Adam did not respond, but he began to smile at the book lying in the air in front of him, and then to speak, and these words were clear and bright.

'In times of chaos, a great division will split the Brotherhood. Faith shall weaken and many shall be lost forever to the void. In this confusion of spirits, darkness shall rise silently and take upon a form known to many. This force shall command the elemental spirits and countless spirits of ill-passage. This evil will take hold whilst others look away, but a trinity shall see all and one shall be triumphant. The one who overthrows shall have known nothing of the wickedness of the living world and shall have died unsullied by the mire of the living. This innocent shall raise a blade, forged in purity and crystal fed, and shall strike down the demons that rise to overthrow the living world. This shall be the Sentinel and their form shall be true and shall be that of a child.'

Edie gasped with pain as sheer white light cut across her vision and she was back in the Reading Room with Adam in front of her.

'I can't feel D'Scover!' she said.

'What d'you mean?' Adam asked. 'I thought it took all that effort just to read my thoughts?'

'Yes, but I could *feel* him even if I couldn't actually catch specific thoughts.'

'And you can't feel him now?'

'No,' she said. 'I saw a blinding flash, a shower of sparks and felt a pain across my chest and then nothing.'

'We know the Vision, but does it make sense to you? Can it help him?'

'I know the words, but I can't quite make sense of it. All that stuff about crystals and swords?'

'Don't you see? Don't you get it? The sword, the innocent child? It's him. It means D'Scover is the Sentinel.' He grabbed Edie by the shoulders. 'The last time the Senior Council put him up for trial wasn't the right time, or the right conditions. We have to help him.' Adam let go of her, his eyes filling with tears. 'We're running out of time. We have to help him. He's all I've got.'

'It's not just you any longer, Red,' she said. 'We'll always have each other now. We'll never be alone again.'

A silence fell between them. Edie forced a smile.

'There must be something from your mind.' She broke the moment. 'I saw you when you were alive, and where you died, and your training with D'Scover and then ...' She hesitated, the image of the child in the garden seemed too private for her to have seen without permission, and so she chose not to mention it. 'Then I saw you in the library ... Hey! That's it!'

'What?'

'The library, you could talk to the books and they responded to you, I saw you. You could do that here.' She looked around at the shelves towering above them, full to bursting with ancient tomes. 'There must be one here that has the answer, but it'll take too long to find it the normal way – but you could *ask* them for help.'

'I dunno.' Adam followed her gaze to the high stacks above them. 'These books aren't the charmed ones in D'Scover's library. It's a whole different thing.'

'They've never been asked; maybe they're all charmed by their content, or their makers, I don't know.' Edie shrugged. 'This all seems crazy anyway and I don't know where the real ends and the unreal begins anymore. In any case, do you have a better idea?'

Adam shook his head and ran to the middle of the room, pushing aside chairs to clear a space right in the centre under the dome.

'Library!' he called out. 'We need your help. We need to know what we can do to defeat the Elementals.'

The room remained still; nothing shifted on the shelves and the silence enveloped them.

'It's too quiet outside; we have to do something quick – ask again,' Edie said.

'But it's pointless.'

'We have no other option,' she pointed out. 'I still can't sense D'Scover. Try again.'

'BOOKS!' Adam called again, shouting this time. 'IF YOU DON'T HELP US, THEN YOUR BROTHER THE VOYNICH WILL BE LOST TO THE HANDS OF DEMONS AND THIS BUILDING WILL BE DESTROYED BY THE ELEMENTALS WHEN THEY COME FOR US. WE CAN'T PROTECT YOU IF WE DON'T KNOW HOW.'

Again silence at first, but this time it was broken by a thin rustling from high up on the top walkway. A black book lifted itself from the shelf and slowly made its way down to Adam like a crow descending on a breeze. It flapped gently, and he stretched out his arms to allow it a comfortable perch.

'Thank you,' he said to the book. 'Help us.'

Hugely relieved, Edie ran over to join him and they both watched as the book skimmed through its pages, searching for the relevant chapter.

'It's a book of myths and legends,' Edie said, her eyes catching bits on the pages as they flittered past. 'Look, elves, faeries, gorgons, piskies – these aren't all real, are they?'

'It's complicated,' Adam said distractedly.

The book had slowed down and was turning one page at a time, settling on a chapter entitled 'Myths of Nature'. They both quickly read down the page and turned over, and there on the next page was a perfect likeness of Fire.

'It says here about her last being seen in sixteen sixty-six during the Great Fire of London.' Adam pointed to a paragraph below the illustration.

'Is there anything about how to get rid of her?' Edie leaned over the book.

'Hold on, I'm getting to it.' He flicked a page over. 'It says that

Fire is the more dominant and aggressive of the Elementals with Earth coming next. Water and Air are usually gentler. Not driven by a destructive urge.'

'So fires and earthquakes are the product of the two evil sisters, but tornadoes and floods aren't?' Edie said. 'Doesn't make sense.'

'I suppose that good can come from wind and flood, but fires and earthquakes are always terrible,' Adam said. 'I mean, you have to think on a world scale and not in terms of people. Plants are helped by wind, seeds carried, rain is moved around the world, and everything would die without water.'

'But things recover after fire – plants and stuff live on,' Edie argued.

'But maybe that's just adaptation to impossible conditions.'

'OK, I get the point,' Edie said. 'You know, Red, you would've been a genius if you'd ever gone to school. But does it say anything we can actually use?'

'That's wrong.' Adam was frowning. 'It says here that the Elementals are *never* seen together.'

'What? But they *are* here together. Does it say why they're not seen together?'

'It says they hate each other because of their conflicting personalities,' Adam explained. 'Maybe that's the key; maybe we can set one against the other – Water against Fire, that kind of thing.'

The book ruffled its pages and began to close.

'Well, the book seems to think it'll work,' Edie said. 'I told you before, I have some power over water and air, and maybe that's why I'm here; maybe it's my purpose all along. I know it's a long shot, but it's our only plan so we'd better go with it.'

The closed book rose up through the air and slid back into the gap it had left on the shelf. Adam and Edie ran towards the doors and stood behind them.

'I'll have a look first,' Adam said. 'I can slip through and see if there's a way to get to one of the sisters.'

'Who shall we start with?'

'Let's try Water first as the book says that she's the gentlest,' he replied quickly.

'What about floods and stuff?'

'It said those are caused by her tears and not by malicious intent,' he said. 'But we're dealing with myths here, so if we *believe* it hard enough, it might work.'

'OK,' Edie said. 'You'd better get on with it.'

She leaned over quickly and, before he had time to react, pressed her lips against his cheek; he was stunned to find he could feel her warm kiss against his skin.

'You take care,' she smiled at him, 'I can't do this alone.'

He beamed at her and shifted his substance to a state where he looked to Edie as if all that remained of him was a pale shadow. He flashed a final grin back at her and began to slide through the door and out into the Great Court.

Chapter Twenty-One – Onslaught

Outside the court was now in almost total darkness. The full moon was wrapped in deep cloud and no longer shone through the glass roof. All that illuminated the space was the light pollution from outside. This gave the court a pale and sickly yellow glow and Adam had to adjust his eyes to see through it. Keeping his substance on the edge of Dispersal, he made his way out on to the floor and hoped he was not noticed. The court was so quiet that at first he thought the Elementals had left, but then he saw a crimson glow from further around the curve of the building.

He raised himself a few centimetres from the floor to avoid causing any noise and slid still further out across the mess and destruction. He could make out Air and Water still standing halfway up the staircases as if hypnotised. The only movement from them was the ebb and flow of Water's gown over the stairs and the soft swirl of the breeze that enveloped Air. Both of them had their eyes closed and they did not notice Adam as he slipped past them at the foot of the staircases, heading towards the glow.

As he rounded the curve of the Court he could see the full damage that had been caused to the building. The floor glittered with diamond fragments of shattered glass, picking up what little light bled in, and the contents of the gift shops had been tossed around by the force of a great wind. A shiny slick of water lay across the floor and dark, muddy smears showed the route Earth had taken over the wet surface. Around the floor on one side of the court a jagged crevasse had opened and split the white floor wide open. Glossy black beetles scurried from the crack and fled across the floor in droves, all heading in the same direction.

Adam followed them with his eyes and could see a dark figure huddled over a small bonfire. At first he thought it was D'Scover and began to rush towards him, but as he got closer, he saw a chilling sight. Earth was kneeling on the floor with her back to him, her long hair slowly crawling around her head and a seething mass of beetles on her back busy scuttling around. In front of her lay the weakly crackling body of Fire, deep gouges showing black across her smouldering chest, stomach and legs.

As Adam watched, Earth reached over her own shoulder and pulled great dark lumps out from inside her own back. As quickly as a hole was made, the beetles rushed forward in a glossy black tide to fill it in. She took the black lump of coal and thrust it deep into the wound on her sister, where it began to glow and burn and fill the gash left by D'Scover's sword.

Adam moved slowly backwards and a pair of dark grey legs protruding from the plinth of a statue stopped him in his tracks. Kneeling down, and with his substance still in a weakened state, he was able to crawl into the plinth and lean over D'Scover where he still lay unconscious. D'Scover seemed to be drifting in and out of Dispersal and Adam could see the shining grey particles that represented him form and burst like tiny bubbles. Adam tried to ignore the grainy particles of the granite plinth all around them and concentrated a ball of energy into his hands before placing them on D'Scover's chest and forcing the red surge into his friend. The grey bubbles stopped bursting and swirled for a moment before beginning to settle into their usual human shape. Adam rolled D'Scover from the plinth just before his substance fully formed once more.

253

'Don't make a sound,' Adam whispered. 'Are you OK?'

D'Scover nodded and automatically reached out, patting the wet floor around him for his sword, and sighed with deep relief when his hand fell on the hilt. He drew the weapon in.

'I don't think that'll do you much good anymore,' Adam said.

The last bolt from Fire had not only damaged D'Scover, but his blade too. The tip of the sword had been melted away, leaving a charred, blunted end.

'It seems to hurt her,' D'Scover told him, 'and it's all we have, it will have to do.'

'If you're sure,' Adam said softly.

'What is happening?'

'Earth's healing Fire. She's still badly injured but healing fast.'

'Then we do not have much time.' D'Scover gripped his sword tightly and tried to stand. 'I think I can stop Fire, but I cannot take her sisters on as well.'

'Don't worry, we've got a plan...sort of..' Adam said. 'Stay here till we signal.'

'What will your signal be?'

'Don't know yet, but I'm sure it'll be obvious when it comes.'

With that, he Dispersed fully with a crimson crackle of light and vanished – reappearing inside the library next to Edie.

'Is he OK?' she asked.

'Yes, he is now; he's waiting for us to make a move. He can handle Fire as he managed to injure her before, but we have to try and do something about the sisters. Earth's healing Fire and is distracted at the moment, so maybe we can talk to the other two.'

'Adam, I have an idea,' Edie said. 'When I realised I couldn't sense D'Scover anymore, I felt something else as well.'

'What?'

'I might be wrong.' Edie looked nervous. 'When I reached out to search for him, I think I could feel them, the Elementals. You said Fire was wounded; was it in the stomach and legs, and further up her body?'

'Yes, across the chest,' Adam said.

'I felt a flash of pain, burning and a white light that was enough to throw me out of your thoughts. I thought it was D'Scover, but it could've been her.'

'How?'

'They are, in a sense, living spirits and part of the living Earth, and witches work on Earth magic,' she explained. 'I couldn't pin it down before because everything was so chaotic, but now it's quieter it might work.'

'Are you saying you think you can communicate with them from in here?' Adam asked. 'Get inside their heads?'

'I managed with you, but with them? I honestly don't know,' she replied. 'But I'm here and so it must be right.'

'You and your destiny rubbish will be the death of me,' Adam sighed.

'I'll ignore the obvious irony in that statement,' Edie said. 'As we've no time to row about it now.'

She sat down on the floor in front of the doors of the library and crossed her legs.

'Where are they?' she asked. 'Air and Water I mean.'

'Still on the stairs.' Adam ran to one side of the doors. 'I'm guessing that Water is here.' He pointed to a space halfway up the wall to the left of the doors. 'And Air in the same spot on the other side.'

'I'll try Air first,' Edie said, and closed her eyes.

At first all she could feel were the still sleeping security guards taking their silent and somnambulistic walks around the building. She stepped lightly through their dreams as she had no desire to wake them and make them face the horror of the battle being played out in the Great Court. She felt a number of other spirits in the building, but could not tell where they were and reasoned that they must be the ghosts who routinely haunted here, driven back by the chaos and confusion.

She concentrated and drew her thoughts closer in and, for a second, she brushed over D'Scover still in his hiding place behind the plinth. She could not make out his exact thoughts, but felt his urgency to get on and she shuddered at the intense, dark anger that wafted over her from him. She felt the raw hatred of Earth crouching over her injured sister and she quickly pulled her thoughts away, afraid of being detected in her roaming. Then nothing, a cold and empty sensation of falling which churned, and she nearly opened her eyes. Then she realised that she had found Air.

All around her wind whistled and the space was cold and vast. Edie felt as if she had stuck her head out of a car window at great speed and struggled to find a rhythm to her breathing. She let herself go and allowed the falling sensation to take her, and the nausea began to subside. Air was asleep.

'Can you hear me?' Edie tried. 'We need your help.'

After the initial shock she felt surprisingly safe in this falling world; no floor rushed up to meet them and she moved as gracefully through the air as a leaf caught in an updraught.

'Can you hear me?' she tried again.

The wind caught her and turned her around and around, tossing her up and down as lightly as if she was made of paper. The sounds around her were a rushing breeze that twisted her hair around her head and toyed with her. For a moment Edie thought she could hear something, a word, and then more, and she realised Air had been speaking, but she had not known how to listen. Her voice was more a collection of rustling noises than words, but strung together Edie could just make them out.

'*Safe, the people, it is good?*' Air whispered in her ear.

'Yes, they're safe, but I don't know for how much longer,' Edie said into the wind. 'You can help us; you can remove your sister Earth so we can defend ourselves from Fire. You could get Water to help you. Please, help us.'

'*Fire, strong, Earth, angry, this is not possible. Not stop, not remove, not possible,*' the voice continued. '*Should not be here, in this place, this is my place, you not here …*'

Air's voice began to fade away and the falling sensation grew less and less until Edie felt as if she was simply drifting in the breeze.

'NO!' Edie screamed. 'YOU CAN'T IGNORE US; IF YOU LET HER BEAT US, THEN SHE'LL BEAT YOU TOO. WE KNOW YOU DON'T MEAN PEOPLE ANY HARM SO TELL ME, WHAT WILL FIRE DO IF NO ONE STOPS HER?'

The falling sensation stopped so abruptly that Edie felt as if she must have hit something hard; instinctively she looked down at her feet, and was amazed to see that she was still in mid-air above a bank of thick white clouds. A cloud in front of her began to lose clumps, which started to stick to each other as if a child was building a person from cotton wool. Within moments, a humanoid shape stood in front of Edie, lumpy and misshapen, but obviously with the form of a woman. Two arms stretched out from the cloud and smoothed the shape as if smoothing a statue made of lumpy white plaster.

The figure leaned forward and, with a flourish, tossed its head back again, throwing fine strands of cloud behind it and revealing a face framed with hair of white gossamer strands. Her face was almost too perfect to look at and Edie was struck by her beauty and could not speak for a moment. Air smiled with a calm and saintly expression that lit her whole face with a golden sunset glow, and in an instant, Edie knew she would help them.

'*Mortals fear sister,*' her voice breathed, '*and right to fear her. Fire wants the living, for food, fear is food, she is hungry, always hungry. She should not take mortals, not right. Too much destruction, upset balance of worlds. Can help. But cannot stop Fire, too strong for Air. Water also not strong. Fire boil Water, kill her – choke Air, kill her.*'

'Can you and Water do anything about Earth?'

'*Earth? Earth angry. Anger is not control, anger can be dealt with.*'

'I'll take that as a yes,' Edie smiled. 'Thank you.'

'*Thank child, pretty witch inside thoughts of Air. Will stop Earth, witch stop Fire, all will balance again for a time.*'

'What do you mean for a time?' Edie called out.

'I never said anything,' Adam replied.

She was back in the library and Adam was crouched down in front of her.

'You all right? You look dead pale,' he said. 'Did it work?'

'Yes.' Edie jumped up. 'We have to get outside.'

They ran out through the doors and already Air and Water were descending the stairs. This Air looked very different from the ethereal, cloudlike one Edie had spoken to. This new Air was bruise-black, churning with storm clouds, and her robe was now decorated with silver flashes of lightning. The moon had split the clouds and now hung in an otherwise black sky, casting brilliant light into the court, illuminating the descending sisters. Water had also undergone a dramatic transformation and now met her sister wearing a robe of churning dark sea set off with tresses of wild waves tipped ice-white. Both of the sisters carried expressions of serious determination and on reaching the bottom step, they turned and walked together towards Earth.

'WHAT DO YOU IDIOTS WANT?' Earth raged as they neared her, standing over Fire's still prone and smouldering body.

'*Enough, this is done, balance is needed.*' Air's voice was still soft and almost intangible, but something in her tone made Edie shudder.

'Balance?' Earth laughed and the court shook so hard that sheets of glass fell from the roof and cascaded around them, shattering into great shards on the floor. 'What do you know of balance? Pathetic waifs – look at you, what can you do to me?'

'*Restore balance, it is time.*'

Air looked to Water who spread out her arms in a slow and languorous movement. A waterfall cascaded from each arm to the floor and began to flow towards Earth and very quickly she was standing in a puddle.

'You think these droplets can hinder me?' Earth laughed.

Water smiled and tipped her head to one side, with a steady drip falling from the rolling waves that made up her hair. Slowly she brought her hands together and, when they were directly in front of her, she raised her palms to the ceiling. The puddle rose too, in a solid, shimmering curtain around Earth, whose eyes now darted nervously about. Experimentally she reached out a long ebony finger and touched the curtain of water that now imprisoned her. She screamed and snatched it back as the water dissolved her finger, leaving only a shower of small, polished-clean stones cascading to the floor at her feet with a rattle.

'Sister,' Earth's voice oiled from within her aqueous prison, 'we can join forces and be stronger than ever, just you and I. We can have this mortal world for our own.'

'*No.*', Water spoke and the gentle ebb and flow of her voice hid the insistence within the words. '*Our sister is correct, we must have balance. It is time for you to take your leave.*'.

She lowered her arms and looked away as the curtain of water closed in on Earth. At first she struggled, but each part of her that touched the water was eroded by it. Screaming, she turned around and about, trying to avoid the inevitable touch of the water, until finally she gave in to it.

'YOU CAN SEND ME BACK THIS TIME, BUT EVENTUALLY I WILL REGAIN MY STRENGTH AND RECLAIM ALL I HAVE LOST,' she screamed.

'*Will take time, time, generations of mortal time, that will be enough balance,*' Air said.

She gently blew and her breath formed a solid column of wind spiralling around her, speeding up the erosion of her sister in a whirling vortex. A maelstrom of stones and earth spun in front of them until all that remained was a small pile of gravel on the floor. Water knelt down and the now filthy puddle rushed back towards her and flowed into her waiting arms. Air cast a small dismissive gesture with her hand and the pile of gravel was swept across the floor where it cascaded down into the crevasse Earth first crawled from.

'And what did you plan for me, my errant sisters?'

The familiar voice of cracking hot bones made them all turn. Behind them stood the fully recovered Fire, burning with a white-hot light that seared and boiled like the surface of the sun. She walked slowly to them, her infernal robe causing the white floor to crack where she walked. Adam and Edie backed off into the ruined remains of the shop and dived behind a smashed display case for cover.

'I am surprised at you, Air,' she said in patronising tones. 'Did you think you could bring me down with your pathetic summer breeze?'

She leaned towards her sister and breathed on her a humid and hot waft that enveloped her in a fierce, churning heat haze. Air clutched her throat, and gasped – her eyes startled and staring. She fell to the floor at her sister's feet, desperate for breath, and gasped short gulps. Fire ignored her plight and rounded on her other remaining sister.

'And did you think I would fall like my ineffective sister to a bit of water?'

She shot out her arm and pointed to Water, casting a flare of such intensity that she vaporised on the spot, leaving only a thin echo of a scream and a wall of steam momentarily filling the court. D'Scover saw his chance and ran from his hiding place, swinging his sword out and casting a thick black gash across Fire's back.

'DAMN IT, BOY, WILL YOU NEVER LEARN?' Fire screamed and turned towards him.

Her gown roared with fire and the trapped souls within it screamed and wailed at D'Scover as she moved towards him.

'YOU WERE LUCKY LAST TIME. THAT LUCK HAS FLED YOU NOW.'

Adam and Edie watched as the wound on Fire's back hissed and began to close and heal with a searing white light. Behind Fire, Air still lay on the floor, gasping in the broken glass, her dark gown fading to a paler blue with each gasp. Her mouth slowly moved as she lay staring towards where Adam and Edie hid and she reached out her hand to them.

'She's trying to say something,' Adam said.

He closed his eyes and shifted his substance once more and slid across to where Air lay on the floor. The space around her was unbearably hot, but Adam knew it was not strong enough to harm his substance; he leaned down as close as he could through the haze and placed his ear close to her mouth.

'*Child, innocent, child, must be child,*' she gasped. '*Belief stronger in innocence.*'

Adam's thoughts reeled in his mind as he instantly realised what she was saying, and what he must do. He stood up and forced himself across the wreckage to where D'Scover was backing away from Fire.

'A CHILD!' he shouted. 'YOU CAN ONLY DO THIS IF YOU'RE A CHILD. IT'S YOU, AND YOU HAVE TO *BELIEVE* THAT YOU'RE THE SENTINEL.'

'NO!' Fire spun round and screamed at them, hurling a bolt of fire in their direction that made Air gasp and vanish.

The distraction gave D'Scover the chance he needed. He closed his eyes and the veil of years fell away from him until he was just as he had been when he died – a skinny boy in faded and poor clothing clutching a sword that stood nearly as tall as he did. His leg glistened with the blood from the ancient wound once more and he limped forward. Taking a deep breath, he lifted the burnt and ruined sword with both hands and stood his ground.

'He's injured!' Edie cried out. 'How can that be?'

'Don't worry,' Adam tried to reassure her, 'it happened centuries ago, when he died. A crucifix shattered and a piece of the crystal ...'

'Crystal,' they exclaimed in unison. 'That's it!'

'We have to tell him that's the key,' Adam gasped. 'The crystal – that's the last part of the puzzle, the missing piece.'

'But we can't get out there. What can we do?'

'Can you put an idea in his head?' Adam said in desperation.

'Possibly,' she shrugged. 'I dunno, but it's worth a shot.'

261

She closed her eyes while Adam stood in front of her to shield her from the heat of the battle. D'Scover still stood in front of Fire, brandishing his sword and slowly circling round in a dance of mutual avoidance. He stared defiantly at her, his face set in an expression of pure concentration and, just for a second, he dropped his gaze. The sword seemed to become heavy and it drifted down as he stared into the distance, momentarily removed from the fight. He took several steps backwards and lowered the blade.

'What is it, boy?' Fire's words flicked round the circle. 'Are you admitting defeat?'

D'Scover looked down at his leg and plunged one partially Dispersed hand deep into the gory, ancient wound; he screamed in agony. Pulling out a blood-covered, sharp-edged scale of crystal, he wiped it on his clothes. The light bounced off it just as it had when it stood within the monastery as part of the crucifix. He took the fragment and held it to the broken tip of his sword. The second the crystal touched the metal a furious wave of silver-blue sparks ran up the weapon and coursed over the blade and the hilt. Sparks spattered and jumped from the blade as they fused the shard to its tip, falling to the floor like a shower of stars. D'Scover raised his new blade and smiled a cold smile at Fire.

'Now, demon,' he said with a placid tone, 'we shall see who triumphs.'

He hefted the crystal tip up over his head and ran forward into the flames. Fire took several steps backwards, but not far enough to avoid D'Scover's attack. As he reached her, he lunged and the glittering sword thrust deep into the blazing Elemental. A solid column of brilliant light erupted within her and burst through the remaining glass of the ceiling which rained down upon them with an ear-splitting roar.

For the briefest moment they all watched the relief on the faces of the souls trapped within her as they spiralled upwards and vanished. Fire slammed herself against the walls of the column, trying to escape the cold white prison it created, but to no avail. The light grew brighter and brighter until they could no longer look and it exploded with a deep, sonic throb that bulged the walls momentarily. Then all was silent.

'Red, are you all right?' a small voice called from the moonlit shadows.

'Edie!' Adam called out her name in desperate relief and ran towards her. 'We did it, we really did it!'

She ran out to meet him, glass crunching under her feet, and was relieved to find that he had enough strength to give her a proper hug. D'Scover walked over and joined them, still a boy and dragging his heavy sword through the debris on the floor.

'What do we do about all this mess?' Adam grinned.

'I THINK THAT IS OUR CONCERN.'

Looking about, they saw that next to them the twelve figures of the Senior Council had silently formed a shadowy enclave. Their chanting voices sounded louder and more solid in the ruined court.

They were not alone. Standing in the middle of the circle of figures stood Sister Goodman. She was wearing her nun's habit once more and was violently struggling against unseen restraints. From the terrible contortions on her face it was easy to see she was in intense pain and screaming, but no sound could be heard.

A low thrum of resonant voices grew from the circle and slowly they began to close in on the writhing figure in their midst. Soon it was almost impossible to see her through the closed ranks of the Council. They raised their hands above their heads and, with a sudden silence that seemed to make Edie's head almost burst with the oppressive pressure of it, they ripped into Sister Goodman. Tearing great clumps of her substance away, they tossed them into the air in a frenzy of movement. Each torn mass rose into the air and crackled with an explosive energy before splitting apart with fierce lilac sparks that cascaded to the floor around them. They could just make out the agonised and twisted face of the sister as she tried again and again to escape the circle, but it was all in vain. Within moments, the last mass was thrown into the air, and she was gone, forcibly Dispersed forever.

'Better late than never,' Edie said angrily, trying to mask the shock she felt at the horrific scene she had just witnessed. 'Couldn't you have been here an hour or two ago?'

'WE DO NOT ANSWER TO YOU, WITCH CHILD. HOWEVER, AN EXPLANATION MAY BE WARRANTED. SISTER GOODMAN HAD HER CO-CONSPIRATORS KEEP US OCCUPIED. WHEN WE WERE MADE AWARE OF THE SITUATION, IT WAS FITTING THAT OUR PRIORITY SHOULD BE TO PURSUE HER. SHE WAS UNDER THE INFLUENCE OF POWERFUL DEMONS AND IT WAS WITHIN THE INTEREST OF ALL CONCERNED THAT THE VOYNICH BE RETRIEVED. OUR PRIORITY WAS THAT SISTER GOODMAN BE FORCIBLY DISPERSED. THE EVENTS PLAYED OUT HERE WITH YOU WERE OF SECONDARY SIGNIFICANCE.'

'You would have just left us to die?' Edie gasped.

'THE IRONY OF THAT STATEMENT SEEMS LOST ON YOU. YOU *CHOSE* TO BE HERE. WE DEAL WITH ISSUES BIGGER THAN THE LIFE OF ONE CHILD AND THE SPIRITS OF TWO OTHERS.'

'Hold on,' Adam interjected. 'How did you know what was going on here at all? I mean, if she had you occupied, how did you know?'

'I told 'em.' Marcus walked out from the shadows to join them on the debris-covered floor. 'I followed Sister Goodman and then contacted the Senior Council, well, me and Emma did.'

'Marcus, you did? We thought you'd run off!' Adam laughed.

'Don't worry about it,' Marcus replied, 'I nearly did!'

'The book, the Voynich,' D'Scover asked. 'Did you retrieve it?'

'THE MONK'S BOOK IS SAFE. NOW YOU MUST ALL LEAVE SO WE CAN DEAL WITH THIS DESTRUCTION IN A WAY THAT THE LIVING WILL COMPREHEND. YOU WILL MAINTAIN SUBSTANCE AND ESCORT THE GIRL TO D'SCOVER'S OFFICE. D'SCOVER, WE WILL SUMMON YOU IN EIGHT HOURS TO DISCUSS THESE EVENTS.'

With that, the shadows turned away and began to drift into the darkness.

'But you can't just …' Edie stammered '… I mean, after all we did they just …'

'Come on,' Adam cut in, pulling her away, 'let's get out of here.'

They walked across the destroyed court, heading out the way they came in, the guards still resting in their undisturbed slumber. D'Scover blended his outward image back into his adult form as he walked, his immaculate suit and spotless black coat looking hopelessly out of place in the mess. Adam wondered what was different about him and realised he could see the crystal tip of the blade poking out from under D'Scover's long coat. He had kept the sword.

'Hold on,' Adam said as they reached the door, 'I forgot something.' He Dispersed quickly and was back in a few seconds.

'Done, let's go,' he said and they all walked out of the door into the chill of the night air.

'What did you do?' Edie asked him.

'Just had to say my thank yous!' he laughed and they both ran on ahead to catch up with D'Scover.

In a dark library standing like an island of calm, cut off by a white court that was now a chaos of broken glass and smouldering rubble, thousands of books ruffled their pages with pride.

Acknowledgements

This book has been a labour of love and only exists thanks to the support of many people. I wanted to take this opportunity to thank a few, but if I miss you out I'm sure you'll understand. You know you are important. Feel free to request cake.

My thanks go to Scott Pack who believed in my ghosts and was their champion right down the line. Thanks to the lovely Rachel Faulkner for putting it all together with patience and grace, and to my agent Ivan Mulcahy and marketing whizz Caitriona Horne for watching my back! You all worked hard to make my book live, and I can't thank you enough.

The research for this book was long and detailed, and required help from many sources. I would like to say thank you to the British Museum for their patience and understanding with my odder enquiries, including having the night guards check the Great Court in moonlight. The same for the Beinecke Rare Book and Manuscript Library at Yale, who answered my questions about their building and the Voynich Manuscript without assuming I was casing the joint.

Thanks are also due to the *Fortean Times* for being an invaluable source of research material and ideas. I could not do all this without the *Fortean Times* to draw on for all the magnificent High Weirdness that would otherwise go unnoticed.

And huge thanks go to all the libraries I've ever used in my life, and for all the superb librarians who run them. I dread to think of a world without free access to books, it's not one I want to live in.

Finally – this is a book dedicated to every freak, geek, nerd, weirdo, storyteller and creative crazy. This is for every person who knows with absolute certainty that there is another world just out of the corner of your eye.

You go right on making worlds that are dazzling and brilliant. Thank you all.

D'Scover's World

D'Scover's office is based in London and the locations featured in the book are all real, as are most of the historical events mentioned. Adam Street (where Adam is discovered), for example, is a street in London that runs between The Strand and the Thames; you can find it easily online and have a virtual wander around.

You can also find out a lot more about this world by using the websites below; but I'm afraid I can't tell you where the office actually is because that is classified information.

If you do find it, keep it to yourself …

John Dee

www.johndee.org
A very complete biography of all things John Dee – real person, real alchemist, but real magic, real angels?

Decide for yourself …

The Voynich Manuscript

The Voynich manuscript is authentic. It is currently held by the Beinecke Library of Yale University in Connecticut. The Voynich is attributed to the thirteenth-century monk and scholar Roger Bacon and was later associated with John Dee. It has never been deciphered and is one of the world's great literary mysteries.

You can have a look at the Voynich for yourself by going to **www.library.yale.edu/beinecke** and searching digital images for the Voynich. You will see the little crinkly beige-coloured book. Click on it and you can browse the manuscript yourself – without having to use your CC at all.

Why not take some time to have a look at the Beinecke building, too? You'll see the marble wall panels that are described in chapter 17.

www.voynich.nu is a fantastic site that allows you to choose how much more you want to know about the Voynich manuscript. You can dip in and just look at the pictures or, like a number of people with a lot of time on their hands, make it your life's work to attempt to decode it!

Other Great Sites

www.thebritishmuseum.org
Here you can search the picture library for some wonderful images of the Great Court or search the online collections for artefacts relating to John Dee, including the obsidian mirror that Adam will need to break the code of the manuscript.

http://cathedral.southwark.anglican.org/
D'Scover was based in the tower of Southwark Cathedral (his room is described in chapter 12) and the Sisters guarded the precious

monastic texts here. Go to this website and click on 'Visit Us', then go to 'History and Architecture' to find out more about the history of the cathedral and Southwark.

www.nhm.ac.uk/
In chapter six, Marcus is re-allocated to the Natural History Museum. Click on 'Visit Us' and explore the various galleries, including the mammal room where the characters play their macabre betting game.

www.forteantimes.com
This is the site that Adam and D'Scover use to search for reports of ghost activity around the world. This website, and the magazine it represents, is a truly wonderful resource for anyone interested in all things 'as yet unexplained'.

www.cottingley.net/fairies.shtml
This is a lovely website from the village of Cottingley where you can read all about the 'faked' fairies.

About the Author

Dawn Finch grew up in a book-filled house on the river's edge of a tough London-overspill council estate. When she was ten her dad gave her a collection of Edgar Allan Poe stories and this launched a lifetime fascination with the macabre and the unexplained. At the age of eleven a fierce librarian refused to lend her a copy of Bram Stoker's *Dracula* on the grounds that she was too young to read it. She vowed that if she was ever a librarian she would never deny a child a great book. At twelve Dawn told her careers advisor that she wanted to be either a writer or a librarian, and she was dismayed to be told to stop 'pointless dreaming'. After many years of study and hard work, and a range of jobs – from reading unsolicited slush-pile manuscripts to dressing as a Benedictine monk to take children on cathedral tours – Dawn carved out a successful career as a Children's Librarian and Reader Development Consultant. With the publication of her first book, *Brotherhood of Shades*, she is thrilled to be able to add Writer to her CV as well.

She knows with absolute certainty that the only time dreams become pointless is when you stop working hard to achieve them.

About Authonomy

Authonomy is an online community of authors, readers and publishers, conceived and developed by editors at HarperCollins. It was launched to provide unpublished authors with a platform to showcase their work. Authonomy is also dedicated to seeking out and publishing the very best new writing talent. To find other exciting new books or to join our brilliant community, visit www.authonomy.com.

Printed by RR Donnelley at Glasgow, UK